Other Books by Susan Lantz Simpson

Plain Haven

Plain Discovery

Plainly Maryland Series

Book II

SUSAN LANTZ SIMPSON

Vinspire Publishing
www.vinspirepublishing.com

In memory of my grandma, Martha Richards,
who grew the most beautiful flowers,
including heavenly-smelling "pinks."

Chapter One

Esther checked her last plant and replaced the small green pot gently in the black plastic tray. The sun heated the greenhouse nicely despite the still cool, late April temperature. Southern Maryland had had an uncharacteristically long, cold, snowy winter, and spring was dragging its heels as if reluctant to make an appearance.

She breathed in the scents of damp earth and fertilizer. She loved the greenhouse and plunging her hands into the moist dirt to care for her plants. Her bopplin. It didn't look like she would have any bopplin of the human variety since she was already twenty-five with no marriage prospects in sight. An old maedel. She shrugged. She did adore kinner and longed for some of her own, but she was happy with her greenhouse and nursery business. Surely springlike weather would arrive soon so she could work outside more. Already, though, customers began to seek her out. They knew she always had healthy plants and could offer them all sorts of advice.

If only she understood her family—more specifically her older sister and her kinner—as well as she did plants and herbs. One look at a sickly plant and Esther would know if it was under watered, overwatered, needed sunlight or shade, or required a good talking to. And, jah, she did talk to her plants. But for the life of her, she didn't know how to help Lydia, David, and Ella.

Something was amiss, but she couldn't quite put her finger on it. She tapped her cheek, forgetting that same dirty hand had recently patted soil around plants, then realized it had probably now left a wide, brown smear on her face. She wrinkled her forehead in that familiar worry frown that her mamm warned her would become permanent one day if she wasn't careful.

Esther stared out the greenhouse door at the cavorting children. They giggled as their spindly legs carried them around the yard. They had begun to look healthy, robust even. Now, in the last week or so, they had grown downright puny again. She couldn't figure out what happened. She knew Mamm had been feeding them right. They were too young at three and five to wander off and get into things they weren't supposed to. Besides, Lydia normally watched them like a hawk.

Things weren't quite so normal now, though. Had they been sneaking into Daed's private stash of goodies in the barn? Had Mamm kept the cookie jar and bread out of reach and out of sight? Were they simply coming down with some childhood malady? Esther had always been good at piecing clues together. She had to figure out this mystery before her niece and nephew faded into oblivion.

Lydia, only one year older than Esther, had married at nineteen and moved to Pennsylvania shortly after her wedding. She had met Amos Kauffman when she was seventeen and Amos was nineteen. He came to St. Mary's County, Maryland, with some other fellows on a scouting mission for farmland. Amos didn't find the land he wanted, but he did find a tall brunette with gold-flecked brown eyes who hung on his every word. Lydia had told her that since Amos stood over six feet tall, he had been thrilled to find a girl he didn't have to stoop down to talk to — or to kiss when the time was right. Lydia had blushed prettily when she relayed this last part.

Lydia and Amos had kept the mailman busy with twice-weekly letters. When they could bear being apart no longer, Amos returned to Maryland to claim Lydia as his bride. Even though it meant leaving her family, she happily accompanied her husband back to Bird-in-Hand where they established their home. A year and a half later, they welcomed David to their family. Ella came along less than two years after David.

From her letters home, Lydia seemed happy being a fraa and a mamm, even if she did miss her family. She updated them regularly on the happenings with her own little family and always said how much she looked forward to the infrequent visits. When Amos was killed in a logging accident six months ago, a distraught Lydia returned home to Maryland. Now she once again occupied her girlhood bedroom, and her kinner took up residence in the smaller guest room across the hall from Esther's room.

Lydia had changed. Esther hadn't expected her schweschder to remain the same happy-go-lucky girl once she married and became a mamm. And, of course, suddenly losing a soulmate would definitely bring about change. But Lydia seemed sharper, prickly, like last year's pinecone that still looked pretty but would stab like a thorn. Esther sighed. It had only been six months since Amos' passing. Lydia needed time. And Esther needed to find a way to help her and the kinner.

She lovingly cleaned her gardening tools and put them away. It wouldn't do to leave pruning shears, clippers, and spades where little hands could grab them. Besides, she always took excellent care of the tools of her trade, as any carpenter or blacksmith or farmer would.

Loud giggles reached her as Esther exited the greenhouse. She smiled, glad to have wee ones around, glad they could laugh again, completely unaware they were looking less than healthy. She'd have to talk to Mamm. Lydia was so touchy lately; she'd think Esther was criticizing her mothering skills.

"Grossmammi sent us to fetch you." David pulled his little sister to a halt in front of Esther.

"She did now, did she?" She stooped down, getting eye to eye with her niece and nephew.

"She said to help her with supper." With his reddish-brown hair, David was the spitting image of his daed, except the little bu's nose was spattered with light brown freckles.

"Ach! Is it that late already?" Esther always lost track of time when tending her plants. Briefly, she wondered why Lydia couldn't help but instantly chastised herself. Maybe her sister had another one of her terrible headaches.

"You have dirt all over your face," Ella said.

Esther tried not to feel prideful, but Ella could easily have passed for her own little girl with her same dark hair and eyes. "I do? Now you will!" She lunged for the kinner, pretending to wipe her face on first Ella and then David.

"Nee! Nee!" they squealed together and ran for the house.

Esther chuckled and headed for the house herself. Better hurry and wash up so Mamm wouldn't have to call her again. For sure and for certain, that wouldn't be a good thing.

Uh oh, Esther thought as she drew close to the house. Daed was home already. It must be even later than she thought. She started to quicken her pace and then stopped short. "Who in the world is he talking to?" she questioned the air. It looked like...

"Esther!" Daed called.

She'd been spotted. No sneaking away now. She rubbed her hands quickly over her cheeks to remove the dirt David and Ella said she had there.

"Look who's here! Andrew's back."

"What are you doing here?" That sounded rude. Esther tried quickly to amend her comment. "I mean, I mean..."

"Gut to see you, too, Esther." A smirk appeared on Andrew's too-handsome face. "By the way, you missed a spot." He reached out as if to wipe her face.

Esther jerked back. "Danki. I'll take care of it." She swiped at her cheek.

"Probably not with those dirty hands." Andrew couldn't quite hide his smile.

She looked at her hands. She'd brushed *most* of the dirt off. She dropped her hands and wrapped them in her black apron. "So what brings you here?"

"You remember at Sarah's wedding I said I planned to move back to Maryland. I'm just a little later getting here than I planned."

Andrew's cousin, Sarah Fisher — now Sarah Esh — married Zeke during the fall wedding season. Andrew's family, who moved from Maryland to Ohio more than ten years before, came for Sarah's wedding. When Andrew hadn't reappeared after the holidays, Esther breathed a sigh of relief. She assumed he had a change in his plans. She suddenly realized she should respond to his last comment. "Oh," was all she could come up with. Esther shifted from one foot to the other. "I'd better go help Mamm." She started for the house again.

"Thanks, Daniel, for hiring me on even temporarily."

"What?" Esther stopped abruptly and whirled to face her daed.

"I need some help in the saw mill." An amused expression crossed Daed's face.

"You have plenty of help." Esther's cheeks burned. She seethed at her daed's obvious delight at her discomfiture.

"Jah, usually, but Mose Troyer is still out."

"He'll be back soon, though, ain't so?"

"Nee. He had a relapse. That pneumonia isn't through with him yet."

"I'm sorry to hear that," Esther mumbled.

"Jah. We'll pray for him, for sure. While he's recovering, Andrew is going to help out. Then he can go to work for Beilers' Furniture like he planned."

"Oh," Esther said again.

Andrew twisted his black felt hat in his hands. The cool breeze ruffled his chestnut colored hair slightly, and the sleeves of the shirt that was the same jade-green as his eyes flapped against his muscular arms. Esther would like to use her dirty hands to wipe that smug look off his face. Instead, she spun on her heel, determined to make it to the house this time.

"Tell your mamm not to rush. I'm early." Daniel paused for only an instant. "And set an extra place."

Esther nodded, ground her teeth, and held back a reply. She was sure any comment she made at the moment would not be Christian or even polite. She stomped up the steps, washed up, and stomped some more into the kitchen.

"Was ist letz? You look like a mad bull." Mamm glanced at Esther before she set a pan of biscuits in the oven.

"That!" Esther sputtered and pointed to the window.

"Why, Andrew Fisher is back. "Mamm peeked out and then drew back from the window.

"Daed hired him!" Esther's voice rose a few decibels.

"I guess Mose won't be back for a while. It's gut your daed got some extra help."

"Gut? Mamm, really? Couldn't Daed have found someone else? Anyone else?"

"I don't recall needing to clear my decisions with you, Dochder." Her father's voice boomed loud and clear. When did he come in?

Instantly contrite, Esther murmured, "Sorry, Daed." She looked around nervously. Even though she was unhappy with his decision, she didn't want to be rude to a guest—even if that guest did happen to be Andrew Fisher.

"He's seeing to the horses," Daniel said, noticing Esther's embarrassment. "And you'll hold your tongue at supper, jah?"

"Jah." Esther scurried to set the table, biting the tongue she promised to tame.

After the silent prayer, she passed a heavy bowl of boiled potatoes and cabbage and an equally heavy platter of ham slices to Andrew. She snatched her hand back as if scalded when his fingers brushed hers when he took the platter from her. Then she busied herself cutting ham up into small pieces for Ella and David before glancing at Lydia who looked pale and distracted.

"Feeling better?" Mamm asked Lydia.

Lydia shrugged her shoulders. "Some." She pushed the food around on her plate without eating it.

"Another headache?" Esther asked.

"Jah."

"Maybe Sophie has something that will help." Sophie, the "medicine woman," had herbs or teas for practically any ailment. Her remedies usually worked as well as or better than the Englischers' pills—most of the time, anyway.

Lydia shrugged again. "Maybe I'll pay her a visit."

For the rest of the meal, Esther focused her attention on the kinner, completely ignoring Andrew unless he asked her to pass a bowl. This was the only way she could be sure she wouldn't say words she'd later regret. She'd let Daed entertain their guest since it was his idea to ask Andrew to dine with them.

After supper, Daed walked outside with Andrew. *Thank goodness Andrew is staying with the Fishers, or Daed may have offered him a room, too.* Esther instantly berated herself for her uncharitable thought. She vigorously scrubbed the plate she'd been washing for the last five minutes.

"That one is clean unless you're trying to scrub the finish off the plate," Mamm observed.

"Sorry." Esther rinsed the plate and plunked it in the dish drainer. She halfway wished Mamm hadn't sent Lydia off with the kinner. At least Lydia was usually too distracted to notice anyone else's mood. She wouldn't be so lucky with Mamm.

"What's got you so riled up? Something to do with Andrew, ain't so?"

Esther dropped the glass she'd been washing, splashing soapy dishwater all over her black apron. "Mamm, don't you remember how mean he was to me when we were in school together?"

"You were kinner."

"Jah, but he knew better. He was always teasing me or picking on me. Once, he put a toad in my lunch pail. That kind of backfired on him, though, since I wasn't scared of toads." Esther smiled at that memory only briefly before her scowl resurfaced. *But that isn't the half of it. Not a soul knows the rest, except for Andrew and his cohorts.*

"I think he must have been sweet on you even then."

Her mouth dropped open. "Mamm! What are you saying?"

"Didn't you notice the way he kept cutting his eyes to look at you at supper?"

"Of course not! I was busy with the kinner. Besides, he probably thought I was going to throw potatoes at him."

"I don't think so, dochder."

"He was a mean boy," Esther began again.

"*Was.* People change, you know. And I know what I see."

Quick! Find a new topic! Her cheeks grew warm. "Mamm, have you noticed Ella and David seem a bit puny again? They were looking right healthy for a while, but now — "

"I'll thank you not to talk about my kinner behind my back." Lydia stomped into the room.

"Lydia! I didn't mean any harm. I'm only concerned about the kinner — and about you, too." She softened her voice and reached out to touch her older sister's arm.

"We're fine!" Lydia snapped, jerking her arm away from Esther.

"You've all been through a lot, schweschder. I want to help."

Lydia released a deep, shaky sigh. "I know," she whispered. "I've been feeding them right. They've been to see that Dr. Kramer more than I'd like. I really wish Dr. Nelson was here. I trust him."

"Dr. Nelson is still caring for his ailing father. I haven't been to Dr. Kramer. I go see Sophie if I need a quick remedy." Mamm picked up the glass and dried it.

"What's wrong with this Dr. Kramer?" Esther asked.

"I can't put my finger on it, but he's very formal or something. David and Ella were pretty sickly before they were diagnosed with celiac disease. Once we got their diet under control, they perked right up. They gained weight and everything. I think they were doing better before they started seeing Dr. Kramer."

"Hmmm, that's interesting," Esther mused. "We've been careful to keep to the gluten-free diet and even use different pans and utensils for the kinners' food."

"Jah, I know." Lydia sighed. "I don't think they've been sneaking any forbidden food. They've always been good fruit and vegetable eaters—no gluten there. They drink milk and eat eggs and meat. They even seem to like the special bread and cookies I got from Dr. Kramer. I don't know what else to do." She rubbed her hand back and forth across her forehead.

"Have you still got that headache, dear?" Mamm tossed the towel on the counter and studied her older dochder.

"Jah."

"Maybe some fresh air would help." Esther swiped at the bubbles that still clung to her apron.

"Maybe *you* need to visit Dr. Kramer." Worry lines snaked across their mamm's forehead.

"I think I'd rather check with Sophie. I'm going to get David and Ella ready for bed."

"I'll kumm tell them goodnight shortly." Mamm retrieved the towel, dried another glass, and set it in the cabinet.

"You know, maybe the kinner are more active here and burn off whatever they eat. Maybe that's why they seem to be losing weight." Esther wanted to be reassuring even though she, too, was concerned.

"We'll try to be even more vigilant about their diet, but we need to get you feeling better too, dochder."

"Maybe I can do some investigating." Esther tapped her cheek, leaving a soap bubble behind.

"Nee, Esther, no more playing detective." Mamm hung up the dish towel and followed Lydia out of the kitchen.

"Why not?" Esther mumbled to herself. "I'm pretty good at it."

Chapter Two

What a difference one day makes! One thing for sure about Southern Maryland weather—it was never totally predictable. The air harbored no nip today. The sun shone brightly from a clear cerulean sky. Not a cloud in sight. Esther inhaled deeply. "It smells like spring—finally!" She quickened her step. Sunshine and warm weather made everyone feel better, didn't they? Even Lydia had actually gotten out of bed early and offered to help Mamm with the noon meal so her sister didn't feel the need to rush with her work this morning. "That wasn't very charitable, Esther," she chided herself. It would be gut, though, for Lydia to keep busy to help her through the grieving process. At least that was Esther's humble opinion.

As usual, she lost all track of time while readying her garden plots. The sun beating down on her from directly over her head told her it must be noon or nearly noon. Her rumbling stomach sent that same message. She turned her head in the direction of approaching voices.

"You might as well take your meal with us since you're already here to refill your water." Daed's voice came loud and clear.

Andrew. Again. Was Daed going to drag him inside for every meal?

"Nee. But danki, Daniel. I did bring my lunch."

"Why have a peanut butter sandwich when you can have a good, hot meal?"

Honestly, couldn't Daed leave Andrew to his own devices? He didn't haul Mose over to the house for meals. *But Mose has a wife to pack him a good, hearty meal,* the little voice of Esther's conscience chimed in. She gritted her teeth.

"Hello, Esther," Andrew called. "Getting ready to plant, ain't so?"

Well, of course. Why else would she be out here in the dirt? "Jah." She curled her hands into tight fists when she saw Andrew's gaze shift to them. He used to tease her about always having dirt under her fingernails.

"Let's wash up." Daed nudged Andrew toward the house.

Slowly, Esther uncurled her fingers. Sure enough, rich black dirt lodged beneath each nail. She shrugged and ambled toward the house. She wanted to give the men plenty of time to clear the washroom. Peering down, Esther was surprised to find herself picking at the caked earth jammed beneath her fingernails. Dirty hands were a hazard of her trade. They couldn't be helped, even if she wore gardening gloves. Esther sighed.

She gobbled what she could force down of her meal as quickly as possible, almost choking on the coleslaw. Again, she focused her attention on David and Ella. "Would you two like to help me after nap time?"

"Actually, Esther, I was going to ask if you'd mind going for a walk and visiting Sophie for me." Lydia rubbed her lined forehead.

"Do you have another headache?" That worried frown creased Mamm's forehead again.

"Jah. Maybe I'll take a nap with the kinner."

"Why don't you kumm walk with me? The fresh air may do you a world of gut. Then you could describe your ailments to Sophie yourself."
"Nee, I-I think I'll rest."

Andrew cleared his throat. "I'll walk with you Esther—if you don't mind, Daniel." Andrew cast a tentative glance at Daed. "I-I'd like to ask Sophie for something for these allergies." His sudden sneeze seemed a bit forced to Esther.

Facing Andrew squarely, Esther exploded. "There's nothing wrong with you Andrew Fisher, that a good swift kick—" She broke off abruptly at Daed's loud cough and Lydia's poke under the table. "Sorry," she mumbled. She dropped her gaze to her still half-full plate but not before catching the twinkle in Andrew's eye and his barely concealed laughter.

"I think that's a gut idea." Daed elbowed Andrew. "You've worked hard and could use a little break. Besides, you need to do something about that, uh, sneezing."

Andrew had the good grace to flush, but his cheeks were not nearly as crimson as Esther knew her own were. She grunted. What was wrong with Daed? It seemed like he kept pushing Andrew on her. She wished she could nudge him under the table.

"I'll help you clean up, Mamm." Esther pushed her plate back.

"Aren't you going to finish eating?"

"I *am* finished. I guess I lost my appetite."

Daed bowed his head for the silent prayer, and the rest of the family followed his lead. Lydia rose to take plates to the kitchen and to herd her kinner upstairs for a nap.

"Kumm get me when you're ready to go," Andrew called as he followed Daniel back to the sawmill.

Esther rolled her eyes and grunted again.

For a brief moment, she seriously considered sneaking out of the house after the last dish had been stacked in the cabinet and the big oak table scrubbed clean, then shook her head. She would definitely get caught. She might be twenty-five years old, but she would still be reprimanded by Mamm or Daed, or both. Esther smoothed her green dress and black apron and patted her head to make sure her kapp was straight and no errant wisps of hair had escaped her bun. *Why do I even care how I look*? She dropped her hands to her sides, forced her fingers to remain straight and not clench into fists, and shuffled toward the door. *I might as well get this over with.*

She hadn't gotten halfway to the sawmill when she heard a shout, "Ach, Esther, are you ready?"

Esther nodded and continued on at a fast clip. Normally, she would enjoy a leisurely stroll and check for buds on the fruit trees or see if the red-breasted robins had built any nests in nearby branches. Today, she was on a mission she wanted to complete as soon as possible.

"If you'd hold up a bit, I'd walk with you." Andrew laughed.

"Why?"

"Huh?"

"Why do you want to go with me?"

"Uh, my…uh, allergies. I told you." He coughed.

"I wasn't born yesterday," Esther muttered only halfway under her breath.

"What did you say? I didn't catch it."

"I didn't know you had allergies. I don't recall that when we were kinner."

"People change, you know."

"So I've heard."

"You don't seem to like me much, Esther. What do you have against me?"

"Maybe your mean spiritedness."

"I don't have a mean bone in my body."

"You've forgotten all the times you made fun of me?"

"We were kinner, Esther. And it was only teasing. I never meant to hurt your feelings."

"Huh! It didn't seem like fun to me." He must have forgotten the rest of the heartache he'd caused — or didn't care.

They walked along in silence a while, though not a comfortable, companionable silence. Esther kicked a stone and watched it roll several feet away. When she caught up to it, she kicked it again.

"Es?"

"Huh?" He spoke so softly, she wasn't sure he spoke at all but answered just in case.

"I'm sorry."

"What?"

"I said I'm sorry I ever caused you pain. I really liked you — then and now."

"You had a strange way of showing it!"

"Little buwe aren't the brightest of creatures the Lord put on Earth."

Esther laughed. "You can say that again!"

"Little buwe aren't the brightest..."

Esther elbowed Andrew, and they both burst out laughing.

Andrew sobered first. "I meant what I said."

"Apology noted, but..." She wanted to add that she still didn't trust him but didn't get the chance.

"I don't mean—"

"You mean you aren't sorry?" Esther stopped walking to face Andrew, her hands on her hips.

Andrew stopped, too. "Nee. Jah. Esther, will you let me finish a thought without jumping in or assuming?"

"Sorry. Bad habit. By all means, please explain."

"I am sorry for teasing you. I also meant I was serious about...about—"

Esther's questioning gaze slid to Andrew's face. She opened her mouth to ask "about what?" but clamped her lips together in an effort to show patience.

Andrew coughed. "About liking you," he finally finished.

This time, Esther coughed. She dropped her gaze hastily to the rock she had been about to kick again, unsure how to reply. "I bet you say that to all the girls you teased in school." She gave a little laugh, attempting to lighten the mood.

"Nee. Only you."

"Then why...oh, never mind." Esther resumed walking. "We'd better hurry along. Lydia needs something for her headaches, and we don't want you to suffer with your, uh, allergies any longer than you have to. Besides, Daed probably needs your help."

"You're probably right."

They continued on in silence. This time, it wasn't quite so strained.

"There's Sophie's place." Esther pointed to the house across the next field.

"Jah. I remember."

"I guess you do. You haven't been gone so terribly long."

"More than ten years."

"Really? That long? Why did you decide to come back, if you don't mind my asking?"

"This has always felt like home to me. I like our small community here. I like Maryland lots better than Pennsylvania. I always wanted to come back. I had to wait for the right time."

They cut across the field as Andrew talked. Right before they climbed the steps to Sophie's porch, he reached out tentatively to touch her arm. "Can we try to be freinden, Esther?"

"Uh, sure, I guess. Jah, I suppose we can *try*." A slight smile tugged at the corners of her mouth. She averted her gaze so Andrew wouldn't see it. As she turned the door knob, she called out, "Sophie!"

"Wie geht's. Kumm. Kumm. It's gut to see you." Sophie embraced Esther and then stood back to look Andrew up and down.

"You remember Andrew Fisher, don't you Sophie?"

"For sure and for certain. You lived here as a bu. You moved away about ten or fifteen years ago, ain't so?"

"That's me." Andrew gave a little bow.

"Well, wilkom."

"Sophie, Lydia sent me to get something—anything—that may help her headaches."

"Is she still having them? I'm thinking it's her grief causing them."

"I'm thinking the same thing, but I can't get her out of the house to do anything. She wouldn't even walk here with me. She took a nap with the kinner."

Sophie clucked her tongue. "I can send her some soothing herbs and teas, but they won't mend a broken heart or wash away grief."

"I know, but maybe if her pain is lessened I can get her to do things. It's worth a try."

"Worth a try," Sophie repeated. She shifted her small dark eyes to Andrew.

"Ach!" Esther slapped her forehead. "I almost forgot. Andrew needs something for his *allergies*." She rolled her eyes heavenward.

"Allergies, you say? I don't recall you having allergies as a bu, but maybe I didn't know about them."

Right on cue, Andrew produced a sneeze. "I must have developed them more recently." He sniffed.

"Have you ever heard of that, Sophie?" Esther asked.

"Well, I guess it could happen." Sophie looked at Andrew, then at Esther, then back at Andrew. "Let's see if I can find something to help."

She rummaged through her shelves, eventually producing concoctions she thought would help. "Have you got a few minutes, Esther?"

"Sure, I suppose I can spare a few minutes. You can go on back, Andrew. Daed probably needs your help by now."

"I guess I've been dismissed." He paid and started for the door. "Danki, Sophie. See you later, Esther."

"Your beau seemed right nice," Sophie began.

"Ach! Andrew certainly is not my beau! He's
helping Daed in the mill while Mose recuperates. He
wanted to come see you, so he pestered me to let him
tag along."

"I think I'm seeing more to it." A sly smile
played on Sophie's lips.

"I don't think so. Don't you remember how
much he picked on me as a bu?"

"He's a man now, Esther. Perhaps he's put away
those childish ways."

Esther shrugged her shoulders. "Can I talk to
you about Lydia's kinner?" Esther plunged in, telling
Sophie how they seemed to be doing so well but here
lately, their health had taken a nosedive.

"They're grieving, too." Sophie shook her head.
"They are probably sad at the changes in their mamm
as well. Let me give you a little something that may
perk up their appetites a bit. I did notice last church
day that they were a bit scrawny."

"That's just it. They eat—you know we have to
be so careful with their foods—but it's like the food
isn't doing them any gut."

"I'll think on it and see what else I can come up
with."

"Danki, Sophie. I knew I could count on you. I'm
sorry. You said you wanted to talk to me and here
I've gone on and on."

"That's quite all right. How would you like to
learn more about the healing herbs and teas? I'd like
to teach you. You'd be a natural at it."

"Well, uh, I guess that'd be fine. But you are our expert."

"I won't be around forever, you know. There is no one I think would be better to carry on—you know, later—and to even help me out some now. What do you say?"

Esther scrutinized the older woman. Her brown hair did look a little grayer. Lines furrowed her brow and ringed her eyes. Maybe she was feeling some effects of age. "I'd be happy to learn whatever I can, Sophie. I'm honored you asked me."

"We can go over a few things today and really start your learning whenever you get some free time." Sophie looked relieved but also excited to share her wealth of knowledge.

"Sure." Esther had wanted to get back to her nursery but didn't want to disappoint her freind. "And I'll try to stop in tomorrow."

That certainly came out of the blue. Esther crossed the field with her purchases a short time later. She hoped Sophie was feeling well. It might actually be fun to learn about medicinal plants. A new spring entered her step as she strode toward home. Now she *did* notice the cloudless blue sky and the leaves popping out on the winter-weary tree limbs.

As soon as she stepped onto the blacktop road, Esther heard the clip-clop of an approaching horse and buggy. She squinted into the sunlight, raised a hand to shade her eyes, and focused on the buggy's driver. A huge grin spread across her face as the buggy pulled alongside her. "Ach, Hannah! School's out already? It must be later than I thought."

"Jah, it's past three," the beautiful woman with pale blonde hair and huge blue eyes confirmed. Two little boys who had been looking out the buggy's back window popped their heads around the driver.

"Jonas, Eli, how was school today?" Esther asked the buwe.

"Gut," they replied in unison. What else could they say? They were riding with their teacher.

"Hop in," Hannah invited. "I'll drop you off."

"Do you have time?"

"For sure. I'd make the time anyway." Hannah smiled.

Esther climbed nimbly into the buggy and perched on the seat beside Hannah. She marveled at how well Hannah—an Englischer who had been sent to Cherry Hill for her safety—had adapted. Even when the crime she witnessed was resolved, rather than return home to Virginia, Hannah had chosen to stay in the community. Esther and Hannah had become almost instant freinden. It had been a year now since she'd been baptized into the Amish Church. She lived with Rebecca and Samuel Hertzler whose little boys were now riding home from school with her. If Esther read the signs correctly, Hannah may even be marrying during the next wedding season. Of course, Amish courting couples didn't let on about their intentions.

"How's Jacob these days?" Esther pretended to be nonchalant.

Hannah gave her freind a sidelong glance, a tiny smile curving her bow lips. "Gut, I suppose."

"You can't fool me, Hannah Kurtz. I'm thinking you'll be helping Samuel and Rebecca plant a fair amount of celery this year." A good celery crop usually indicated a young maedel in the household would wed soon.

"Hmmm." Hannah didn't admit any such thing. "So I hear Andrew Fisher is back." Hannah turned the tables on Esther.

"Seems that way."

Hannah poked Esther playfully with a pointy elbow. "Could be a gut thing, ain't so?"

"I doubt it."

"Time will tell, I'm thinking." Hannah laughed softly. "He seems like a nice man."

"I don't know about that."

"Don't write him off too quickly, freind."

"I try not to think of him at all, actually, but he's working for Daed at the sawmill while Mose is out."

"Maybe you'll get to know him better."

"Maybe not."

"Ach, Esther, we never know what the Lord Gott has in store for us."

"I'm hoping it's not Andrew Fisher! Danki for the ride." Esther practically leaped from the buggy before it came to a complete stop beside the Stauffers' house.

"See you soon, Esther."

"Jah. Soon," she called over her shoulder before disappearing into the two-story white house.

Do I look that desperate that everybody is trying to match me with Andrew Fisher, of all people? Did I really tell him we could try to be freinden? After the way he treated me, I must need my head examined!

Chapter Three

"Do you really need me to go with you?" Esther asked Lydia a week later as she set plates of eggs, bacon, and pancakes on the table. Lydia plunked down plates of special gluten-free pancakes and scrambled eggs at Ella's and David's usual places at the big table.

There goes my plan to spend time with Sophie today. She enjoyed learning about Sophie's herbs and teas. She planned to grow some of the special herbs and to learn how to prepare them under Sophie's tutelage. But she had grown quite concerned about her niece and nephew. They had begun to look so pale and frail. Bouts of nausea and diarrhea left them fatigued. She *would* like to hear what this Dr. Kramer had to say.

Lydia rubbed a hand across her forehead. "Jah. I'd really like another set of ears there. Maybe I'm missing something." She cast a worried look in the direction of the doorway where her kinner had entered.

"I'll go with you. Maybe you should ask the doctor about your headaches while you're there."

"Nee. They do seem to be fewer now. I think Sophie's concoctions help me relax and sleep better."

"That's gut to hear."

"Can we leave right after breakfast?"

"As soon as I help Mamm clean up the kitchen."

After the silent prayer, Daed ate as ravenously as usual. Mamm and even Lydia appeared to have healthy appetites this morning. Esther sneaked glances at her niece and nephew. They both dug into their syrup-covered pancakes with gusto, but their interest fizzled after only a few bites. Ella rubbed her belly. David began to play with his food, swirling eggs in the sticky syrup.

"David, stop playing with your food and eat." Lydia used her most serious voice. "You too, Ella."

"I'm not hungry, Mamm," David said.

"Not hungry, Mamm," Ella repeated.

"Can you eat a few more bites for your aenti?" Esther hoped she could coax them to ingest a few more calories.

"You aren't doing so great there yourself, dochder." Daed nodded at Esther's plate.

Surprised, Esther glanced down at her untouched plate. "Ach! I'd better eat." She made a huge display of scooping up a forkful of eggs and shoveling them into her mouth. "Mmmm. Yummy!" She looked directly at the kinner. Truth be told, her own appetite had vanished with her concern for Ella and David. She struggled to swallow the mass of semi-cold eggs in her mouth and was relieved when Mamm and Daed began talking, thereby shifting the focus from her. *Now if Daed would hurry and signal for the end-of-meal prayer, I can dispose of this unappetizing mess glued to my plate.*

"It looks like it's going to be a beautiful day." Esther gazed at the clear, blue sky before she, Lydia, and the kinner climbed into the buggy Daed had hitched for them. "Maybe spring is here at last."

"I hope so." Lydia grew quiet, and a faraway expression crossed her face.

Ella and David, oblivious to their mamm's suddenly quiet demeanor, clambered into the back of the buggy, excited to be going on an outing — any outing, even a visit to the Englisch doctor.

"Was ist letz?" Esther touched Lydia's arm in concern.

"I'm worried about my kinner."

"We'll get them healthy again with the Lord Gott's help, jah?"

"I hope so."

Esther clucked to the horse who took off at a trot, apparently as eager for an outing as David and Ella. The morning commuter traffic had, for the most part, already journeyed through the area, heading for Washington, DC, or some other town further north. Fewer cars on the highway always made for a more pleasant trip. They didn't have too far to travel distance-wise to get to the doctor's office in nearby Maryville, but by horse and buggy, the trip took a good thirty to forty-five minutes.

Some of the children's enthusiasm waned as they drove into the parking lot at the medical office building. In fact, they got downright quiet. Esther feared she and Lydia might have to drag them out of the buggy. But, obedient children that they were, when their mamm said, "Kumm," they came. Esther grasped Ella's small, cool hand as Lydia took David's hand.

"You have cold hands for such a nice, sunny day." Esther held Ella's hand little tighter. The little girl nodded her head.

"She's probably anemic again," Lydia explained. "It always makes them feel cold. David's hand is cool, too."

"I don't understand why." *I wish I could figure out what was going on here.*

Lydia shrugged her sagging shoulders. These days, she seemed to be carrying the weight of the world. Esther wasn't sure how much more her schweschder could bear. She sent a silent prayer heavenward, asking the Lord to help Lydia and these precious little ones and to show her what to do to help them all.

"Whenever we used to come see Dr. Nelson, the room would be full," Lydia said. "Since I've been back and bringing the kinner to Dr. Kramer, there haven't been a lot of patients here. That at least makes the wait shorter. Maybe since it's spring, people aren't sick as much."

Maybe it's the doctor, Esther wanted to say but didn't. She needed to be fair, she scolded herself. No jumping to conclusions.

A door creaked open. "Mrs. Kauffman, you can bring the children back." The medical assistant who called them wore cartoon-character scrubs. A purple stethoscope dangled around her neck. Esther doubted that either of these would allay David's or Ella's fears.

Esther stood Ella on the floor. "Do you want me to come back with you?"

"Please." Lydia took David's hand again. She shepherded her kinner toward the open door.

"The doctor wants you to stop here first to get their blood drawn so he can have the results before he sees them." The young medical assistant led them into the lab.

Lydia merely nodded and guided David into the room where another young woman wearing a white lab coat waited. Ella squeezed Esther's hand in a death grip. Esther murmured reassurances to the little girl in Pennsylvania Dutch. "You can get the results right away?" she asked the woman selecting tubes from a tray.

"We can get certain results right here, like whether the children are anemic. Other tests we have to send out. Can you hop up in this chair for me?" She turned to David and patted the chair with the folding padded armrests on either side. She gave David an encouraging smile but didn't realize that Amish little ones usually didn't learn much English until they started school, so he understood little of what she said. Lydia repeated the request in Pennsylvania Dutch and led David to the chair. Hesitant but obedient, he hopped onto the chair. Lydia removed his jacket and pulled up his sleeves so the lab tech could decide which vein to use. Even though the day promised to be sunny and warm, Lydia had put jackets them since they had been so cold lately.

Please, Lord, let this go quickly and easily for them. Esther sensed their fear even though they remained quiet. She felt certain this was a fairly familiar procedure for them but still scary and unpleasant at best. She lifted Ella into her arms and whispered to her to draw her attention away from her bruder, even though the woman in the white coat blocked much of her view. Over Ella's head, Esther saw David squeeze his eyes tightly shut as the tech punctured a vein and gathered several tubes of blood. *At least she seems gut at her job. That's a plus.*

David didn't have to be told twice to jump down from the chair. He moved quickly to stand beside Lydia.

"Next." The lab tech smiled at Ella.

Ella clung tighter as Esther carried her across the room. To her relief, the little girl released her hold when she deposited her gently in the chair. She removed Ella's black cape, a miniature of her own cape hanging on the hook at home. She continued to murmur to her as the tech selected a vein and gathered her sample. Ella's lip trembled, and tears welled in her big, brown eyes, but she did not cry out.

"Gut girl," Esther whispered into her ear when she gathered the child in her arms again.

The cartoon-clad lady reappeared and led them to an examining room. She took temperatures and recorded vital signs in the charts, then left them to wait. "Dr. Kramer will be with you shortly."

"I'll finally get to meet the man," Esther mumbled.

"Behave," Lydia mouthed.

Both women turned at the knock on the door. They watched the doorknob turn and the door slowly swing open before they could utter a response to the knock.

"Good morning," a deep, gravelly voice boomed before the man had even gotten inside the room. The doctor was younger than Dr. Nelson. Esther guessed he was in his late thirties. His light brown hair was in desperate need of trimming, and she suddenly wished she had her scissors with her to at least snip off the strands of hair that fell over the man's brown, thick-lensed glasses. Small, almost shrewd eyes took in the children and both women. Apparently, the man was also in need of an iron since his green shirt looked a bit rumpled beneath his white lab coat. Esther had the urge to straighten the crooked brown-and-green tie around his neck. The man smiled a smile that curved his lips but failed to reach his eyes.

"Hello," Lydia began. "This is my sister, Esther Stauffer. I asked her to come with us today."

"Nice to meet you." The doctor extended his right hand to Esther.

She shook the man's rather cool, clammy hand briefly and mumbled some pleasantry. For some reason, she had the feeling Dr. Kramer scrutinized her the same way she assessed him. She barely managed to keep her hands from smoothing any stray strands of hair under her black bonnet. *Maybe this is how a lab rat feels.* It was an uncomfortable feeling, for sure. Relief claimed her when the doctor turned his attention to David and Ella.

"How are they doing?" Dr. Kramer looked at Lydia.

Esther wanted to shout, "Look at them. Can't you see they are wasting away?" She didn't want to embarrass her sister, so she held her tongue. She would behave as Lydia wished her to — as long as the man didn't do or say anything else foolish.

"Let's take a look. Who's going first?"

Esther plunked Ella down on the paper-covered examining table while the doctor studied her chart.

"It looks like she's lost weight. How is her appetite?"

Esther feared she would lose the battle with her tongue. She looked at Lydia, who had suddenly turned mute. "She starts out eating her meals but then says her tummy hurts," she answered for her sister. "She gets a few bites in and stops eating. Same with David." Esther nodded toward her nephew.

"Hmmm," was Dr. Kramer's only response.

She raised questioning eyebrows to her sister. Lydia scowled back at her.

The doctor turned his attention to Ella. "Well, Miss Ella, can you tell me where your tummy hurts? Can you point to the spot?"

Ella simply looked at the doctor with wide eyes.

"She doesn't understand." Either the man didn't try to communicate with the kinner during previous visits or he forgot they didn't understand English. Esther repeated the doctor's question for Ella. The little girl nodded in understanding and rubbed her lower abdomen with a tiny hand.

"Hmmm," Dr. Kramer said again. "It hurts all over?"

Again, Esther translated, and Ella nodded.

The doctor pressed his black stethoscope to the girl's chest and back. When satisfied her heart and lungs sounded okay, he looked into her mouth, nose, and ears. He motioned for her to lie down so he could press around on her belly. Ella complied and stoically endured the probing.

Lydia found her voice. "Sometimes she vomits and sometimes she has diarrhea." Lydia blushed but continued. "She seems tired a lot—listless, actually. David does too. They have the exact same symptoms." She was interrupted by a knock on the door.

The medical assistant cracked the door open wide enough to pass slips of paper through to the doctor. She withdrew her hand and clicked the door closed.

"CBC results. That's the blood test we just ran," he said to Lydia.

"Jah, I know. I'm familiar with that by now. Are they anemic?"

"I'm afraid so. Both children are anemic. We need to make sure they take a vitamin with iron."

"We can pick up some on the way home if you've run out," Esther mumbled. Lydia bobbed her head in silence.

Dr. Kramer finished up with Ella and repeated the same examination with David. "I'll want to see them back in a month—sooner, if they have other problems. We need to make sure they eat some high calorie foods—without gluten, of course."

"We've been watching their diet like hawks," Esther blurted out. "We even use separate plates, cooking pans, and utensils."

"Good. Good." The doctor nodded his head. "Can you try giving them milkshakes and adding butter to their vegetables? Any extra calories to help them regain their weight would be good."

"Jah. Jah. We can do that." Esther wanted to tell the man they'd been doing that but saved her breath.

"Do you have any more of that special bread and cookies?" Lydia asked. "They liked those, and I've run out."

"I'm sorry. Uh, I haven't...uh, received any new shipments."

"Oh." That single word captured all Lydia's frustration and disappointment.

"When was the last time the children had any of those foods?" Dr. Kramer asked.

"Maybe two days ago. Why? Should they not eat these either?" Lydia sounded worried.

"Oh, uh, no. They're fine. I merely wondered about their diet, that's all."

Lydia sighed in relief. Esther knew she wanted so much for her kinner to be healthy and to do the right things for them.

"I'll ask Kathy to drive us to the health food store in Lewistown. I'm sure they'll have ready-made cookies or the flour we need to bake some." She would do anything to ease Lydia's worries. Kathy Taylor was the middle-aged Englisch neighbor who gladly drove the Amish to places that would take too long to reach by horse and buggy. Esther felt sure Kathy would drive them as soon as she could schedule the trip.

"Those foods are very costly," Lydia said. "I've checked before when we lived in Pennsylvania."

"Leave it to me. Aenti Esther can help out."

Dr. Kramer scribbled some more in the children's charts. He asked them to wait for a moment while he briefly left the examining room. He returned right away with four small bottles of pills. "Here are some vitamin samples. This will save you a trip to the pharmacy. Maybe we'll have the bread and cookies next time." He repeated his diet instructions and re- minded Lydia to schedule the children's next ap- pointment.

Esther grabbed the bottles of pills before Lydia could reach for them and stuffed them into her hand- bag. She wanted to read the labels. A quick glance told her the bottles were sealed. *Now why did I want to know that?* It must be because of her suspicious nature or maybe because of all the mysteries she read.

Lydia straightened the children's clothes and helped them into their outerwear. Esther opened the door to the waiting room at the same instant that an older Amish man opened the outer office door.

"Mose!" Poor Mose Troyer looked years older and pounds thinner than he had when Esther last saw him. Was it only a couple of weeks ago? She hurried to his side. "How are you doing, Mose?"

"I can't seem to shake this cold or whatever it is." Mose turned his head before barking out a deep cough.

"Is there anything we can do for you and Martha?"

"Nee. Martha's been taking gut care of me. I've kumm to see about more medicine and to have Dr. Kramer listen to these lungs." A wheeze escaped at the end of Mose's speech.

"Mr. Troyer," the medical assistant called from the doorway. "I signed you in. You can come on back."

"That's gut. You won't have to wait," Esther said.

"Jah. I'm sure they don't want me coughing on anyone."

"You take care, Mose, and get better soon. Daed sure misses you at the mill."

Mose nodded and headed in the direction of the waiting medical assistant, his gait a little wobbly.

And the sooner you get back to work, the sooner Andrew Fisher can leave!

The sun felt almost hot shining into the gray buggy as they clip-clopped toward home. Ella's head bobbed then crashed against Esther's arm. A quick glance toward the backseat showed her that David was about to lose the battle with sleep as well. Lydia, sitting beside David for the return trip, stretched an arm around her son, pulling him close. He resisted initially but soon gave up the struggle and let his head loll against his mamm.

Esther smiled. "They're tuckered out."

"Jah," Lydia agreed. "I feel about done in my-self."

"How's your headache?"

"A dull pain."

"That's better then, ain't so?"

"I suppose."

"Is it okay if I stop at Kathy Taylor's and ask for a ride whenever it's convenient for her?"

"*Jah*." Lydia paused momentarily. "I've been wracking my brain to remember if the kinner might have been eating something they shouldn't and to come up with ways to help them gain weight if they can't eat breads and treats."

"It's hard to gain weight eating fruits and vege-tables. Maybe we can get some ideas at the health food store."

"Maybe."

The kinner never awoke during the ride home, even though Esther had to reposition Ella gently when she stopped to talk to Kathy Taylor. Lydia had been so quiet, Esther had to turn around when they got home to make sure she was awake.

Ella tried to focus her heavy eyes. "Home, Aen-ti?" she croaked in a sleep-raspy voice.

"Jah, dear one. I'll help you out."

Of all people, Andrew appeared out of nowhere to lift Ella out of the buggy. He reached to help Esther who tried unsuccessfully to resist his attention. "You could say danki," he whispered, keeping hold of her hand a bit too long. She extracted her hand from his and muttered, "Danki"

"Let's go help Grossmammi with the noon meal." Esther tugged Ella toward the house as An-drew assisted Lydia and David.

Esther felt like smacking herself. *Dummchen*! *I forgot the horse*! She felt certain her face flushed crimson if the heat was any indication. Why should she even care if she appeared foolish to Andrew? She raised her voice and shouted "Danki!" to the man who busily unhitched the horse.

The Stauffers were one of those families that rarely ate in silence—after the silent prayer, that is. Some families in the community did not converse as they ate. Esther had visited in some of those homes and had always been a little unnerved by the lack of voices. Forks scraping plates and belching were the only sounds if you didn't count the ticking of the wall clock. She much preferred her family's meal times. Someone always had something to share. What did unnerve her here at her home today was Andrew Fisher sitting across the table from her. Daed invited him again! He didn't haul Luke Troyer or his other helpers in, though, Esther noted wryly.

"How did the kinners' check-up go?" Daed paused between forkfuls of macaroni salad.

Lydia filled her parents in on the trip to see Dr. Kramer—what there was to tell.

"Kathy Taylor is going to drive me to the health food store tomorrow morning so I can find other gluten-free foods to help these little ones fatten up." Esther chucked Ella under the chin. The girl giggled. Her nap seemed to have given her some energy. She made a fair attempt to eat her meal. "Then we'll bake some bread and some cookies." Esther smiled at her niece sitting beside her.

"Gut. I'll send Andrew along to pick up some things I need at the hardware store." Daed set his fork on his plate and raised his glass of iced tea to his lips.

"What?" Esther's head snapped around to face her father. Her mouth stayed open in shock. Even Andrew had the good grace to look surprised.

"I'll make out my list." Daed totally ignored the expressions on both their faces.

"I can pick up what you need, Daed, like I've done many times before. I'm sure you need Andrew here to help you." Esther wanted to spend as little time with Andrew as possible. If she could get out of these cozy meals Daed kept arranging, she would certainly do so.

"The hardware store is new since Andrew lived here. It will be good for him to be familiar with the layout of the store in case I need him to make later trips on his own. I want you to show him where things are, dochder, since you are used to going there for me."

Daed's tone left no room for argument. If it weren't for the kinner, she'd cancel the whole trip. Then Daed could show Andrew the many sights in the hardware store. Instead, Esther hung her head and focused on her suddenly unappealing food.

"I think *you* should go tomorrow, Lydia. I'm sure you know more about the proper foods for David and Ella than I do," Esther whispered to her sister as they washed dishes and straightened up the kitchen.

"Nee. You're quite knowledgeable about their diet. Besides, Daed wants *you* to help Andrew at the hardware store." Lydia was unsuccessful in keeping the smirk from her face.

If it wasn't at her expense, Esther would rejoice that Lydia found something to smile about. "Pshaw!

You've seen one hardware store, you've seen them all. Besides the store has signs up as big as day to point you in the right direction. Andrew doesn't need any help."

This time, Lydia laughed out loud. "Why, Esther! I don't think you want to spend time in the company of handsome Andrew Fisher."

"You've got that right, schweschder."

"Are you bearing a grudge?"

"I'm trying not to. You have to admit, though, Andrew used to be mean to me."

"Used to be. Past tense. He was a mischievous bu, but I think he's probably changed."

"People keep saying that."

"You aren't convinced?"

"Nee, not really. But people don't always change for the better, you know. We've sort of called a truce, but that doesn't mean I want to be alone with him or at the same table with him or in the same room with him or…"

"Okay. Okay." Lydia elbowed Esther.

"I don't know what's gotten into Daed."

"Jah. It sure isn't like him to play matchmaker."

"Maybe he doesn't want to be responsible for an old maedel. Maybe he wants me out of the house."

"That's narrisch. Daed and Mamm love having you here. You're a big help to them."

"They have you and the kinner now, so maybe they think it's time I left the nest."

"I'm sure they simply want you to have a family of your own and be happy."

"You don't think Daed is throwing me to the wolves, so to speak?"

Lydia laughed again. "Are you saying Andrew is a wolf?"

"He could be, you know, a wolf in sheep's clothing. Maybe he hasn't changed, and he's pulled the wool over Daed's eyes."

"Ach, Esther!" Lydia laughed harder. "You read too much. I think you are worrying for nothing." Lydia raised her apron to wipe the tears from her eyes.

"Well, it is gut to see you laugh, even if you're laughing at me."

"I'm not laughing at you, Esther. I'm laughing with you."

"I'm not seeing much humor here myself."

Lydia burst out laughing again. This time, Esther joined in. She was so happy to see Lydia's face crinkled in laughter instead of puckered in a frown of pain or sadness.

It's for the kinner. You can survive Andrew's presence for a little while for the kinner. It would be the fastest hardware store visit ever!

Chapter Four

Esther muttered under her breath as she wiped down the kitchen table and countertops after breakfast the following morning. The happy, bright sun mocked her. How dare it be such a beautiful morning when she felt so grumpy and out of sorts!

"Cheer up, Esther." Lydia patted Esther's arm after she hung the checked dish towel on the hook near the sink.

"I still think *you* should go pick out foods for the kinner."

"But then who would show Andrew around the hardware store?"

"Ridiculous!" Esther spat out. "Utterly ridiculous!"

Lydia patted Esther's arm again. "It looks like your ride is here." Lydia nodded toward the window.

"Best get this over with." She washed and dried her hands, smoothed wisps of hair under her kapp, and snatched her handbag off the chair.

"Have fun." Lydia's lips twitched.

"Right. And wipe that smirk off your face."

Lydia choked back a laugh. "Here's some money. Let me know if you spend more than this." She pressed some dollar bills into her schweschder's hand. Esther wadded up the money and stuffed it into her handbag without bothering to look at it. Lydia sobered. "Danki, Esther. I appreciate your help."

Spontaneously, Esther reached out to hug her older schweschder briefly. "I'd do anything for you and the kinner. You know that." *Even spend time with Andrew Fisher.*

"Danki," Lydia said again.

"Well, here goes." Esther looked out the window at Kathy's minivan. She sighed when she saw Andrew bound across the driveway. He shaded his eyes with his hand and looked toward the house. Esther nodded, not sure he could see her in the doorway. Somehow, though, she got the impression he could see right into the house — and right into her heart and soul. She immediately shook off that crazy notion and trotted down the porch steps and out to the light green van.

"Gude mariye." Andrew slid open the van's back door and stepped aside for Esther to climb in.

"Gude mariye." She had hoped he would sit up front with Kathy, but apparently, he planned to sit in the back with her. Esther bent her head and crawled into the van. She scooted all the way across the seat, positioning herself behind Kathy, her shoulder touching the window. Kathy's fingers drummed on the steering wheel in time to the song that played softly on the radio. "Gude mariye," she repeated to the Englisch driver.

"G'morning, Esther."

"Do you remember Andrew?" she asked.

"Andrew Fisher? The little boy who always ran through my flowerbeds in a hurry to get some place or another?"

"That would be him," Esther confirmed.

"Hey! I didn't mean any harm. I always had lots to do. I'm sorry about your flowers." He did his best to look contrite.

"Jah, Kathy. He didn't know a daffodil from a dandelion. He probably still doesn't." Esther added that last bit while sneaking a peek at him out of the corner of her eye.

"Ach, Esther, I think I've learned the difference by now."

Kathy smiled at the sparring couple. "Ready?"

"Jah," Andrew and Esther responded simultaneously.

"Your dad mentioned needing things from the hardware store." Kathy glanced at them in the rear-view mirror.

"That's right. I'm sorry about the extra stop."

"No problem. It's right on the way."

"Danki, Kathy."

Esther clicked her seatbelt in place as Kathy started the engine. She stared out the window as if completely absorbed in the trees lining the road and the occasional oncoming car. Andrew lapsed into silence as well. Kathy hummed along with the radio after attempting to make small talk and receiving only one-word answers or grunts from the couple behind her. Andrew tapped his foot in time with the music. Esther wished the van would go faster so she could get this whole ordeal over with.

"Here we are." Kathy pulled the van alongside the sidewalk in front of the hardware store. "I'll park and watch for you to come out."

"Danki," Esther replied.

Andrew slid the door open then jumped out. He turned to assist her.

"I can manage."

"I'm sure you can. I'm trying to be gentlemanly, that's all." He tipped his straw hat at her and gave her his best smile. He grasped her arm lightly as she stepped out onto the sidewalk. "Danki would be the appropriate response."

"Right," she muttered through clenched teeth. Maintaining a truce would be much more difficult than she thought. She stepped away quickly, leaving a good distance between herself and Andrew.

The automatic doors opened as they approached the entrance. "The items Daed needs will be over here." Esther headed across the store. "As you can see, the signs tell you exactly where everything is located. Lighting and electrical supplies are over there." She pointed to the left. "Plumbing things are next, then seasonal stuff and so on." She felt like a tour guide.

"I see. Even my shallow little brain can comprehend."

"Gut to hear. I know what Daed usually needs. Did he give you a list?"

"Jah. Here." He produced a crumpled piece of paper with barely legible handwriting smeared across it.

"Where has this been?" She snatched the list from his hand and tried to smooth out the wrinkles.

"I put it in…" He patted the waistband of his broadcloth pants.

"Never mind." Esther felt heat rise to her face. "I can read it gut enough." She flounced down the aisle, anxious to gather what Daed needed and to get out. Hardware stores were not her favorite places. She'd rather be at a nursery or even a yarn shop. Though her knitting and crocheting skills were not the greatest, they at least surpassed her quilting ability. Mamm had been tutoring her on her domestic skills all winter. She was ever so glad spring had arrived and she could escape outside.

Andrew paid for the few items Esther was sure her daed did not really need, and they headed for the door. Kathy must have had her eyes glued on the front of the store. The van appeared seemingly out of nowhere the moment they stepped onto the sidewalk.

"Do you need to go anywhere else before the health food store?" Kathy asked.

"Nee, not for me," Esther replied.

"Me either," Andrew agreed.

"Alrighty. We're off." She stepped on the gas, propelling the van through the parking lot.

The scents of herbs and spices greeted them as soon as they entered the health food store. Esther had never been in there before. They grew their own healthy food. A sign reading "organic" hung over the refrigerated case of vegetables and fruits near the back of the store. Tall bins filled with wheat, rye, and buckwheat flours; assorted coffee beans; cinnamon sticks and ground spices; whole wheat pasta; shelled walnuts, almonds, pistachios, and pecans; and dried apples, pineapples, and cranberries occupied two outside rows of the store. Cereals, soups, and other ready-made packaged foods filled the center rows. Vitamins and supplements occupied most of the back part of the store. Glancing at the neat rows of bottles and vials, Esther recognized some of the same herbal preparations Sophie sold. The others she didn't even have a clue how to pronounce let alone know what they were used for.

There weren't any overhead signs to indicate the products shelved on each row as there were in the grocery store or even the hardware store. This place wasn't nearly as large, though, so Esther figured it wouldn't take her too long to wander the aisles to find what she needed.

Before she could take another step, a pleasant young woman wearing jeans and a t-shirt covered by a long, dark-green bib apron approached her. The woman's faded blonde hair was pulled back into a braid that hung halfway down her back. She smiled broadly, showing even white teeth. Her big green eyes crinkled at the corners. "May I help you find something?"

"Jah, I believe you can. My little niece and nephew have celiac disease, and I'm trying to find foods or ingredients they can eat."

"Well, you came to the right place. Our gluten-free section is right over here." The young woman walked a few aisles over, her white tennis shoes silent on the tile floor. "We have some ready-made foods like cereal, crackers, and cookies. We also have flours and even mixes that are gluten free. While you're browsing, I can print some information off our computer system about gluten-free diets and foods, if you like."

"Danki—I mean, thank you. That would be ever so helpful."

"Great. It will take me only a few minutes. Here is a basket if you need one."

Esther nodded and smiled as she accepted the green plastic basket from the clerk. She picked up one product after another, reading the ingredient lists and directions for cooking. *These foods are rather pricey. The kinner need to put on weight fast. I'll get a package of these cookies and then learn how to make them myself.* With that decision made, she plopped a package of cookies and a box of crackers in the basket.

The young woman's voice reached her from the computer across the store. "Your wife is right over there." When Esther heard, "Danki," she realized the girl spoke to Andrew. She almost dropped the basket to race around the store to tell her this man was definitely not her husband, but she didn't want to create a scene. Evidently, the woman didn't know that Amish men grew beards once they married. Maybe she thought they were Mennonites. Old Order Mennonite men remained clean-shaven even after they married.

When Andrew came into view, his wide smile irritated Esther to no end. He strode quickly down the aisle where she stood perusing labels. "Why did you let her think we were m-married?"

"No use making a big deal." He shrugged. "No harm done."

"Oooh, you!"

"Calm down, dear." He patted her arm.

Esther moved out of his reach, shooting a ferocious scowl at him. *Glad he's so amused.* She quickly added a couple cans of soup, packages of buckwheat and potato flour, and certified gluten-free oats to her basket. She wondered which other products would be best for baking when the mistaken, but nice, young woman brought over the computer print outs. She explained some of the information and even suggested which items to purchase. She didn't try to push the most expensive items, which increased Esther's already favorable opinion of her. "Danki so much for all your help." She truly would have been at a loss otherwise.

"No problem. I'm glad I could help. I'm a celiac, too, so I've had to learn all about this stuff. Please feel free to come in any time. I'll share whatever information I can."

"You're so kind."

"Are you ready to check out?"

"I believe so."

"My name is Patty," the young woman called over her shoulder, her braid swishing from side to side as she walked. "I'll write it on a store card. You can always come by and ask for me or call if—" She broke off, obviously unsure if Esther could make phone calls.

"I could call from a public phone," she assured her.

"Good." At the counter, Patty scribbled her name on a little white store business card and began ringing up the order. Esther left some space between herself and Andrew, still a bit miffed that he let this woman think they were a couple. She counted out the money Lydia had given her and added some of her own money to make up the difference.

As if reading her mind, Patty said, "It will really save you money once you start making as many foods from scratch as you can."

"Jah, I hope so," Esther replied then worried she seemed rude or unappreciative. "I—I mean, I—we would like to make the food from scratch anyway, b-but these things are a bit, uh, costly."

Patty chuckled. "They sure are. It's hard for me to afford them. I bake muffins and breads from scratch myself. I hope you don't mind, but I included some recipes with the information I gave you in case you're interested."

"I'm very interested. I'm sure they will be a big help. *You* have been a big help. I'm ever so grateful."

They finished their transaction, and Andrew lifted the full brown paper bag with "recycled" stamped in green in its center. "I can take it," Esther said. She was accustomed to doing things for herself.

"I've got it." He did not relinquish the bag. "Let's find Kathy. She should be finished at the bank by now."

Like the ride into town, the ride home was mostly silent. Kathy's radio played catchy tunes and her fingers again tapped out the rhythm on the steering wheel. Andrew's foot wiggled in time with the music, and Esther stared out the window, lost in thought. Her brain tried out various combinations of ingredients to concoct edible recipes for David and Ella. She felt sure Mamm and Lydia would be much more knowledgeable about baking and cooking. She had always plotted to be out of the kitchen at meal preparation times unless Mamm caught her before she could escape the house. Now she wished she had paid more attention. *Never too late to learn.*

"Are you going to the singing on Sunday?" Andrew asked in Pennsylvania Dutch, breaking into her reverie.

She had always thought it was a little rude to converse in Dutch in the presence of their Englisch drivers. It was like deliberately leaving them out of the conversation. Despite her tendency to be outspoken, she didn't want to hurt anyone or to have her

Englisch neighbors think she was saying anything bad about them. "Probably not," she answered in Englisch. She slapped her forehead. "Ach. I forgot. I did promise Hannah I'd help her. Church is at Rebecca and Samuel Hertzler's place so they're hosting the singing."

"That means Hannah is pretty much hosting the singing, ain't so?" Andrew took Esther's cue and spoke in Englisch.

"Jah, I suppose so. It will be her first time since she was baptized almost a year ago."

"Then you will go?"

"Ummm. I guess I have to."

"Don't sound so excited about it!"

Esther elbowed him in the ribs. Maybe she could think of some excuse to get out of going.

They thanked Kathy when she stopped the van beside the Stauffers' house. Esther reached into her handbag for money to pay her, but Andrew was quicker and produced a wad of bills he thrust out to Kathy.

"I have the money." She still fumbled inside her purse.

"I've got it. Besides, your daed is paying me pretty well even if I am just learning about the sawmill business."

"Maybe Mose will be back soon and you'll be able to work for the Beilers and build furniture like you planned."

"Maybe. This is fine for now, though." Andrew shot her a wink and a smile.

Hurry and get well, Mose.

Esther spent the next morning with her plants. She still kept her more delicate, weather-sensitive plants and seedlings in the greenhouse. Hardier plants had been moved outside. She was reasonably sure the danger of frost was over. It seemed spring had finally arrived in Southern Maryland. She'd already had many customers drop by to purchase flowers and vegetables. And she had already planted her own garden, looking forward to all the fresh food that would soon grace their table.

After cleaning up the kitchen from the noon meal and with Ella and David down for their naps, Esther, Lydia, and Leah began brainstorming and devising recipes to try out using the newly purchased gluten-free products.

"I think the suggestions from Patty may save us some time and experimenting." Esther handed the recipes from the store clerk to her mudder. "What do you think, Mamm?"

"Jah. If she already knows these ingredients combine well, there's no use trying to reinvent the recipes."

"Maybe we can tweak them a bit to add different fruit to the muffins," Lydia suggested.

"I don't see why not." Mamm scanned the papers.

Each woman chose a different baked good to mix up. Since Mamm was the most experienced baker, she experimented with the bread recipe. Lydia substituted home-canned peaches for berries in a muffin recipe. Esther tackled a cookie recipe, adding cocoa powder since David was especially fond of chocolate.

The women baked all afternoon until time to prepare the evening meal. Esther thought she had finally produced palatable cookies. The real test would come when David emerged from his nap.

She held out a chocolate cookie for the little boy. "Tell me what you think, David." Esther smiled at her nephew. She held her breath, waiting for David's verdict.

He reached for the cookie, raised it to his lips, and bit off a chunk. A huge smile broke out on his face. "Mmmm. Wunderbaar." He quickly shoved the rest of the cookie into his mouth.

"Hurray!" Esther sang out. She picked up a second cookie and handed it to Ella. She, too, smacked her lips when she tasted the cookie. "It looks like this recipe is a keeper!"

"Ach! We've got to get supper going." Mamm glanced at the wall clock. "I didn't know it was so late."

"I'll help, Mamm. It looks like you have a customer, Esther." Lydia nodded toward the window. A white van had stopped near the greenhouse.

"I'll take the kinner out with me."

Supper time was more pleasant than it had been in a while. David and Ella ate without complaining about tummy aches. And they actually liked the new bread their grossmammi had baked for them. Esther thought the pinch of bread she had sampled tasted more like cardboard than bread, but she kept her opinion to herself for fear the kinner wouldn't try it. Of course, the thick homemade strawberry jam Mamm smeared on each slice for the little ones probably greatly enhanced the flavor.

Adding to Esther's delight over David's and Ella's heartier appetite was the fact that Andrew Fisher returned to his aunt and uncle's house for his evening meal. She would not have to feel his jade green eyes watching her from across the table. She would not have to see his smile or endure his teasing—even though it was not done with a mean spirit. She would not have to worry about him stretching his long legs and accidently touching her foot. Was it accidental? A little voice in her head nagged at her. Of course it was! Oh great; now she had voices warring in her head, all because of Andrew Fisher! She shouldn't even be thinking about him. He was out of sight so should be out of mind as well.

Esther relaxed and actually enjoyed her meal. "Gut, Ella. You've eaten all your food. You, too, David." Both children beamed.

"It looks like your appetite has improved as well, dochder." Daed pointed his fork at Esther's nearly empty plate.

"Jah, I guess it has. I'm so glad the kinner are eating and feeling better. You wouldn't think a couple doses of the vitamins and iron and the new foods would perk them up so much."

"I've been noticing a gradual improvement the last couple days. Now maybe *you* can put back on the weight *you* lost." Mamm wore a concerned expression.

"Weight loss? Me?"

"You hadn't noticed?"

"I haven't paid any attention, I suppose."

"Hmm," was all Mamm said, but she gave Lydia a knowing look, and the two exchanged smiles. Esther deliberately ignored them and scooped a forkful of coleslaw into her mouth with gusto.

After Daed read from the big family Bible and the family had prayed together, he and Mamm retired for the evening. Lydia tucked David and Ella into bed and rejoined her schweschder in the living room. Esther's frown deepened into a scowl as she examined the afghan she was knitting. "Whoever de-

signed this system of twists and turns on two needles? Crocheting is much easier." She prepared to rip
out stitches.

Lydia placed her hand on the soft, dark-blue
yarn. "Wait. Let me see before you destroy it." She
scrutinized the stitches. "You do nice work when you
take your time. Here is your problem. Take out these
last few stitches. Don't go ripping it all apart."

"I guess I get frustrated too easily. I don't know
why Mamm insists I master the art of knitting. I can
crochet passably. And she spent the entire winter tutoring me in quilting."

"She thinks Amish wives need to do all three."

"I'm not an Amish wife."

"Don't you want to be?"

Esther shrugged her shoulders. "I'm happy with
my life. I like growing my plants and learning about
medicinal herbs from Sophie. It's amazing how much
she knows. I don't think I'll ever master it all."

"Don't change the subject."

"I thought that subject was talked out."

"Hardly. I know how much you love David and
Ella and all kinner, actually. Don't you want some of
your own?"

"I'd have to find a man I could tolerate first—or one
who could tolerate me."

"I think I know one who would like to apply for
that position."

"Really?"

"Jah. He's right under your nose. His feet have
been under our table a lot lately."

"Andrew Fisher?" Esther squealed. "That's narrisch."

"Shhh! You'll wake everyone. I don't see any craziness in that at all. He's considerate, helpful, and pleasant to look at."

"Looks can be deceiving. I still don't trust him."

Lydia clicked her tongue in exasperation. "Well then, there's always Ol' Silas."

"Ach, Lydia! You are narrisch, for sure. You know, you're older than I am. Maybe Ol' Silas would be a better match for you."

"I'm not looking for a husband."

"That makes two of us then."

"You're impossible, schweschder!"

"You are, too. I guess we're two peas in a pod."

"All the same, I think you should let Daed or me drive you to the singing on Sunday so you can accept a ride home."

"I don't plan on riding home with anyone but that old horse out there. If the Lord Gott wants me to be an old maedel, then that's what I'll be."

"And if He doesn't?"

The question hung in the air and pierced Esther's heart. "Gut nacht, Lydia." She stood, stretched, and hugged her sister briefly on her way out of the room.

"Gut nacht," Lydia called after her.

Chapter Five

Esther sat beside Hannah Kurtz on the backless wooden bench at Sunday preaching in the Hertzlers' swept-clean barn. She was impressed with how eagerly and thoroughly her freind had embraced the Amish faith and way of life after having been raised Englisch. Hannah hardly squirmed on the hard bench anymore and seemed to understand most of the sermons spoken in High German.

Esther pretended not to notice her companion's blue eyes dart their gaze across the barn to Jacob Beiler, who sat beside none other than Andrew Fisher. She also pretended not to feel the butterflies flapping around in her stomach when she realized Andrew's gaze had shifted to her. This time *she* wiggled, smoothed an imaginary wrinkle from her black apron, and forced herself to concentrate on the minister.

The three-hour service seemed six hours long today. Esther wanted to bolt from the barn but forced herself to walk with the other women who would be serving the common meal. She wasn't quite sure why she was so jittery. She almost didn't trust herself to carry any heavy platters or cups of hot kaffi.

She inhaled deeply to calm her nerves and told herself to focus on the cloudless blue sky, the bright warm sun, and the twittering robins and blue jays. The men had made quick work of setting up tables under the towering oak trees. Esther snatched up bowls of beets and pickles—foods she figured she could transport without making a mess—and set them on a table. She avoided making eye contact with the men seated at the table and steered clear of Andrew Fisher altogether. She was heading back to the kitchen when Hannah caught up with her

"Was ist letz? You don't seem like yourself."

She shrugged her shoulders but kept silent.

"Are you upset with me about something?"

"Ach, Hannah, of course not." She raised her eyes to meet Hannah's cornflower-blue ones. "How could I ever be upset with you?" Esther had been Hannah's staunchest supporter and had even defended her to the school board and to Jacob when the true reason for her presence in St. Mary's County became known.

"Is it the singing tonight, then?"

"Nee, jah, I don't know. I haven't been to one since—since—"

"Since Andrew was here the last time?"

"Jah. And that didn't go so well."

"You seemed like you had a gut time then."

"Hannah, don't you remember? He teased me most of the time."

"As I recall, you gave it right back to him. Jake and I were pretty amused."

A sly smile replaced her frown. "I guess I did keep right up with him."

"I'll say!" Hannah laughed. Esther surprised herself with a chuckle of her own. "I really appreciate your helping me with the singing. Don't worry. Everything will be fine."

"That's easy for you to say." She hoped her hands were steady enough now to carry a pitcher of iced tea out to the table full of men. Maybe she should ask Hannah to take it. She turned to ask when she spied Martha Troyer entering the kitchen. The older woman looked frazzled and worn out, as if she hadn't slept in a very long time. She swayed slightly as she crossed the room.

"Are you all right?" Hannah rushed to take one of Martha's arms and lead her gently to the big oak table.

Esther slid the pitcher of tea further back from the table's edge and quickly took Martha's other arm. "Was ist letz?"

"I'm tired, girls." She panted as if out of breath. "I've been at the hospital all night."

"Is Mose worse?" Esther was almost afraid to ask. She recalled how ill Mose looked when she ran into him at the doctor's office.

"He wasn't getting any better, though he's taking his pills. Yesterday, I could hear all the rattling in his chest when I wasn't even standing right beside him. Of course, the doctor's office was closed on a Saturday, so I asked Kathy to drive us to the Urgent Care Center. She took one look at Mose and drove us straight to the hospital."

"Is-is he okay?" Hannah ventured.

"They gave him some medicine in his veins and put an oxygen mask on him. He was resting much easier when I left."

"Gut. I'm glad to hear that." Hannah patted Martha's thin arm.

"He'd been taking his medicine all along, hadn't he?" Esther asked.

"Jah. It was the strangest thing, though." Martha lowered her voice.

"What's that?" Esther leaned closer to hear better.

"I had some of his medicine with me. The doctors at the hospital kept telling me they wanted to see his medicine, not his vitamins. But, Esther, he didn't have vitamins. Those were the pills Mose had been taking for the pneumonia."

"How odd!" Hannah exclaimed.

"Very odd..." Esther's voice trailed off. Her face took on a faraway expression.

"It's gut Mose is getting help and is starting to feel better now." Hannah patted Martha's arm.

"Jah. Kathy will drive me back to the hospital later. Bishop Sol didn't have a problem with that, even though it's Sunday and all."

"I'll go with you, if you like." Esther suddenly tuned back into the conversation.

"Danki, dear, but I'll be all right. Luke will go with me, I'm thinking. Let me go help serve."

"We can manage, Martha," Hannah assured her. "Why don't you rest up?"

"Nee, it helps if I keep busy." To prove her point, Martha lifted the pitcher of tea and headed for the door.

"At first, I thought you wanted to get out of attending the singing, but now, upon closer scrutiny..."

Hannah paused and looked right into her friend's eyes. "I see you are hatching some sort of scheme. What are you thinking, my detective freind?"

"I'm not sure yet."

"Don't even think of planning something that will get you out of the singing." She poked Esther's shoulder playfully with her forefinger.

"Me?" She gasped in mock horror. "I would never dream of doing such a thing."

Hannah made a face at her and thrust some napkins into her hands. "Here, take these out for the second table. The first group has finished."

As always at singings, girls lined one side of the barn on wooden benches, and boys lined the other. Most of the girls chattered, awaiting the start of the first song. Most had hopeful expressions on their faces as they stole glances at the boys opposite them. Would this be the night a special young man asked to drive them home?

"I'm getting too old for this," Esther grumbled to herself handing, her horse off to one of the young men who had been assigned the task of seeing to the horses and buggies. *All the people are younger than I am. They're probably all seventeen or eighteen, maybe twenty or twenty-one.* Surely no one had attained her advanced age of twenty-five. Hannah was close to that, but she didn't really count since she had been Englisch up until a little over a year ago. It seemed the Englisch waited longer to marry and start families.

Esther had been raised expecting to marry by age twenty or so. She should already have one or two kinner by now. Even Sarah Fisher, the school teacher prior to Hannah who had married Zeke Esh last fall, was expecting her first boppli. She might be all of twenty years old.

"I don't belong here." She sighed. She hadn't even particularly enjoyed singings when she was younger and Lydia had dragged her to them. Her shoulders slumped. She ducked her head. If she turned and fled now, no one would even notice. No one except Hannah. Esther sighed more deeply. Hannah was counting on her. She couldn't let her freind down. She could endure a few hours of misery, she supposed. She straightened her shoulders and attempted to paste on a pleasant expression or at least some expression to mask the scowl she felt certain had taken up residence on her face.

"Ach, Esther! You're here!" Hannah rushed to the entrance as she approached.

"Jah. I do keep my word."

"Don't look like you're being sent to the gallows." Hannah laughed. "You'll have a gut time."

"I think you mentioned that before."

"But you don't believe me?"

"Let's just say I'm skeptical." Her gaze roved the barn.

"He's not here—yet," Hannah whispered behind her hand.

"I'm not looking for anyone in particular."

"Uh huh!" Hannah elbowed her freind playfully. "Kumm on. We'll be starting soon."During the third song, Esther began to relax. The tension eased in her shoulders, the frown lines smoothed out on her forehead, and her breathing became even and regular. She might have a good time after all. She enjoyed the music, and her singing voice wasn't half bad. She could even easily return Hannah's smile. Until the newcomers entered the Hertzlers' barn, that is.

The singing was almost over and the socializing ready to begin when Andrew Fisher strode into the barn with Luke Troyer on his heels. *Almost made it.* The two latecomers stole across to the men's side to perch beside Jacob Beiler. Right away, her shoulders tightened, and her voice faltered on a song she had sung since childhood. *There goes the evening.* She did want to find out from Luke how Mose was doing, though.

Near the end of the last song, Hannah tapped her on the shoulder and tilted her head in the direction of the refreshment table. Esther bobbed her head affirmatively and rose to follow Hannah. They would make sure everything was in order for the young people who would be very thirsty and ravenous.

As the young folk began mingling, Luke became the center of attention. His face, framed by golden-blond hair, blushed a bright crimson. Esther abandoned her post to maneuver her way through the crowd to talk to Luke. Though a few years younger than Esther, he towered over her at about six feet tall. Firm muscles in his arms had become well defined from his work on the farm and at Jeremiah Yoder's machine shop. Eyes flecked with gold and green hues shifted from one to another of the young people gathered around him.

"How is Mose doing?" Esther asked before anyone else could form the question. "Is he any better?"

"Jah, I believe he is. The new medicine seems to be working. He ate some supper and even walked in the hallway a little with Mamm and me."

"Gut news, for sure and for certain. Thank the Lord."

"He may be able to come home tomorrow or Tuesday if he keeps doing well, the lung doctor said."

"We're so relieved." Rebecca had entered the barn to check on the young people and to see if they needed anything. Ten or eleven years ago, she would have been at singings. Now she was a married fraa with two young school-age sons, two preschool daughters, and twins not yet a year old. She smiled at Hannah. "I'm glad the singing is here. It doesn't seem possible I attended singings not so very long ago. Now I'm ancient."

"You're far from ancient," Hannah assured her.

"The children are all in bed and Samuel is reading the Budget, so I thought I'd take a few moments to step outside and greet everyone." Rebecca arrived right in time to hear Luke tell about his daed.

"We'll keep Mose and Martha and all of you in our prayers." Esther spoke the group.

"Danki." Luke tried to step back from the center of the crowd.

From the corner of her eye, Esther caught Andrew watching her as she talked to Luke. An aggravated expression crossed his face until he looked her in the eyes. Then a sly smile tugged at his lips. *Now what is that all about?*

"Refreshments are ready." Hannah pointed to the table.

She didn't need to call twice. The group around them dispersed. The singers snatched up cookies and juice before pairing off to talk. Luke grabbed a handful of cookies and retreated to the shadows where Andrew chatted with Jacob. Rebecca grabbed a one to nibble on her way back to the house.

When the group had all helped themselves to cookies, brownies, chips, and juice, Hannah moved away from the table and waited for Jacob to join her. Esther remained rooted to her spot near the table, not sure what she should do. She didn't want to be paired up with anyone. Besides, the men there, with a couple of exceptions, were too young for her. Maybe she could sidle over to the door and slip into the night unnoticed.

Esther's eyes roamed the barn. Gut. No one paid any attention to her. Satisfied, she turned her back on the group to make her exit. She gasped and clutched her chest as though to push her heart back down into its proper place when a strong hand clamped down on her shoulder. She didn't dare open her mouth to scream for fear her heart would go flying out.

"Going somewhere?" a deep, familiar voice questioned.

"Probably to the hospital now." Esther patted her thumping chest. "You nearly scared the life out of me." She tried to shrug his hand off, but his grasp was too firm.

"You're not leaving so soon, are you?"

"Well, jah, I had thought about it."

"The night is still young."

"I—I'm tired."

"Would you like me to drive you home? I wouldn't want you to fall asleep and let the horse stumble into a ditch."

"Danki, but I think I can make it. How did you know I was leaving? I didn't even see you."

"I've been watching from over there." Andrew nodded to the shadowy corner.

"You've been watching *me*?"

"Jah. I was watching you weasel your way to the door." Now Andrew did laugh out loud.

"I'm certainly glad I kept you entertained, Andrew Fisher!" Esther stomped her foot very near Andrew's toes.

He stepped back quickly to protect his feet. "Now, Essie, don't go getting riled up."

"It's Esther!"

"I know. I know. I liked your nickname, but I guess we're not kinner anymore."

"Nee, some of us have grown up."

Andrew wiggled his eyebrows. "Are you saying I haven't grown up?"

"If the shoe fits…"

"You know, *Essie*, sometimes it's a gut thing to retain some child-like qualities. It's gut for the soul to have fun and laugh. It keeps us young in mind and spirit, ain't so?"

"Hmmm. Having child-like qualities and being childlike are two different things, I'm thinking."

Andrew laughed. "Are you always so hard to get along with?"

"Me? I don't think so." When had they left the barn? Suddenly, she noticed a half moon and stars smiling down from the inky sky. Crickets chirped, and other insects chattered and sang their evening songs. Should she run back inside? Only moments ago, she had wanted to escape. Now she was outside and wanted to run back inside. How did things get so complicated in a matter of minutes? Andrew. He turned everything topsy turvy.

"Beautiful night." Andrew gazed at the clear, star-speckled sky.

"Jah. I-I'd better get back inside."

"You were the one inching your way toward the door. Now you want to go in?"

"Well, I…uh, better help Hannah."

"Hannah has everything under control. Besides, Jacob is there to help her."

"I suppose so, but I promised to help."

"And you have helped. You're allowed to have some fun. I'm sure Hannah would be the first to agree with me."

"Fun? With you?" Esther blurted the words before she could censor them or her change her tone. The lantern light from the barn highlighted his dejected countenance. She had to try to make amends. "I-I mean, I should be cleaning up or something."

"Couldn't you stay outside for a few more minutes?"

"I-I guess. I don't want to give anyone the wrong impression that we're, uh...you know...uh, a couple."

"Is there anyone in particular you're concerned about? Is there someone else you'd rather be outside talking to instead of me?"

"Of course not! I don't want to be the subject of gossip, that's all."

"I can't help but think maybe if someone else was out here with you it would be different. Maybe you'd let that someone else drive you home."

"Andrew Fisher!" Esther exploded. "The buwe here are just that—buwe. I'm older and not interested. Besides, I drove myself here. Am I supposed to tie my horse to the back of someone else's buggy to pull my buggy along or let him find his own way home?" Esther folded her arms across her chest and glared at him.

A mischievous grin spread across his face.

"And exactly what are you grinning at?" She knew her checks must be tomato red and was glad for the dark of night.

He tried to wipe the smile from his face but did not succeed. "Don't go getting all mad, Essie..."

"Esther!"

"Essie! You look, uh..."

"I look what?"

"Uh, you look...uh, well, you look funny—but in a gut way—when you get all puffed up. Your eyes look like big chocolate drops, and—"

"I am not all puffed up!"

"You know what I mean."

"You are incorrigible!" Esther turned and started to stomp back into the barn.

"Wait, Esther." He put a hand out and touched her arm tentatively as if afraid she'd snap it off and smack him with the bloody end of it. She did stop and turn back to face him. "Don't be mad at me. Okay?"

She exhaled noisily, shrugged her shoulders, and let the aggravation drain out of her. "Jah. Okay. I'll try."

"Gut. I'll help you clean up if you like."

She shrugged again. "Suit yourself."

Andrew trudged along behind her like a duckling following its mother.

Couples had been slipping away one-by-one. A few singles were still mingling when Esther entered the barn several paces ahead of Andrew. She did not turn to look back at him, nor did she speak to him for fear of giving the impression they were a courting couple. Luke Troyer still lounged at the shadowed fringe of the barn.

"Hannah, let me help you," she called as she neared the refreshment table where Jacob helped Hannah clean up the few leftovers. She pretended she didn't see the smile and nudges the two exchanged as they watched her approach.

"I'm gut, Esther. It looks like everyone enjoyed all the cookies and brownies. There isn't much to do, and Jake has been helping. Go and enjoy yourself."

"I'm not—I wasn't—"

"Enjoying yourself?" Jacob prompted.

"Well, *I* was," Andrew interjected. He snatched up a leftover oatmeal raisin cookie and popped it into his mouth.

Esther turned her back on the threesome and strode purposefully toward the shadows.

Andrew had hoped Esther wouldn't get upset with him, that their truce meant something to her. He had watched her inch her way to the door from his shadowy corner earlier and had been amused by her escape attempt. He hadn't wanted to ruffle her feathers, as he seemed to do without even trying. He simply wanted to talk to her. Apparently, he had inadvertently irritated her again.

Now, his shoulders sagged in dejection as he watched Esther approach Luke. He nearly choked on the cookie that suddenly tasted like the sawdust he swept up daily at the mill. He knew Luke was younger than her. After her speech about everyone being younger and her lack of interest, was she really considering a relationship with Luke? Why should he care? He shouldn't, but his heart hurt anyway.

Watching her converse with Luke, Andrew shifted his weight from one foot to the other. Subconsciously, his hands clenched and unclenched. He noticed the worried look Hannah exchanged with Jacob. As Jake took a step in his direction, probably to divert his attention, Andrew headed across the barn with long strides. He had to do something. He'd reached the end of his endurance.

"So is Mose going back to see Dr. Kramer when he is released from the hospital?" Esther apparently had more questions for Luke. What was she up to?

"Nee. The lung doctor said he would take over the case," Luke replied.

"Hmmm. Interesting." She tapped her cheek. Andrew could almost see the wheels turning in her brain. "I'm glad Mose—"

"Luke, do you need a ride home or are you going with Esther?" he interrupted, his voice harsher than he'd intended.

Obviously startled, she whirled to face Andrew. "Whatever made you say that?"

"I...uh, in case you two want to talk more." *Alone*, he almost added.

"Nee, if you don't mind dropping me off, Andrew, I need to get home so my sister Linda can get home to her family."

"No problem." Andrew attempted to soften his brusque tone.

Luke looked at Esther, shrugged his shoulders, and followed Andrew to the door.

"Tell Mose we're thinking of him," she called.

Luke nodded and lengthened his stride. "Wait up, Andrew!"

"What's with him?" Esther asked Hannah once Luke and Andrew were out of earshot.

"You honestly don't know?"

"Nee. How would I know what goes on in that pea brain of his? All of a sudden, he got all grumpy."

"Jealousy," Hannah mumbled.

"Huh?"

"Andrew was jealous. You were talking to Luke."

"So?"

"Esther, really, can't you see that Andrew obviously has feelings for you?"

"Ach, Hannah! That's ridiculous!"

"I don't think so."

Esther's mouth opened into an 'O' but no sound came out. She stared at the doorway through which the two men had disappeared.

Chapter Six

"Mamm, I don't see why I have to stay inside and make strawberry jam. I've helped you with that a zillion times."

"*Helped.* That's just it. You always help with household chores. You don't do them from start to finish on your own."

"That doesn't mean I don't know how to do things."

Mamm raised her eyebrows and studied her younger dochder's pouty face. "Let's see about that."

"Mamm, I have a business to take care of."

"Lydia and I can keep an eye out for any customers. This isn't a market day, so business should be slower."

"Mamm!" Esther didn't like the sound of her wail, but she was helpless to prevent it.

"Esther, your daed and I did you no favors by letting you do so many outside chores instead of learning how to run a household on your own."

"I know enough, Mamm. It's not like I'll have my own home anytime soon."

"You never know what the Lord Gott has in store for you. Now, what are you going to do first to make the jam?"

"First, I have to wash and cap the mountain of strawberries over there that David and Ella helped me pick yesterday."

"Jah."

"Ugh! That will take forever. I'd rather pick the berries than process them." Esther continued to mutter. She exhaled forcibly, setting the ribbons on her white kapp aflutter.

"Kumm, kumm, dochder. Let's be cheerful. Think how much you'll enjoy the jam on a slice of fresh-baked bread — that you baked, by the way."

Esther heaved a deeper sigh and cast a dirty look in the direction of the plump, red strawberries before filling the sink with hot, soapy water. She washed the pint jars and lids thoroughly, rinsed off the soap, and placed them in the huge pan of boiling water to keep them clean and hot until she was ready to fill them.

When all traces of soap had been rinsed from the sink, Esther filled it, this time with cold water. She eyeballed the jars and fruit to try to determine the number of berries she would probably need for this batch. She plopped a bunch of them into the water and looked questioningly at her mudder. Of course, Mamm's expression was blank. Behind Mamm, Lydia motioned for Esther to add more berries. Esther scooped up a couple more handfuls and tossed them into the sink. She stopped adding berries when, out of the corner of her eye, she saw Lydia curl her thumb and forefinger into the okay sign.

She washed, capped, and sliced berry after berry and filled the waiting large kettle with the slices. Red juice ran up her arms, nearly to her elbows. Red berry fragments lodged under her fingernails. *No dirt under my nails, now, Andrew Fisher.* Now why would *he* invade her thoughts?

Esther drained the sink after slicing the last berry, rinsed and dried her hands, and lifted the heavy kettle onto the hot stove. She poured in several cups of sugar. Before she could set the canister of sugar down on the counter, she caught sight of Lydia's raised index finger.

She threw in one more cup of sugar, snapped the lid closed on the big plastic canister before sliding it across the counter, and picked up the long-handled wooden spoon. Now she'd have to stand beside the hot stove, mashing and stirring the berries until the precise consistency was reached. She sighed again. She'd much rather be outside with her plants where at least there was the hope of catching a breeze.

Finally, the time had come for Esther to fill the pint jars with jam and to set the jars in the hot water bath to process. Now, she could clean up the kitchen and escape outside as soon as the jam was through processing.

"That batch looks pretty good, dochder. Now you can get the next batch ready."

"Next batch?" Esther wanted to scream and run.

"Jah. There are lots more berries there." Mamm nodded to the remaining pile of fruit. "After the next batch, you will probably have enough berries left over to bake a pie for supper."

"Bake a pie, Mamm? This will take all day!"

"Probably." Mamm turned away to pull food out to throw together a simple noon meal, but not before Esther saw her grin.

She stuck her tongue out at the pile of berries before gathering up more jars to wash. She couldn't believe Mamm expected her to make another batch of jam and to bake a pie afterward. Honestly, she'd never get outside.

Esther nibbled at a ham sandwich with no real desire to eat as everyone else — even Andrew — sat at the oak table to enjoy a break from the day's work while eating the noon meal. She, on the other hand, continued to work without a break. She had watched out the window when Lydia waited on her two customers at the nursery and wished it had been her outside with her plants — or orbiting the moon or anywhere else but in the stifling kitchen.

She finally screwed the lid on the last pint jar and started timing the final hot water bath. Maybe there wouldn't be enough berries left for a pie. She thought briefly about throwing some out before Mamm could see them but couldn't bear the thought of wasting any of the tasty fruit.

"I think you'll have enough for a pie." Mamm glanced at the pile of berries before she put the leftover food away.

"Great!" Esther groaned. Her back ached. Her fingers ached, but that didn't seem to matter to anyone. She rolled out dough for a pie crust three times before meeting her mudder's approval. She washed and cut up the remaining berries, stirred in sugar, and prepared the filling. By the time she slid the pie into the oven and all the jar lids had popped one by one as they sealed, the day was practically gone. She didn't care if she never saw another strawberry. She didn't

care if she never had her own home or family to provide food for. Her hands and fingernails would probably be permanently red, and the cramp in her right
hand would most likely last a week.

Wearily, she pulled the pie from the oven and set
it on the hot pad on the kitchen counter to cool. She
glanced around the kitchen to make sure there was
nothing Mamm could find fault with. She knew she
was not supposed to entertain thoughts of pride, but
those little jars of strawberry jam lined up in neat
rows on the counter looked mighty nice. Esther was
pleased with her day's work and hoped the jam and
pie tasted as gut as they looked. She snatched a paper
napkin to mop her brow and prepared to escape outside for a breath of air.

"Gut job." Mamm smiled her approval. "We'll do
blueberries and blackberries and peaches the same
way in a few weeks. The apple butter in September
will be a bit more complicated."

Esther turned a horrified look on her mudder
and fled from the kitchen. She heard Mamm and Lydia laugh as the screen door slammed behind her. *Am I
too old to run away from home?*

Esther awoke on the second Tuesday in June to
the sound of rain pounding on the roof. *Gut thing the
wash was done yesterday.* She yawned and stretched
before swinging her legs over the side of the bed.
"Guess I won't be working outside today."

She wasn't sure if the total darkness in the room
was due to the cloudy, rainy day or if she had awak-
ened much earlier than usual. Her hand fumbled
around on the nightstand until it located her battery-
operated clock. She turned it to face her and leaned
over closer to read the numbers: 3:45.

She was early. Oh well. She'd get kaffi and breakfast started. Maybe today would be a good day to experiment with some of the gluten-free recipes that had been rattling around in her head. She thought she'd try making some peanut butter cookies. With enough peanut butter, any other strange flavors would be easily masked. What could she do about that dry, tasteless bread, though? She'd try adding applesauce to increase the moisture and enhance the flavor. She was certainly no expert in the culinary arts, but her ideas were definitely worth a try. She still had plenty of the necessary ingredients left from the last attempts. It was a certainty that no one else in the household wanted to eat them!

Kaffi bubbled, eggs sizzled, and biscuits baked by the time Mamm appeared in the kitchen doorway. "What? Can this be my dochder Esther in here cooking up a storm? I thought the smells of kaffi and food were my imagination."

"See, Mamm. I can cook and do a few things in the kitchen."

"So I see indeed. What are you getting ready to bake?" Mamm nodded toward the blue ceramic mixing bowls on the counter. Esther explained her ideas. "They might work. It certainly can't hurt to try."

Lydia bustled into the kitchen with David and Ella, who both sported huge yawns. Lydia handed them napkins and silverware to set at each place at the table. Breakfast was ready right as Daed washed up after completing morning chores.

"I sure am glad to have Mose back, even if he does work shorter days for the time being." Daed forked a bite of eggs and bacon into his mouth before continuing. "Andrew will still help out a couple days each week, but now he can build furniture with the

Beilers. I hear he is a gut furniture maker." His gaze
slid over to encompass Esther.

She shrugged her shoulders and wiped her
mouth on the white paper napkin. "I wouldn't know
about that," she mumbled into the napkin while
avoiding her daed's eyes. *Why does he always talk about
Andrew around me? What's his agenda?*

Esther helped clean up the kitchen after breakfast
and then proceeded to mess it up again. She baked
peanut butter cookies using the gluten-free flour and
chunky peanut butter. They weren't half bad, she decided after sampling a tiny cookie fresh from the ov-
en. If only the breads and muffins were as simple to
create. She tried adding mashed banana to the bread
recipe and applesauce to the muffin recipe. The batter
mixed up better than before. That was a plus. A pinch
from the finished products told her the flavor was
marginally improved. She sighed. Butter and jam
would no doubt render them more palatable to the
children.

"Ach, Esther! Look at you!" Lydia clapped a
hand over her heart as she entered the kitchen shortly
before noon.

"Look at the kitchen — the once clean kitchen!"
Mamm added.

Esther looked down at her flour-covered apron
and batter-encrusted forearms. Then she glanced
around at all the dirty bowls and pans. "I'll clean it
up quick."

Lydia began gathering up wooden spoons and
mixing bowls. She paused to brush flour out of the
front of her schweschder's dark hair.

"I think I've made some improvements." Esther
hoped to atone for her mess.

Lydia cut a thin slice of bread, broke it in half, and shared it with Mamm. They both took small bites and chewed pensively.

"What do you think?"

"Definitely better," Lydia pronounced.

"You may be on to something with these." Mamm licked crumbs from her lips.

"Gut." She smiled, but it faded quickly when she surveyed her mess. She ran water into the sink to begin washing dishes. There was scarcely a clean spot to be found at which to prepare the noon meal.

"Here, I'll help. You wash and I'll dry." Lydia grabbed a dish towel.

"Hurry, girls. Daed will be in for the noon meal, and I don't have anything ready."

"There's leftover casserole," Esther suggested.

"That will have to do." Mamm whirled around the kitchen as if an idea or two would be engraved on the wall somewhere. "I'll open jars of beets and pickles and heat up the leftover green beans, too."

"Sounds like a plan to me." Lydia dried bowls and pans vigorously.

Later in the afternoon, the rain slacked off a little, so Esther ventured outside to check on her plants. The kinner had liked the bread and, of course, the cookies. Maybe they would have a muffin for a snack when they awoke from their naps.

Esther sniffed. She liked the smell of damp earth after a spring rain, especially when it mingled with the strong, flowery scent of the magnolia blossoms from the two tall trees in the back yard. She couldn't wait for the mimosa trees to bloom. They were her absolute favorite. Several grew at the edge of the woods. Because they were often shaded by taller trees, they bloomed a little later. Their delicate, feathery pink blossoms gave the sweetest fragrance ever. She often wished she could bottle that scent to savor it throughout the year. She was so happy Daed had built her a potting shed not far from those special trees.

She decided to take a detour to the mill to see how Mose was doing. She hadn't had a chance to talk to him since he returned to work. The sawmill had a smell all its own, a smell she liked and always associated with Daed. Esther learned to identify the scent of oak, pine, maple, or cherry wood. She knew the type of lumber being sawed simply by sniffing the air. For some reason, the Lord Gott had blessed her with an extra sensitive nose. She often thought that even if she was blindfolded, she would be able to discern where she was as long as she could smell.

Esther stepped inside the noisy mill. She spotted Mose but waited until he looked up and saw her. She waved at him and started in his direction. She didn't want to sneak up on him and cause him to injure himself. He switched off the saw when she drew near.

"Wie bist du heit?" she asked as soon as her ears stopped ringing.

"Much better, danki."

"You look better." She smiled. Mose still looked a lot thinner. Martha had not yet succeeded in filling out his usually robust frame. His beard and hair had a few extra gray strands that hadn't been there before his illness, but his cheeks had a slightly pink tinge. She wasn't sure if the color was from returning health or exertion. "You had a pretty rough time, jah?"

"Jah. Once I got the right medicine, though, I started to perk up."

"The medicine Dr. Kramer gave you wasn't right?"

"Well, now, I don't want to say anything against the man, but it seems what he gave me didn't help none."

"Then I'm glad you went to the hospital and got what you needed." She had been concerned about Mose. She always had a particular fondness for the older man who had willingly taken the time to talk with her, even when she visited the mill as a curious little girl.

"That hospital stay was pretty costly, though."

"That's what the benevolent fund is for, Mose, to help in emergencies, ain't so?"

"I suppose. I never figured I'd need any of that. I was able to cover most of the bill, though. Those hospital folks were gut about working with me on it."

"I'm glad to hear that. It's wunderbaar to see you back at work. Just don't work too hard."

Mose pulled out a handkerchief to wipe his brow and oblong peach-colored pills flew out of his pocket in Esther's direction.

"What are these?" She scrambled to recover the pills."

"Ach! They must have been wrapped in my handkerchief. These were the pills Dr. Kramer gave me."

"You aren't still taking them, are you?"

"Nee. I finished up the pills from the lung doctor. I guess I forgot to throw these away."

"I'll get rid of them for you."

"Danki, Esther."

"So you really are feeling better?"

"I'm getting my strength back, but I should be back to normal soon." Mose flexed a muscle in his arm and smiled at her.

She returned the smile. "I'm sure you will. You take care."

Mose nodded and turned back to the log he was sawing as she made her way back outside. She waved to Daed as she passed through the mill. *I think I'll hang onto these pills.*

Chapter Seven

Wednesday dawned warm and sunny. Esther's fingers twitched, wanting to dig into the moist earth and tend her plants. Her fingers would have to be content with hitching the horse to the buggy since she had promised to accompany Lydia and the kinner to their doctor's appointment. As she waited by the buggy, she inhaled deeply and let the breath out inch by inch. The air smelled so clean and pure after yesterday's heavy rain. The damp earth gave off its own special scent that overtook even the strong fragrance from the big, wide-opened, white magnolia blossoms. The grass fairly sparkled in the sunshine with water droplets still clinging to each blade like crystals. The birds chattered in the tree branches, happy they did not have to hunker down in their nests today.

"We're finally ready." Lydia rubbed a hand across her forehead as she approached the buggy.

"Another headache?"

"Jah."

"Why don't you ask Dr. Kramer about them?"

"He's too busy with really sick people. I can deal with a headache."

"You've been dealing with them a long time now, ain't so?"

"I suppose, but they've been fewer and not as severe. Maybe some of the stress is easing."

"I hope so." She patted her older schweschder's arm, then lifted Ella into the buggy. David, determined to be a little man, did not want to be lifted into the buggy like a boppli, he'd said, but he did accept a boost up from his aenti. Esther waited for Lydia to climb in and get settled before claiming her own seat. With everyone finally situated, they could begin the trek.

More cars filled the parking lot than on the previous visit. Esther hoped all the people from them weren't there to see Dr. Kramer, and she hoped the wait would not be long. She was anxious to get to her garden and greenhouse. There would probably be more customers today, too, and she didn't want her mamm to have to wait on them on top of all her other chores. She also hoped to squeeze in a visit with Sophie Hostetler to see how Sophie's lavender was coming along and to learn more about its uses.

The door squeaked open, allowing another family to exit as they entered the medical office. Several patients sat scattered around the room in the hard, plastic chairs, but there were still vacant seats to accommodate the four of them.

"Please, Lord, let all be well." A little prayer escaped from Lydia's lips.

"There's Joanna King." Esther jerked her head toward the far corner of the room where the only other Amish patient sat waiting to be seen by the doctor. "I hope she's all right. She looks thinner."

Lydia nodded in agreement before settling David and Ella at the low children's table with a puzzle.

"I'm going over to speak with her."

Lydia nodded again as she stroked her wrinkled brow.

"Gude mariye, Joanna. Wie bist du heit?"

"Ach, Esther? It's gut to see you."

"Jah, it's been a while." Joanna King lived in a different district several miles from Esther's community. She grew flowers to sell so the two women knew each other from their plant businesses. Joanna was nearly twenty years older than Esther, but her face was still unlined, and her hair was light brown with no streaks of gray. Usually a plump, smiling, energetic woman, today she looked thin, tired, and worried. "Are—are you well?" Esther ventured.

"I'm struggling to get this blood pressure under control. I've stopped using salt and lost weight. I even go for a brisk walk every day on top of all my other chores and still the blood pressure stays up."

"I'm sorry to hear that. One of your parents had that problem, ain't so?"

"Jah. My daed. He—he died in his late forties after a stroke. I—I don't want that to happen to me. I've still got kinner at home." Joanna's voice grew quieter and a little shaky.

Esther grasped Joanna's hand in an effort to comfort her. "Are you taking any medicine?"

"Dr. Kramer put me on some pills, but they haven't helped so far. I guess he'll increase the dose if my pressure is still up today."

"I'll pray it is down."

"Danki, Esther. You're such a dear girl." Joanna blinked back tears.

I'm hardly a girl, but I guess I'll be thought of as a girl until that title is taken over by old maedel. She mentally shook herself and tried to think of a way to distract Joanna from her health worries so she'd be calmer when she was called back for her appointment. "How are all your kinner?" If she remembered correctly, the older woman had ten.

Joanna smiled, and her shoulders relaxed a bit. "They are all gut. Mary, my oldest, is probably a little younger than you. I think she'll mar—well, let's say I'm putting in a good celery crop this year." Joanna gave a little laugh.

"Really? That's wunderbaar."

"And you? Any special fellow? I know I'm not supposed to ask, but you are such a kind person. Surely there is a young man…" Joanna's voice trailed off.

"Nee. Nee. There is no one."

"I'll pray on it."

"Danki." Esther wanted to tell Joanna to save her prayers and not to pester the Lord Gott with such a thing. He most likely had already decided she'd be alone. And she was okay with that. Most of the time. Some of the time? "How old is your youngest now?" She again sought to divert Joanna's attention—off of *her* this time.

"Ach, Little Ruth is three now. Such a delight. Who'd have thought she'd come along after I was forty and my youngest was six?" Joanna's smile was broad and genuine now. Ruth obviously was the apple of her mamm's eye. She continued talking about her little one's antics. She briefly mentioned all her other children but returned to Ruth time after time.

Esther grew wistful. This was one of the times she minded her single status. She'd probably never talk of her little ones with others. And how she loved kinner!

"Mrs. King." The same assistant as before, dressed in a different set of cartoon character scrubs, stood in the doorway that opened into the examination area.

"Here goes." Joanna jumped up so quickly she dropped her open handbag. Her wallet and tissues spilled onto the floor. A bottle of pills rolled under the chair.

Esther dropped to her knees to retrieve the bottle. "Ach! The lid popped off." She stretched her arm back nearly to the wall. She captured the bottle and lid, pulled them out, and then picked up two pills that had escaped from the bottle. Peach-colored oblong pills. "These are dirty now, I'll throw them away. You go ahead." She snapped the child-proof cap on and handed the bottle to Joanna.

"Danki, Esther." Joanna dropped the bottle into her purse and headed for the doorway.

Esther folded her fingers around the pills. They looked familiar. They looked like Mose's pills. Never having the need to take much medication in her life, Esther wondered if all pills looked alike. She crossed the room to sit beside Lydia. She reached for her own handbag and felt around inside to locate a tissue. As inconspicuously as possible, she wrapped the two peach pills in the tissue and stuffed it down into the corner of her purse. She needed to think on this. Later. When she was alone.

Lydia raised her eyebrows questioningly. Esther shrugged and shook her head. She rose abruptly and moved over to watch David and Ella fit giant puzzle pieces together at the little table by the window.

The children played quietly and patiently while two other patients were called back to the examination area. When the second one disappeared, Joanna King reappeared. She stopped at the receptionist's window to pay her bill and schedule her next appointment. Esther slipped across the room and touched Joanna's arm. "How'd it go?"

Joanna turned watery eyes on her. "The blood pressure is still high. He increased the dose of my medicine." She sniffed and looked ready to burst into tears.

"I'll pray. I'll try to get over and visit you. Maybe I can help with something."

"Danki." Unable to speak further, Joanna patted her arm and attempted to smile. She nodded at Lydia and fled from the room. Esther sighed and returned to the hard little chair next to Lydia.

"What's wrong?" Lydia asked. "Is Joanna okay?"

Esther described Joanna's situation briefly before the cartoon-clad woman called for David and Ella. The children quickly put the puzzle pieces in the box and followed their mudder. Obedient children, the only visible signs of their reluctance to follow were their downcast eyes and the slight dragging of their feet.

Lydia looked at the floor as the lab technician withdrew tubes of blood from each child. Esther cringed. It wasn't that she was squeamish at the sight of blood. She just hated seeing David and Ella have to get pricked with a needle so often. The little ones endured the procedure stoically though they scrunched up their faces and squeezed their eyes shut as soon as the tourniquet was tied around their arms. Who could blame them?

The children marched over to the scale and climbed on one at a time. Esther saw Lydia suck in a breath and hold it.

"Yes!" the assistant cried. "David gained a pound and a half, and Ella gained a pound."

"Thank you, Gott," Esther whispered.

Lydia released her breath in a long, shaky sigh. She gathered her kinner to her in a quick hug and released them to follow the assistant into the examining room. Lydia sat in one chair and pulled David onto her lap. Esther scooped Ella up and sat in the only other chair._After taking temperatures, asking a few questions, and scribbling in charts, the assistant slipped out of the room with a promise the doctor would be in soon.

"It's gut they've begun regaining weight." Esther poked Ella's belly.

"Very gut. Maybe they won't have to come back for a while."

Lydia barely finished her sentence when the door creaked open to admit Dr. Kramer. He again wore the ink-stained white lab coat with a rumpled shirt beneath. He swiped unruly brown hair off his forehead and with one finger, pushed his glasses up on his nose. "Well, things are looking up," he announced in his gravelly voice. Esther wished the man would clear his throat. Maybe then his voice wouldn't sound so rough. He smiled a tight sort of smile. Apparently, his lips did not let his eyes know about the smile. Though not hard, they did not exhibit warmth. Maybe the man was shy. Esther tried to give him the benefit of the doubt.

"I picked up their lab results. The anemia is much improved. The hemoglobin is still a little low, though, so—"

"They should stay on vitamins, ain't so?" Esther interrupted. Lydia frowned at her, but for some reason, Esther felt fidgety around this man with his beady brown eyes.

"Right." Dr. Kramer asked Lydia some questions about the children's diet and activities and nodded at her responses. He scrawled something in their charts. "I'd like to check their progress in a month."

Lydia's shoulders slumped, but she nodded assent. Esther knew her schweschder hoped they could go longer between appointments, especially since they were doing better. These frequent doctor visits would definitely be biting into her savings. Dr. Nelson didn't hesitate to accept homegrown or homemade goods or services as part of his payment. Even Esther was reluctant to approach the topic of payment with the substitute doctor, so she knew Lydia would never mention it.

"Oh, before I forget," the doctor began. "I got in some of those cookies and bread for the children."

"We've been baking things for them," Lydia replied.

"Oh, well, this can give you a little break. As before, they are totally free. I'll be right back."

Lydia looked at her and raised her eyebrows. Esther shrugged her shoulders. Before they could say anything, the doctor returned with several packages of cream-filled chocolate cookies and two long loaves of brown bread. All were sealed in clear, plastic wrappers.

She first picked up one package of cookies and then one loaf of bread. She turned them every which way in her hands. "Where is the list of ingredients? I was hoping to get ideas of things we can add to the foods we bake for the kinner."

"Oh, uh—you see, the food comes to me, uh, in bulk. You know, a lot of packages in one big container. I...uh, took the individual packages out. I, uh, guess the ingredients were, uh, listed on that outside container." Dr. Kramer again adjusted his glasses.

Could the man speak without stumbling over his words? Esther instantly chided herself for her mean thought. "I see. I had hoped we could make improvements in our own concoctions."

"Well." The doctor cleared his throat at last. "I hope the children like these." His voice didn't sound any better after the throat clearing, still thick and gravelly. Esther decided it must be his normal voice.

"They surely do like them," Lydia mumbled. "Danki—thank you—Doctor."

The man practically shot out of the door before either Lydia or Esther could rise from their chairs. "Don't forget to make the next appointments," he tossed over his shoulder.

Lydia signed again. "At least we can take a little break from the extra baking." David's and Ella's eyes latched onto the cookies with longing. They never asked, but their hope was obvious. Lydia chuckled. "You may both have one cookie on the way home."

Esther glanced hastily around the room on her way out. She even peeked under the exam table and into the trash can. She really wished she could find that list of ingredients. For some reason, that seemed important. *I'll figure this out yet.*

Chapter Eight

After such an unusually long, brutal winter for Southern Maryland and a spring reluctant to make an appearance, Esther welcomed the warmth of the early June day. Back in February, she vowed not to complain about the summer's heat and humidity, even when the air became thick and oppressive. She hoped she'd be able to honor that vow.

Today, though, she enjoyed the sun beating down on her. With the laundry flapping gently on the clothesline, the garden weeded, the nursery work completed, and the customers waited on, Esther was ready for a break of sorts. She washed up and set out for Sophie Hostetler's place. She had wanted to visit before now, but there had always been a host of other things to do.

She decided to walk to Sophie's since the day was so fine with only a very few white, filmy clouds in the blue sky. It would, of course, take her longer, but she liked walking. Besides, she didn't want to waste the time it would take to hitch up the horse and wagon. She set off at a brisk pace and allowed her mind to wander at will. Her nose picked up the almost sickening sweet scent of the honeysuckle still blooming along the side of the road. As kinner, she and Lydia would pluck off the blossoms and suck out the tasty nectar. She smiled at the memory.

I wonder if David and Ella have tasted honeysuckle. Merely thinking of the precious little ones made her feel warm inside. How she loved them! She hoped and prayed their little bodies continued to be healthy. She had thought of baking this afternoon since the kinner had eaten their way through the homemade cookies and breads, but they had the stash from Dr. Kramer, and they seemed to like those foods well enough. Not to mention the fact that Esther really didn't want to spend such a gorgeous afternoon trapped in the hot kitchen.

Besides, she'd tasted a pinch of that bread and a few of the cookie crumbs. They were actually quite good for store-bought. In fact, they tasted like regular baked goods, not at all like the usual gluten-free products she had sampled. What was the secret?

Esther hummed as she strode across the field leading to Sophie's house. Wild flowers—purple ones and blue ones and yellow ones—lifted their heads in greeting. As she drew closer to the house, she saw the purple blooms on the lavender Sophie had planted. The slight breeze broadcast their gentle fragrance. The crop looked like it was growing well. She knew that making her own lavender oils, balms, and teas was Sophie's dream. She said she had always ordered her lavender products and hadn't previously tried growing her own plants. After studying the soil and climate, she decided to give it a try. If anyone could be successful at growing lavender and making things from it, it would be Sophie.

Esther crossed the front porch to the side door leading to the shop. A little bell tinkled as she pushed the door open. "Sophie? It's me, Esther."

Sophie popped up from where she had been stooping to search through a bottom cabinet. "Ach, Esther. It's gut to see you."

"Your lavender seems to be coming along nicely, ain't so?"

"So far. I don't think we're in danger of any more cold weather as long as the precipitation cooperates. That's all in the Lord Gott's hands."

"Jah. So show me what you're working on or what you want me to learn next."

"You're a gut girl, Esther, to oblige an old woman like you're doing."

"You are not old, Sophie."

"Well, I sure ain't young! Gideon and I were never blessed with kinner so I had no one to pass my herb business to."

"I don't think you need to worry about passing it on right now."

"That's what Gid says, too. He says, 'what's your hurry woman? You ain't going nowhere.'" Sophie chuckled.

"I agree with him, but I'm happy to learn all you can teach me. I'm really interested in herbs and their uses. And you know how much I enjoy growing things. I'm honored you want to pass your knowledge and skills on to me."

"You are exactly the right person, my dear Esther. Are you ready to learn more about peppermint?"

"Jah. I remember it's good for digestion, sore throats, coughs, and even headaches."

"That's right. You can even make toothpaste with it. You can use peppermint capsules, ointments, or teas."

Sophie went on with the lesson, growing more and more animated with each tidbit she shared, flinging her hands about in emphasis. Esther soaked up the knowledge as a dishcloth soaked up spilled milk. She didn't know how much time had elapsed when the little bell jingled. She had been so absorbed in the lesson that she never heard anyone approach despite the open windows.

"Sophie?" a soft voice called out tentatively.

Esther smiled. She knew that voice. She looked up at the tiny young woman with the corn silk hair peeking out from beneath her kapp and the big, sky blue eyes. "Hello, Hannah." Her smile widened. "It's gut to see you."

"Ach, Esther. Fancy meeting you here. Hello, Sophie." Hannah crossed the small room to stand near her two freinden.

Esther happily acknowledged the fact that she was the first freind Hannah had made when she moved to Southern Maryland, not counting Rebecca and her kinner. And they had become very close in a short time.

"What brings you by?" Sophie asked. "Not that you can't drop by whenever you like, but I wondered if there was any special reason for your visit."

"I always enjoy visiting with you, Sophie, but I am on a mission today as well. Rebecca sent me to see if you can offer some advice. The twins are working on those stubborn molars and are quite fussy. Two irritable babies are about to send her running into the woods for peace and quiet!"

"Not to mention that you and the rest of the household will be trotting along right behind her." Esther chuckled at that image.

"I'm afraid you're right about that. Cranky little ones can make life miserable."

"Let me see what I can find for the bopplin and also something to calm Rebecca's nerves." Sophie looked at Esther. "What do you suggest?"
"Is this a test, Sophie?"

Sophie laughed. "Maybe. Do you have any ideas?"

"Well, we could definitely send Rebecca some chamomile tea. Maybe some lavender tea or oils would help? I don't know about the bopplin, though."

"Excellent suggestions for Rebecca. Lavender sachets or oil in the twins' beds may help them sleep better. Now, for the teething, you can put a tiny bit of clove oil on the gums to ease the pain. Only use a tiny bit, though, mind you. Too much clove oil could upset their little tummies, and we don't want that. I'm sure Rebecca has tried teething rings and biscuits and cool cloths to bite on. She's an experienced mamm. I also have some natural licorice sticks. The little ones can chew on them. They are cool and also numb the gums."

"Licorice?" Hannah looked surprised.

"Not the candy. The herb. They're different."

"I'm sure it's worth a try. No one is getting much sleep and the older kinner are running around with their fingers in their ears."

"And you?" Esther teased.

"Let's just say that cotton balls do not block sound." All three women had a good laugh. "It feels gut to laugh about it." Hannah wiped tears of mirth from her eyes.

"Well, Esther, let's find some help for these folks." Sophie turned to one of the shelves along the wall but stopped abruptly. "Do you remember where the teas are?"

Esther nodded. "Jah. I believe I do know that."

"Why don't you find her the chamomile? There should be lavender there, too. I'll round up..."The sound of a wagon pulling up the gravel driveway practically drowned out Sophie's words.

"It sounds like you have another customer," Hannah observed.

Sophie peeked out the window. "It's Andrew with the new cabinet I ordered. That bu must be a fast worker."

Esther's heart did a funny dance at the mention of Andrew's name. Now why was it behaving so crazily? Her breathing became shallow for some unknown reason. *Was this what a panic attack felt like*? A character in one of the novels she read not long ago suffered panic attacks whenever she was in high places. Maybe she was having one now. *I wonder which herb is good for those.* She also wondered if she could drop to her knees and slither out the back door before Andrew could enter.

Too Late! Sophie marched to the screen door and called out, "Andrew, do you need to get Gid to help you unload?"

"I think I can get it. Let me see." He slid the cabinet toward the end of the wagon.

Esther had crouched on the floor, pretending to search low cabinets for the items she needed.

"Psst? Esther? I doubt the teas are down there."

"Funny, Hannah. I, uh, think I dropped something."

"What was it? I'll help you look."

"Uh, that's okay. It's, uh, a little black bottle cap." She practically flattened herself on the floor as Andrew's deep voice and heavy footsteps grew closer to the screen door.

"Esther," Hannah whispered.

"Huh?"

"You've got it."

"Huh?"

"The black bottle cap is in your hand."

"Oh."

"You can get up now."

She didn't move.

The screen door banged shut behind a grunting Andrew. "Where do you want this, Sophie?"

"Over near where Esther — where is Esther?"

"I-I'm here," she croaked. She forced herself to stand. "I-I dropped something." She held up the bottle cap as if to prove her words. *Dummchen*! she admonished herself. Her fingers trembled so much she had to struggle to screw the cap on the bottle. She set the glass bottle down quickly before she dropped it or squeezed it so tightly it shattered into a million pieces. She ran damp palms down the sides of her blue dress.

"Hello, Hannah. Hello, Esther," Andrew said.

"Gut to see you, Andrew," Hannah replied.

Esther couldn't echo that sentiment. "H-hello," was all she could manage. She was usually a confident, easy-going, happy person. Why did this one man unnerve her so much, reduce her to a bumbling, fumbling idiot, and put her in a surly mood?

"Where exactly do you want this positioned, Sophie?" He set the obviously heavy cabinet down to catch his breath.

"I had it made so it would fit about anywhere, but the best place, I'm thinking, will be right over here." Sophie moved over to where Esther still stood as though in a trance. "It will fit here fine, ain't so?"

He took a deep breath, flexed his arms twice, hoisted the large five-shelf cabinet, and followed Sophie. He deposited it where she indicated and wiggled it back and forth until it was level and snugly in place.

"It's perfect!" Sophie declared. "How ever did you construct it so quickly?"

Andrew shrugged. "I was able to work on it in between other projects. Jake was going to bring it tomorrow, but I said I could come by here on my way home today."

"Danki. I appreciate that. I have Esther here to help me move things."

"Can I help with anything—maybe move any heavier items for you?"

"Let's see." Sophie glanced around the room. Andrew's gaze followed hers. Esther still stared at the floor.

"Ach, Sophie! I nearly forgot." Hannah tapped her chin. "Rebecca told me to be sure I got you to show me that quilt you're working on for next fall's auction."

"Quilt?"

"Jah."

Out of the corner of her eye, Esther caught Hannah's nod toward first herself and then Andrew and saw Hannah mouth, "leave them alone." She made a note to strangle Hannah later.

"Sure, Hannah. The quilt." Esther glanced at Sophie in time to see her wink at Hannah. A smile crinkled her face. "Let's go. I'll show you now. Esther, could you get Andrew to help you move those heavier jars there?" She paused and pointed to the jars she meant. "You can put them on the bottom two shelves of the new cabinet. I'll only be a few minutes." She grabbed Hannah's arm and hustled her into the house before Esther even had a chance to respond. "I'll package up your items as soon as we get back from looking at that quilt, Hannah."

I'm not totally dense. I know what you two are up to. She caught Hannah's sly smile and chewed the inside of her cheek to keep from threatening some type of retaliation. Now to get out of this awkward situation! "Y-you don't have to stay, Andrew. I-I'm sure I can move things by myself." She turned her back on him and reached for a large jar on a high shelf. She felt him close behind her, so close he nearly touched her. She not only heard his breath, but she also felt it on the back of her neck, tickling along the little hairs that had escaped her bun.

"Let me get that." He reached over her for the jar.

"I can do it! I'm not helpless."

"I know that for sure, but the jar is in an awkward spot."

She moved aside quickly to allow him better access to the jar. She frowned, angrier with herself more than with him. Why did she allow him to turn her into a prickly porcupine? Maybe if she sucked on one of those licorice sticks if it would numb her sharp tongue. She snagged the offending creature between her teeth to keep it from uttering another disagreeable word.

"Where should we put this?" Andrew removed the jar easily from the shelf.

We? Esther almost uttered the word aloud but clamped down harder on her tongue. She expected it to spurt blood any minute. She should be grateful that Andrew was a good five or six inches taller than her five-feet, five-inch stature and could easily reach up to grasp the jar. "Danki." She cleared her throat. "I guess we can put the larger jars on the bottom shelf since Sophie wants them moved to the new cabinet." There was that word *we* again. This time she used the word. "I don't want to keep you from your business. I can grab a chair to stand on to move the other jars." She hoped she didn't sound unappreciative, but his presence did set her on edge.

"Nee. You could fall. Even though you aren't very big, I'm not sure the chair in here is safe to climb on."

"Oh." She couldn't think of an intelligent reply.

"Besides," he continued. "I've finished work for the day. I was on my way home, so I have plenty of time."

Esther gazed into Andrew's jade green eyes fringed by dark lashes and nearly lost her train of thought. She forced her attention back to the conversation and hoped she hadn't really been staring into those mesmerizing eyes. "You're sure the Fishers don't need your help with something?"

"Nee. Joseph usually has the chores done by the time I get home, and Ada is probably still working on supper. I think she was planning to spend the afternoon with Sarah, sewing things for the boppli or something."

"I guess Sarah's boppli is due to arrive soon."

Andrew shrugged his shoulders. "I assume so. I don't really know for sure."

How would he? Such things wouldn't be discussed around a single man, even if he was Sarah's cousin and lived with her parents.

"If you like, I'll reach up and grab the jars and hand them to you. Is that okay?"

She got the impression he was treading lightly to keep from saying or doing something to offend her. When he looked into her eyes with such sincerity in his expression, she felt more flustered than ever. "That—that would be fine," she agreed at last. She stole a quick glance at her hands before reaching up to retrieve a jar. She wanted to make sure no dirt lurked under her fingernails. *He has teased me about dirty fingernails all my life. That was hurtful enough, but has he truly forgotten the worst pain he caused me? Surely he doesn't think I've forgotten. If I didn't have to be around him, maybe I could forget!*

They worked in a surprisingly companionable silence. Esther gradually relaxed as she got into the rhythm of receiving the jars of teas and herbs and settling them on the shelves where she thought Sophie would want them. Where in the world had Sophie and Hannah gone? Did it really take so long to examine a quilt?

"Are you going to become Sophie's apprentice?" Andrew broke into her reverie.

"Huh? Well, sort of. I guess." She felt the heat in her cheeks as she stumbled over her reply. "She's teaching me about different herbs and their uses. It's interesting."

"Are you thinking you could grow these plants yourself?"

Esther bristled. Was he thinking she couldn't grow the necessary plants or was he poking fun at her? "Why do you ask?"

"I've heard you have a green thumb and if anyone could grow the herbs, you could."

She peeked at her thumb. Was he alluding to all his teasing of her grass-stained hands and dirt-caked fingernails or was he sincere in thinking she was gut at raising plants? "I-I like growing things."

"Jah. It shows. You have a real gift. I hear you always have the healthiest plants and flowers."

"I-I try." Were Sophie and Hannah ever going to rescue her?

"How are Lydia's kinner doing?"

Maybe he sensed her discomfort and chose a safer subject. Everyone knew Esther loved her schweschder's little ones. She couldn't keep the love and enthusiasm out of her voice if she tried. "They are such gut kinner. Poor dears have had a rough time with losing their daed and then their medical problems." Funny, she didn't stammer or hesitate when talking about her niece and nephew. She wondered if he noticed.

"Are they well now?" He smiled down at her.

"They were doing much better, but here the last few days, they've begun to look a little peaked, I think. I haven't said anything to Lydia yet." Esther grew suddenly pensive. She continued almost to herself. "I simply don't understand these ups and downs when we watch their diet so closely."

"It's a strange thing," Andrew agreed. "I hear Mose is fit as a fiddle again."

"Jah. He seems fully recovered now. Ach!" She sucked in a sharp breath.

"What is it?" He looked quickly at her hands as if checking for any telltale wounds from a cut or smashed finger.

"I forgot the pills."

"What pills?"

"Mose had been on some peach-colored pills that didn't help him at all. At the doctor's office last time, we ran into Joanna King. Do you remember her from when you lived here as a bu?"

"I believe I do. She had seven or eight kinner, ain't so?"

"Ten, now. Anyway, she dropped her purse and peach pills spilled out. They weren't helping her either. I wonder if they were the same pills."

"Did she have pneumonia, too?"

"Nee. That's just it. She has high blood pressure, so she wouldn't need the same medicine as Mose."

"Maybe the pills looked similar but weren't exactly the same."

"Hmmm." Esther snapped her fingers. "I saved the pills Joanna dropped and one Mose dropped. I'll compare them."

"You might not be able to tell anything simply by looking at them."

"You're right. But a pharmacist might..."

"Esther, what are you thinking?"

She ignored the question and asked one of her own. "How well do you know this Dr. Kramer?"

"I don't know him at all." Andrew shook his head. "I never met the man. Why?"

"Just curious."

"Esther, you're hatching some sort of plot. What is it?"

"I'm not sure yet."

"Don't go getting yourself involved in something—"

"Don't you worry about me, Andrew." When she looked into Andrew's face, though, he did appear worried. Why would he be worried about her or even care what she did or did not do? He certainly wasn't concerned years ago when he made a fool of her.

"Esther, promise me you won't—" He didn't get to finish his request as Hannah and Sophie bustled back into the room.

Esther abruptly turned her attention to them, putting extra space between herself and Andrew. "That must be some quilt! It sure took you long enough to look at it."

"You know, I'm only now getting the hang of quilting. Sophie was explaining her...uh, her pattern and, uh, technique." Hannah's eyes slid to her co-conspirator's face.

"Jah." Sophie nodded in confirmation.

"Right," Esther muttered.

"Esther, the cabinet looks wunderbaar. That's exactly what I had in mind. Danki. And danki to you, too, Andrew." *Either I'm overly suspicious or Sophie changed the subject a mite fast.*

"Sure thing, Sophie. Glad I could help. I'd best be heading out now, though."

"Me, too," Hannah chimed in. "Danki for your help, Sophie. See you, Esther."

"Can you wait a few minutes, Hannah?" Esther asked. "I need to leave soon, too. I'll walk a ways with you."

"Okay. I'll wait on the porch for you."

Ten minutes later, after helping Sophie rearrange a few more items and promising to return later in the week, Esther joined Hannah on the porch. When the screen door creaked open, Hannah jumped up from the top porch step where she sat petting a fuzzy orange and white cat. "Such a nice kitty." She gave the cat one more pat on the head.

"You've made her happy. I think they can hear her purring across the road. Are you ready to leave the kitty?"

"Jah, I need to get these herbs home and hope they bring some relief to the twins."

"And to everyone else, too, I imagine."

"That's for sure and for certain. I've about run out of cotton balls to stuff into my ears!"

Both young women began walking. They remained silent for a while, comfortable together. Finally, Esther could resist no longer. "What was that about?"

Hannah shook her head in confusion. "I'm not privy to the goings on in your head, Esther. What was what about?"

"That excuse about seeing some quilt."

"Rebecca really did tell me about a quilt Sophie was stitching. I *did* want to see it."

"Right then and there at the precise moment Andrew appeared?"

"It seemed a gut enough time. Besides, I don't get over to Sophie's house that often."

"And why did it take you so long to merely look at a quilt?"

"Well, she, uh, was explaining the pattern. And she told me why she chose the colors she used. And I asked her about the piecing. And—"

"All right. All right. I simply think you had an ulterior motive that your babbling lends credence to."

"What other motive could I possibly have?" Hannah drew in an exaggerated breath, turned wide, innocent-looking eyes on her freind, and batted them twice. Her lips twitched as if she struggled to hold a smile at bay.

"Breathe!" Esther elbowed the smaller woman. "You're going to burst, and your eyeballs are going to bulge out of your head."

Hannah exhaled in laughter. Unable to remain serious, Esther joined in. "Why is everyone so determined to set me up with Andrew Fisher?"

"Who is everyone?"

"You, for one. Lydia, my daed—"

"Daniel?"

"That's my only daed. He's been devising ways to throw the two of us together."

"So what do you have against him?"

"My daed?"

"No, silly, Andrew?"

"I've told you before."

"If you mean the teasing when you were kinner, that's over and done with. It's in the past, Esther. Let it go."

"He still teases."

"But not in a bad way. He's fun to be with. And he seems really nice."

"Then *you* pair up with him."

"Ach, Esther, you know I already have someone I'm perfectly happy with."

"Don't I know it!" Under her breath, she added, "Must be nice."

"I heard that! It is quite nice, actually. I think you'd find that out if you gave Andrew a chance. It isn't like you to hold a grudge."

"I'm not holding a grudge. I'm, uh, wary. That's it; I'm wary."

"Wary of what?"

"Why, of getting hurt again, I suppose."

"I don't believe Andrew would hurt you, not intentionally, anyway."

"Hmpf!"

"What aren't you telling me about the past?"

"Who said there was anything else to tell?"

"Well, I think you really like him, whether you want to admit that or not."

"How can you say such a thing?" Esther pressed her palms to her cheeks.

"You're blushing right now, for one thing." Hannah began counting on her fingers. She held up a second finger. "You start fidgeting and stammering whenever Andrew is around." She held up a third finger and took a breath before continuing.

"Enough!" Esther grabbed Hannah's hand.

"I'm going to cut through the field here. Think about giving him a chance, Esther. We all change, you know." She squeezed her hand.

"See you." She squeezed back.

"You know I'm only saying these things because I care, ain't so?"

"Jah. I know." Esther released her hand so they could go their separate ways.

She pondered her freind's words the rest of the way home. Could Hannah be right? Had Andrew really changed from the mischievous, pesky, hateful youngster into a kind, caring, funny young man? Did she truly care about him already? Why did she turn into a stammering and, jah, mean person when he was around? Was she so hurt by his actions when they were kinner because she really wanted him to like her? Was there some perfectly acceptable reason why he didn't show up to meet her at the promised time that day? He moved right after that, so maybe something had happened at home. Had she been trying to punish him now or was she simply afraid to trust that he could be different? Oooh! Life could be so confusing!

Esther shook her head to clear the tangled thoughts. She'd been so preoccupied she passed by her own home. She doubled back across the field, praying no one saw her miss her own driveway. She needed to concentrate on her business and on how to help David and Ella stay healthy. She needed to forget about Andrew Fisher.

She picked up her pace as she neared the edge of the field. She had a sudden inspiration about growing lavender and wanted to check out the available space in her garden and greenhouse. According to Sophie, lavender was in high demand. Seemed these days, all Englischers wanted something to calm them down and induce a peaceful sleep. As for herself, after a hard day's work, she usually dropped off to sleep the instant her head sank onto her pillow. Usually.

Sophie said lavender was pretty easy to grow, so Esther shouldn't have any problem adding it to her repertoire of plants. She was learning so much from Sophie. And that was another thing jumbled up in her mind. Why was Sophie suddenly so eager to pass on her knowledge? She hoped the wise woman wasn't secretly ill. She would not allow herself to dwell on that thought. "Give it to the Lord Gott," she said aloud and immediately sent a prayer up for the older woman.

Chapter Nine

Esther rushed around the kitchen early the next morning, helping to prepare breakfast. She had already loaded the plants she hoped to sell at the market. She tried to set up at least once a week at the smaller market in the library parking lot. Other times, customers came to the house. Business had been good so far this year. She opened the oven and grabbed a hot pad to pull out the pan of biscuits.

"They look perfect!" Lydia exclaimed leaning over Esther's shoulder. "Much improved."

"What you mean is we won't have to throw this batch against the wall to break them into edible-sized chunks."

Lydia burst out laughing. "Your last batch wasn't *that* bad, but your cooking skills are improving."

"Nowhere to go but up!"

Lydia laughed again. She reached into the small breadbox where she stored the gluten-free bread and cookies. She slathered creamy butter and thick strawberry jam on two slices of bread, one for each of the kinner.

Mamm slid the last sizzling fried egg onto a plate and set it on the kitchen counter next to a plate of crisp bacon. "Here," she said, handing Ella a handful of forks to arrange at each place at the table. Always happy to help, Ella took the forks and shuffled to the table without her usual enthusiasm. Mamm watched her and then turned to Esther with raised eyebrows. She shrugged and shook her head.

She placed the biscuits on the table as Ella laid down the last fork. Esther hugged her little niece. "Are you feeling okay?" Ella nodded but laid her head against her *aenti* and sighed a weary, grown-up sigh. Esther gave her a gentle squeeze. "Are you hungry?" Ella nodded again. "Gut." She released the little girl and helped her get situated in her place at the table. "Your mamm is fixing you some yummy bread with jam."

Moments later, David entered the kitchen with Daed, his face and hands freshly scrubbed. He, too, looked a little tired. Esther exchanged a worried look with her mamm. She wondered if Lydia noticed her kinners' pallor or if she was pretending nothing was amiss. Should she say something or would Mamm mention any concerns to Lydia? She especially didn't want her schweschder to bite her head off if she truly was in denial and didn't want to face the reality of the little ones' situation.

Mamm set David's and Ella's plates—that had not come into contact with gluten-containing foods—in front of them. They each had an egg and a strip of bacon cooked in special pans and a slice of their special bread. After the silent prayer, the only sound was that of forks scraping against china.

After a few bites, David moaned. "My tummy hurts."

"Me too," Ella echoed.

"Not again." Lydia reached to place her hand on first one little forehead and then the other. "No fever. I don't understand this. We're so careful." Tears welled in her eyes.

"Can you eat a few more bites for me, maybe of the eggs?" Esther coaxed. "And drink some of your milk?" Both reluctantly ate their eggs and drank their milk to the obvious relief of the adults at the table.

Mamm and Lydia enlisted the kinners' help in putting the kitchen in order following breakfast, so Esther was free to travel to the market to spend much of the day there. She liked being home, but she did enjoy the chance to mingle with other members of her own district and neighboring districts at the market. She also secretly hoped to carry out another mission.

The bright sun radiated heat off the blacktop parking lot at the Cherry Hill library, making Esther glad the vendors' booths were situated well back in the shade. The horses must be grateful to be in the shade, too. They flicked their tails and munched happily on grass.

She kept busy; it seemed a lot of Englischers were eager to buy plants and flowers this fine summer day. She barely had time to chat with the other Amish vendors. She spied Hannah flitting around, helping first one vendor and then another as needed. Just as she was about to give up on her plan, Esther spotted Kathy Taylor wandering through the maze of vendors and customers. She beckoned for the short, plump Englischer to join her.

"Hello, Esther. How's business?" Kathy greeted her.

"Business has been real gut today. Um, Kathy, I was wondering if I could get you to drive me up to the drug store for a minute if I can get Hannah to babysit my plants here." Esther paused to survey the crowd for Hannah. "I'll pay you, of course."

"No worry, Esther. I actually need to go there myself, so I won't charge you anything. I can drop you back off here on my way home."

"Danki, Kathy. Let me see if I can get Hannah's attention."

"I'll fetch her for you. You get your purse. I'll be right back." Kathy disappeared into the crowd as Esther waited on another customer.

"Do you need me?" Hannah gasped moments later. Kathy was slower in making her way back to Esther's booth.

"Jah. Do you think you could mind the business here for me for a few minutes while Kathy runs me up to the drug store?"

"Sure. I think I can manage that."

"Ready?" Kathy huffed and puffed. "I've really got to get in shape."

Esther snatched up her purse and joined Kathy. "Be back soon, Hannah. Danki."

"Take your time. I'll be fine here, as long as you've priced everything."

"It's all marked."

"Okay. Shoo!" Hannah waved them off.

Kathy chattered away during the short drive to the pharmacy. Esther interjected an occasional "uh huh" but was mainly preoccupied with her mission.

She slid the van door open as soon as they rolled to a stop in front of the store. "I'll try to be fast."

"Not to worry. I have to get a birthday card for my mother-in-law. It could take me a while." Kathy rolled her eyes, making Esther smile.

She glanced neither right nor left but headed straight for the back of the store. Relieved to find no one else waiting, and especially no one around who knew her, she approached the counter.

"May I help you?" a pleasant young woman asked.

"C-could I speak with the pharmacist if h-he's not busy?"

"Let me check. I'll be right back."

Thirty seconds later, the woman returned with an attractive fortyish woman with every strand of auburn hair perfectly in place. She wore a white lab coat over her stylish black slacks and print blouse. A lady pharmacist. For some reason, Esther felt relieved. She'd be much more comfortable talking to a woman.

"What can I do for you?" The woman had a soft, pleasant voice. Her smile crinkled the corners of her eyes. She moved away from the counter so they could have a bit of privacy.

"I-I was wondering if you could identify some medicine for me."

"I will certainly try."

"I have two freinden—uh, friends, who dropped their medication. I picked the pills up for them, but I'm confused. The pills look alike to me, but these people had different things wrong with them." Esther rummaged through her purse to locate the pills she had put in separate small, plastic sandwich bags, one labeled "M" and the other labeled "J."

"Do you know why they were taking the pills?"

"*Jah*. One had the pneumonia, but the pills didn't help and he ended up at the hospital. The other has high blood pressure. She said the pills weren't helping her either. So they can't be the same medicine, can they?" She produced the two baggies and passed them to the pharmacist.

The woman turned the baggies different ways. "They look like the same...same numbers and markings, but these wouldn't−" she broke off. A deep frown replaced her earlier smile. She suddenly looked agitated. "Were your friends prescribed these pills by a doctor and did they fill the prescriptions here?"

"Uh, actually, the doctor gave them both the pills from his office."

The pharmacist's eyebrows shot up. "Really? The same doctor?"

"*Jah*. They had the same doctor." Her voice dropped so low she was practically whispering. Her goal wasn't to get anyone in trouble. She only wanted to figure out what the pills were and why they didn't help. Esther couldn't let a mystery go unresolved. It was simply her nature. She used to think if she had been born Englisch, she would have been a detective.

"Can you wait a moment to let me double check that I am right about these pills?"

"Sure. I can wait."

The pharmacist sped off toward the back lab area. Esther wandered around the small healthcare section of the store near the drug counter. She feigned interest in the brochures about diabetes and heart disease and prayed the pharmacist would return before Kathy found her and overheard any exchange of information. She liked Kathy very much and trusted her but did not want to air any suspicions or be the originator of any rumors. Preoccupied with her thoughts, Esther picked subconsciously at her nails. She nearly jumped out of her skin when a voice spoke close to her ear.

"I'm so sorry I startled you," the pharmacist apologized. She lowered her voice before continuing. "It's exactly as I thought." She inched over to the far corner of the store, beckoning Esther to follow. "These pills are identical, and they are prenatal vitamins."

"Prenatal vitamins?" She frowned in confusion. "Then they wouldn't help pneumonia or high blood pressure at all."

"Absolutely not." The woman paused a moment as if trying to sort out her thoughts. "Are you sure your friends were given the pills by the doctor, or were they given a prescription that perhaps was filled wrong? If I had their names I could check our computer files to see if a mistake was made at this pharmacy."

"Nee, I do not believe you made a mistake here. Both people said the doctor gave them the pills. He told them it would save them a trip to the drug store."

The pharmacist's frown matched Esther's. "Hmmm. That's interesting. Do you happen to know who the doctor was?"

Esther dropped her gaze to the floor. She gave a slight nod. "I do, but I don't want to get anyone in any trouble."

"I understand. But your friends need the correct medicine. These vitamins won't improve their medical conditions."

Esther looked up briefly and then back at her shoes. "Mose already went to the hospital and got antibiotics. He's better now. Joanna lost weight, goes for walks, and cut out salt but hasn't gotten better," she mumbled, grappling with the discovery. "Why would a doctor not give the needed medicine?" She ventured a peek at the pharmacist's face.

"Why indeed!" She was obviously troubled. "Joanna has the high blood pressure, right?"

Esther hesitated and then nodded. She hadn't intended to reveal their names.

"She won't get better on vitamins. She needs the correct medication. Can you get her to talk to this doctor or, better yet, get her to see another doctor?"

"I don't know."

"High blood pressure can be dangerous, even deadly. She needs treatment — the right treatment."

"Jah, I know. I'll surely try to talk to her."

"Are you certain you can't — or won't — give me the doctor's name?"

"I'll think on it. Danki, er, thank you for your help."

"You're welcome. Please let me know if I can do anything else or if you need my help with...well, with anything."

Esther nodded and reached for the baggies the woman still held in her hands. She wanted to stuff them back into her purse before Kathy located her.

"May I keep these?" The pharmacist had not yet relinquished the bags to Esther.

"I guess so." Esther wasn't sure about giving up the evidence but was even more unsure what she would have done with it anyway.

"There you are," Kathy called, walking down the aisle toward them, a greeting card and a magazine in her hand.

The pharmacist closed her hand around the baggies and jammed her hands into the pockets of her lab coat. "Let me know if I can help you or your friends." She kept her voice low.

Esther could practically see the woman's thoughts. It wouldn't be too difficult for her to determine which doctors the Amish usually visited and possibly determine which one was responsible for giving the wrong medicines. She nodded and hurried down the aisle to meet her driver. "I'm ready if you are."

Kathy must have sensed something was amiss. She didn't attempt to elicit much conversation on the drive back to the market after her first few tries were met with blank stares or mumbles. She hummed along with the radio and tapped her fingers on the forest green steering wheel, keeping the beat of the music.

Esther stared unseeingly out of the van window. She mulled over the information she had gleaned but could make no sense of it. Why would a knowledgeable doctor deliberately give his sick patients the wrong medicine? Actually, it wasn't even the wrong medicine; it was *no* medicine. How did he expect them to recover with no medicine? Surely he knew he gave them vitamins—vitamins for pregnant women. Why? Why would he jeopardize their lives?

Mose had recovered only after being rushed to the hospital for treatment. She had to talk to him and Joanna to make sure Dr. Kramer hadn't given them any other medicines they might have mixed up. Joanna was still sick and could get sicker. She had to somehow convince her to seek out alternative care.

And what about David and Ella? Some niggling little voice had told her to check the bottle of pills the doctor had given them at their appointment. She had and found they were truly vitamins. They were in a sealed bottle with a label detailing each vitamin and its amount. They must be the real thing, unless the good doctor could somehow tamper with the bottle and then make it all look authentic. Maybe she should bring that bottle to the drug store to have the pharmacist check it out, just to be on the safe side. David and Ella didn't take any other medicine, thank goodness. The kinner were healthy when they first came to St. Mary's County to live. Now, they kept relapsing despite Lydia's, Mamm's, and her own vigilance.

Esther rubbed her hand over her forehead, trying to relax the frown that had formed. Who could she discuss this with? She needed to confide in someone, get another perspective. She couldn't talk to Lydia or her mamm without upsetting them. Maybe Hannah could help her make some sense of this whole complicated mess. After all, she was an Englischer until recently. She may have heard of some similar happening in her former life. Maybe even Sophie would have some ideas. This was a real, honest-to-goodness mystery, not one of her beloved fictional mysteries neatly resolved by the end of the novel. Somehow, she had to fit the pieces of this puzzle together to help her people.

Esther bit her lip and frowned again. It would be easy enough to talk to Mose. She'd simply wander out to the sawmill to visit a bit. Nothing unusual about that. She used to spend a lot of time at the mill until Mamm decided she needed to become more proficient in the domestic arena. Getting over to see Joanna would be a little trickier. She'd have to invent some need concerning the nursery in order for her reason to be plausible.

"Are you okay?" Kathy raised her voice over the radio.

Esther looked up and met Kathy's eyes in the rearview mirror. Apparently, the older woman had been observing her. Esther forced the muscles in her face to relax. "Jah. I'm just thinking."

"Must be some serious thoughts."

"I suppose so." Should she confide in Kathy? Kathy was a good-hearted soul, but she did like to talk. Esther didn't want tales to get started so she kept mum. "Did you find a nice card?" She figured she'd better try to make small talk to throw off any suspicion or speculation on Kathy's part.

"Finally, but it wasn't easy. I didn't want one of those mushy, lovey-dovey cards. My mother-in-law and I aren't that close. And I certainly couldn't get one of those funny growing older cards. She'd come through the mailbox and strangle me. I settled on a general card with flowers on it and a simple verse."

Esther gave an understanding nod that she realized Kathy probably couldn't see. "It doesn't sound like she could take offense at that."

"I certainly hope not. I sure don't want to rattle her cage."

Esther smiled. The Englisch had some funny sayings. She supposed the Amish did too.

Kathy signaled and pulled the van into the library parking lot. Esther could see Hannah waiting on a customer and another Englisch woman looking at the potted flowers. Near her plant stand, an Amish man and an Englisch man unloaded a wagon. It looked like a heavy, Amish-made table. It looked like… Esther's heart skipped several beats in a row, causing her to pat her chest. Why did it have to be Andrew? Why did he always seem to show up wherever she was?

Kathy waved off Esther's offer to pay for the ride. "I was going anyway."

"Okay. Danki, Kathy." Esther slid out of the van, contemplating a way to sneak to her booth undetected. With any luck, the Englischer would keep Andrew busy at least for a few minutes.

Hannah was completing her transaction when Esther squeezed in beside her. "You're back. That didn't take long."

"Nee, I guess not. Have you been busy?"

"Jah. Pretty steady, actually.

"Gut." Esther stared off into space.

"Is everything all right?"

"Jah. Nee. I…" Esther almost revealed her dilemma.

"Hannah, are you ready to leave? I need to get back home." Naomi Beiler's breath came in little gasps as she strode toward the two younger women.

Hannah glanced at her. Esther knew her freind sensed she was troubled and would like nothing more than to wheedle the details out of her. Hannah squeezed her hand. "I'd like to stay and talk, but since I rode here with Naomi, I need to leave now. And I did promise Rebecca I would be home early to give her some respite from the twins' fussiness." She looked at Naomi and back at Esther.

"Go ahead. I'm fine." She tried to sound confident, but she really wasn't feeling too fine. She had worried her intestines into a knot and wasn't sure if the apple she had munched on earlier would work its way around the knot or travel back up the way it had gone down. She offered a tremulous smile. "Danki for your help. I'm sure Rebecca needs a break by now."

"We'll talk later?"

"For sure." Esther sighed as she watched Hannah dash off with Naomi. So much for getting Hannah's input. She watched until they were swallowed up by Naomi's gray buggy.

"Wie bist du heit, Esther?"

A deep voice pulled Hannah back to the present. "Andrew!" Esther assumed—had hoped—he had left after unloading the table. She had momentarily forgotten all about him. "I'm, uh, gut."

"You don't sound so sure about that. Was ist letz?"

"N-nothing is wrong."

"You don't sound so sure about that either."

"Ach, Andrew, I don't know what to do." The words burst out of her mouth before she could stop them. Now they were hanging out there, and she couldn't call them back.

"Do you want to tell me? I can be a gut listener." "Really?" She wasn't convinced of any such thing.

"Really. Try me. You can trust me."

"Really?" She mentally kicked herself for sounding like she had a one-word vocabulary.

"Jah." He nodded his head as if to further confirm his trustworthiness.

Esther's voice dropped to barely above a whisper. Andrew leaned close to hear her words. "You have to promise not to tell anyone until I figure out what to do. Can you do that?"

At his hesitation, she started to turn away from him, but he grabbed her arm to force her to face him again. "I promise."

She almost felt sorry for him. He looked as if he regretted his offer to listen and would take that promise back if he could.

Chapter Ten

Esther moved closer to Andrew so she could keep her voice low. He hoped she couldn't hear the pounding of his heart at her nearness. He wished she moved closer to him because she wanted to and not because she had to in order to reveal her secret. He looked down from his six-foot height at the beautiful dark-haired woman by his side. *Concentrate, Andrew! Concentrate on what she's saying, not on her creamy complexion, big brown doe eyes, raspberry colored lips, soft lilac scent...enough!* He mentally doused his thoughts with ice water and forced his brain to focus on the words whispered from those lips.

"I think that new doctor who's taking Dr. Nelson's place is giving people the wrong medicine."

"Huh?"

"Andrew! Aren't you paying attention?" She raised her voice a bit and stomped her foot, clearly frustrated with him.

"Jah. Jah. Calm down, Essie."

"Esther!"

"Okay. Sorry." He lassoed his wandering mind. "Who? What? Wrong medicine?"

"Do you remember Dr. Nelson from when you lived here as a bu?"

"Sure."

"He's been away taking care of his sick daed. Dr. Kramer has been here to take his place." She paused and put a hand to her face as if to prevent her words from becoming public knowledge. "I think...well, it seems Dr. Kramer is giving the wrong medicine."

"How do you know?" Did she think learning about herbs from Sophie made her an expert in medicine now?

Esther gave Andrew a brief overview of Mose Troyer's and Joanna King's problems and described the same peach-colored pill both had been given by the doctor. She relayed her earlier conversation with the pharmacist. "Mose is better, thank the Lord, but I have to talk to Joanna."

"Should you get involved in this, Esther?"

"Andrew Fisher! How can I not get involved? I have to help our people if I can." Her voice rose in volume again.

"You make it sound like this doctor is targeting the Amish. It all seems very strange." It sounded like Esther may be onto something, not merely a whim.

"Shady dealings, I'm thinking."

"Maybe. I-I wouldn't want you to get hurt in any way."

"Me? How could I get hurt? It's Joanna and who knows who else that I'm concerned about."

"What if this man is doing something 'shady' as you say? He might not take too kindly to your inter-

Plain Discovery   133

fering. He might do something to hurt you." How could he get her to consider her own safety?

"I have no intention of seeking his medical advice for myself or of taking any of his pills. It's my family and freinden who could suffer dire consequences. Ach! I should have kept my mouth shut." She turned as if to leave.

"Your schweschder's kinner see this doctor, ain't so?"

"Jah and I'll make sure to attend all their appointments. I intend to watch the man like a hawk. I'm also going to make sure David and Ella don't take any pills from him except for the vitamins. They were in a sealed bottle, but I'm going to have the pharmacist take a look at them anyway. In the meantime, I've got to talk to Joanna."

"I'm worried—" Andrew broke off when Barbara Zook sidled up to the booth.

"You two are looking kind of cozy," Barbara teased.

Esther immediately took a giant step away from Andrew. "Did you sell any quilts today?" Andrew almost smiled at her attempt to divert Barbara's attention.

"I took an order for a queen-sized quilt and sold a gut many smaller quilted items."

"That's wunderbaar. I hope they gave you a lot of time to make that quilt."

"I can get it done pretty fast once I get going on it. Ah-ah-choo!" Barbara reached for the tissue stuffed in her sleeve and dabbed at her runny nose and red, watery eyes.

"You don't sound too gut," Andrew remarked.

"It's nothing contagious. Ah-ah-choo!" Barbara paused to wipe her nose again. "These allergies seem to be a lot worse this year. I guess I need another medicine."

"What have you tried?" Esther asked. He nearly laughed aloud at the image of her as a hound dog with ears perked up at a new scent.

"About every herb Sophie has and a few drug-store medicines. I even saw that Dr. Kramer and tried his pills. They haven't helped either."

"He wrote you a prescription for allergy medicine?"

"He started to but then changed his mind. He gave me some pills from his supply to save me some money."

"How thoughtful." Andrew glanced at Esther, who shot him a dirty look that made him glad he was not within striking distance.

"Do you know what the pills were?" Esther probed.

"I don't know the name of them. They're kind of oblong and are a peachy color." Barbara used her thumb and forefinger to indicate the approximate size of the pills.

"And they haven't helped at all?"

Andrew could almost see the wheels turning at top speed in Esther's head.

"Nee. They haven't done a thing for me. I guess I'll have to go back to the doctor, but I don't really want to do that."

"Didn't you like this Dr. Kramer?" He figured he might as well help investigate.

"I don't know that it's a matter of liking him. There's something about him. He's...well, he's not Dr. Nelson."

"For sure," Esther agreed. "You know, you could ask the pharmacist to recommend something. The lady pharmacist at Tideview is very helpful. It might save you a doctor visit."

"Gut idea. Danki, Esther." Barbara turned away to sneeze again. "I'm going to pack up and call it a day."

"I suppose I will, too. I think business is about over for today." Esther reached for a hanging pot of petunias and called after Barbara. "Don't forget to talk to the pharmacist."

"Overkill," Andrew mumbled.

"I don't want her to go back to that man. She needs to get some medicine that will help her, not vitamins for expectant mothers. So, now what do you think?"

"I think you may be onto something. There really does seem to be a problem."

Esther nodded. "I told you so." She began carrying plants to her wagon. Assuming he'd probably be turned down if he asked, Andrew simply grabbed some plants and helped her pack up.

"I wonder who else is taking those vitamins." She stared off into the distance.

"Be careful, Esther."

Talking to Mose was not a problem at all. In fact, Mamm made it easy. Esther intercepted her mamm the next afternoon as she was on her way to the sawmill with a big thermos of lemonade and paper cups.

"I'll take that for you, Mamm." She had come inside for a cold drink herself. "Let me wash the dirt off my hands first."

"Danki, dochder. It has gotten pretty hot today. I know the men have water, but I thought they could use a little lemonade about now."

"Whew! You're right about the heat. It feels like an August day instead of late June." Esther poured herself a cup of lemonade and downed it in two gulps. "That hit the spot." She threw the paper cup in the trash can. "It's awfully quiet in here."

"Jah, blessed silence." Mamm sighed. "The kinner are down for naps. Lydia had another headache and went to bed, too."

"I thought her headaches were getting better."

"Jah, they were. Maybe it's the heat." Mamm fanned herself with a dish towel. "Maybe she needs to make a doctor appointment for herself."

"Not with Dr. Kramer," Esther muttered under her breath.

"What's that?"

"I'll take the lemonade out." Esther snatched up the thermos and cups and headed for the door. She'd have to be more careful about thinking aloud.

"Wie bist du heit?" She asked as Mose wiped his mouth with the back of his hand after guzzling a cup of lemonade.

"Gut, Esther. I'm feeling fine now. I've almost got my weight back." He patted his belly.

"You aren't taking any medicine now?"

"Nee. I don't need it."

"I'm ever so glad to hear that. Say, Mose, were you ever on any other pills before you went to the hospital—other than those peach-colored ones, I mean." Esther feigned a casual interest and prayed Mose wouldn't ask why she wanted to know.

"Nee. Only those pills you saw that day, the ones that didn't work at all for me."

"Well, I'm happy you're well now." She smiled.

"That makes two of us. Three, if you count Martha." He chuckled.

Esther laughed along with him. "I'm sure she's glad you're better. I'll let you get back to work now."

She scooted around the mill, greeting other workers briefly. She didn't want it to appear she had singled Mose out for any reason. She was working hard at being a gut detective. All those mystery novels she'd read over the years were certainly coming in handy now.

Esther scurried about, putting away hoses and gardening tools so she could assist Mamm to get supper on the table. If Lydia still had her headache, she wouldn't be much help. Leaving the greenhouse, she breathed in deeply the sweet fragrance wafting over from Mamm's lilac bushes. Such a heavenly smell. No wonder the bees and butterflies loved those bushes.

The sudden sound of wheels on the gravel driveway claimed her attention. Would daed have a customer this late? She knew he would be finishing up for the day, too. Esther shaded her eyes with her hands and gulped as recognition set in. Andrew. What on earth was he doing here?

Esther was certain she was covered with dirt. Maybe he was here to see Daed about some lumber. Just the same, she wiped her hands on her filthy apron and picked at the dirt caked under her fingernails. She stood still, hoping he would continue on to the mill. That was not to be, though. He pulled his horse and wagon right alongside Esther and stopped there.

"Hello, Esther."

"Hello, Andrew. I think Daed's probably about to close for the day."

"I didn't stop by to see your daed."

She shot him a questioning look but said nothing. She watched as he leaned down closer to her. "I came to see you."

Esther still said nothing. She swatted at a fly buzzing too near her face.

"Jacob needs me to pick up some tools he had repaired at Timothy Zimmerman's over in Joyville tomorrow. I thought, maybe…that is, uh, I wondered if you'd like to ride along. We could stop at Joanna King's place."

Esther had been about to refuse the offer until Andrew mentioned Joanna. She *had* to talk to Joanna. Maybe she could tell Mamm and Daed she needed cuttings from some of Joanna's plants. That would certainly be plausible. She and Joanna often traded cuttings when they had the opportunity. Esther looked up into Andrew's eyes so full of hope. "That might be a great idea. I *must* talk to Joanna. This may be my only opportunity. Danki, Andrew. I'll kumm along."

"Gut. I'll be by around nine. Is that okay?"

"Sure."

"Uh, well, I guess I'd best get home. See you tomorrow, Esther." He straightened back up in his seat and clucked to his horse to get him moving.

"Okay," she called out. She probably should have asked him to stay for supper or at least offered him a cold drink. But this wasn't a social call. She didn't want to encourage that, for sure and for certain. Did she? She shrugged and hurried to the house.

Esther heard whistling over the clip-clopping of a horse's hooves on her way back to the house the next morning. She had gone to her greenhouse right after breakfast to collect a basket full of cuttings to take to Joanna King. She wanted her excuse for going to see Joanna to be authentic, so she had selected some of her more unusual and exotic plants to snip cuttings from. Truth be told, though, Mamm didn't seem to care why she was making the trek over to Joanna's. She simply seemed glad that a man was driving her there. Honestly, was her family so eager to marry her off that they'd pair her up with the first man that came along? It was a gut thing they didn't believe in arranged marriages or they would have had her hitched to crusty old Silas Hostetler long ago. Esther shivered despite the warm morning. Now there was a scary thought.

The whistling grew louder. As Esther suspected before the horse and wagon even pulled into the Stauffers' driveway, the whistling came from Andrew. She quickened her pace to the house so she could let Mamm know she was leaving. The cloudless, blue sky and bright sunshine foretold another hot day. She was glad they were getting an early start before perspiration had a chance to trickle down her back and mar her dress.

She set her basket on the step and hurried inside to scrub her hands and smooth her hair. Why should she care about her appearance? It was only Andrew. She didn't want Joanna or anyone else along the way to think she was an untidy person, though, she told herself.

"Mamm, I'm leaving now. I'll be back as soon as I can," she hollered.

"Not to worry, Esther. We'll mind the nursery." Mamm entered the kitchen with a dust rag in her hand. "Lydia is feeling better today, thank the gut Lord. You, uh, have a nice time."

Esther raised her eyebrows. "Exchanging plant cuttings?"

"Jah and, uh, whatever."

"Right, Mamm." Esther walked quickly through the kitchen to hug her mudder before heading back outside. No use making Andrew start searching for her.

"*Gude mariye.*" Andrew smiled broadly as he prepared to jump down to help Esther climb into the wagon.

"Hello, Andrew. Don't bother to get down. I can climb up just fine." She set her basket of cuttings in the back of the wagon before clambering up to sit on the wooden seat. She left as much space as possible between them. He guessed she didn't want to set any tongues wagging.

He nodded. *Stubborn woman. She never wants to let anyone help her. She's too independent.* He forced negative thoughts away. "Beautiful morning." Surely she couldn't find fault with that remark, could she?

"Jah, it is." She sighed softly and lifted her head to gaze at the sky.

He glanced sideways at her. Did she really agree with him? Maybe the day would be okay after all. "You brought the plants for Joanna, I see." Of course she did. He saw her put them in the wagon. Dumb comment.

"Jah. I told Mamm I needed to exchange cuttings with Joanna. I didn't want to be untruthful, so I snipped some of my plants."

"Gut." Andrew shook the reins so the horse trotted a little faster. Traffic on the road had thinned since most of the rush-hour traffic had already cleared the area. That would certainly help make the drive more relaxing. Now if Esther could actually relax. From the corner of his eye, he could see that she sat straight and tall, stiff as a plank of wood. How could he put her at ease? His brain searched for a neutral topic. "So have you been back to Sophie's?"

"Not recently, but I hope to get there later in the week."

"Tell me what you are learning from her."

"It's really fascinating. Who would have thought there are so many uses for simple plants?" Her face brightened, and her hands spoke along with her mouth. He hit pay dirt with this topic. She chattered away happily about plants and herbs.

"Do you think you'll grow some of the plants Sophie uses?"

"Jah. I'm already planning to grow lavender and more rosemary and basil and...well, all sorts of things. I've always stuck with mostly flower and vegetable plants with a few herbs. Now I hope to branch out."

"It sounds like a great plan. Do you think Sophie's getting ready to give up her business?"

"I surely hope not. She's so wise. She did say since she had no kinner she was glad I was willing to learn from her. I do hope everything is okay with her. She's pretty tight-lipped about personal matters."

"We'll have to keep her in our prayers."

"For sure."

"Do you want to see Joanna first?"

"Whatever you want to do will be fine."

He couldn't believe his luck. Again, she was agreeable. And she had relaxed a whole lot while talking about her plants. She was so pretty when her face lit up in excitement. *Better not go there, Andrew, my man.* "Well, then, I'll stop at Zimmerman's real quick and you can take your time at Joanna's."

"Okay. Danki, Andrew."

She smiled a real smile, one that reached her doe eyes. He allowed himself a grin so wide he feared it would split his face. He'd have danced a jig if dancing were permitted—and if he wouldn't fall off the rolling wagon.

Andrew completed his business as quickly as he could and placed Jacob's newly repaired tools in the back of the wagon. The morning was still young when they drove up the Kings' long gravel driveway. Children of assorted ages hoed gardens, weeded flower beds, and watered the flowers that bloomed in terracotta pots. Mary, Joanna's oldest, swept the front porch with a vengeance, obviously determined to chase away any spider web or speck of dust.

Esther looked over at the huge garden and chuckled. "Celery."

"What's that?" Andrew asked.

"Celery. Lots of celery. I guess Mary is likely to marry her beau come fall."

"Or someone likes a lot of celery."

She jumped down from the wagon as soon as the wheels stopped rolling and leaned over to snatch her basket of cuttings. "Thank goodness the temperature hasn't soared yet. The cuttings still look fine."

"I would have helped you, you know."

"That's okay, Andrew." She had already started for the greenhouse where they had seen little Ruth disappear. If Ruth went in there, most likely Joanna was there. "I'm used to doing things for myself."

"Jah, too used to it." Would she ever want to change that? Would she ever want to let someone into her life? Would she ever want to share the load with someone, to share her life with someone? With him? Would Esther ever see him as anything other than the pesky, mean, little bu who teased her mercilessly? He had been trying to show her he had changed. The man he now was had changed for the better, he hoped.

He shook his head to scare those thoughts away as he'd done on numerous occasions. The trouble was they never fully vanished. They just hovered around the edges of his brain so they could pounce and take over whenever the mood struck them. He'd better go see if Joanna's husband was in the barn. Maybe he could help with something while he was there. He'd do anything to occupy his hands and his mind.

"Joanna!" Esther called as she neared the greenhouse. A little dark head popped out the open door. "Hi, Ruth. I'm Esther. Do you remember me?" The little girl nodded her head before retreating like a turtle drawing into its shell. A split second later, Joanna appeared, wiping her hands on a cloth that was nearly as soiled as her hands. Little Ruth clutched Joanna's green dress and hid behind her mamm the best she could.

"Esther! It's gut to see you. What brings you by?" Joanna reached around to extract the little hands clutching her. "Now, Ruthie. You stop this. Esther is a freind." Finally freeing herself, she added, "She's a mite timid at times."

Esther stooped down to be at Ruth's eye level. "Do you know my schweschder and her little kinner live with me now? Ella is about your age. Maybe you could play together some time." She talked to the little girl and told her a funny story about Ella and David until she smiled and then broke into giggles. Ruth sidled up to her to peer into her basket. "Kumm. I'll show you and your mamm what I've brought."

"Looks like you've made a freind." Joanna smiled at her, then bestowed a special loving, motherly smile on her youngest.

"Gut. I love kinner."

"You need a house full of them, Esther. You'd make a wunderbaar mamm." She swiped a stray strand of hair off her face, leaving behind a brown streak of dirt. *Exactly like me.*

"I'm not sure the Lord Gott has that in mind for me," she confessed.

"I wouldn't be too sure of that, Esther." Joanna's eyes twinkled and darted in the direction of the barn before returning to her.

She pretended she didn't notice that not-too-subtle gesture. Instead, she carried her basket into the greenhouse with little Ruth trotting along beside her. "Do you want to see what I have?" Joanna joined them and peered over Ruth's head. "You probably already have many of these plants, Joanna, but I wasn't sure. Here are several varieties of succulent plants. They've become quite popular in arrangements and corsages. My pinks have reproduced like crazy, so I brought you some. I have several types. Some produce small flowers and others have larger, ruffly flowers. All of them smell heavenly. You may have some already, but I think they smell better than roses."

"Me too," her freind agreed. "It's a gut thing you brought some. Mine sort of fizzled out last year, so I need to start some new ones. They'll spread out fairly rapidly."

Esther continued pulling plants out of the basket and identifying them, more for Ruth than for her muddere. She was pretty certain Joanna knew what most, if not all, of the plants were.

"I have some wunderbaar new petunias I'll share with you. I had them last year, and they were big sellers." Joanna pointed to her flats of the purple, white, and pink flowers.

"That sounds fine. Ruthie, can you run get some of those black plastic trays I saw by the porch, please?" The little girl sped off, obviously happy to help.

"I have some trays right here." Joanna pointed to a stack.

"I figured you did, but I wanted to talk to you without—"

"I understand. Was ist letz?"

"I-I'm wondering how you're doing, Joanna. Really. Don't say 'fine.' It looks like you've lost more weight."

"Well, I needed to lose some weight." She chuckled and patted her midsection.

"Not so much, I'm thinking. Is your blood pressure better?"

"Nee. I've been walking in the evenings as much to relax and calm down at the end of the day as to exercise. I don't salt my food or eat salty meats. I follow a pretty bland diet, actually, and still my blood pressure is high."

"Did Dr. Kramer change your medicine?"

"He only doubled my medicine like I said that day in his office. He told me to return next month."

"Those same peach-colored pills"

"Jah."

Esther wasn't quite sure how to proceed, but she had to try to be as persuasive as possible. "Joanna...uh, have you thought of seeing a different doctor?"

"I've thought about it, but most of us are used to going to Dr. Nelson."

"Dr. Nelson, for sure, but not this Dr. Kramer. I-I just think someone else may be able to help you more."

"Why is that?"

"Well, Mose Troyer didn't get better from the pneumonia until he went to the hospital and got a different medicine from the one Dr. Kramer gave him."

"Maybe he had an especially stubborn case?" Joanna's voice was laced with uncertainty. "You're biting your lip, Esther. What are you thinking?"

Her voice dropped to barely over a whisper. "Mose was taking oblong peach-colored pills that didn't help. The pharmacist said..." She paused, uncertain how much information she should reveal.

"Go on," her freind prodded.

"I-I...well, you know me, Joanna. I'm more curious than ten cats."

Joanna smiled and nodded encouragingly. "That's what makes you, you."

"I—please don't be angry—I took a pill I had from Mose and your pills that you dropped in the doctor's office to Tideview. The pharmacist said...uh, she said they were the same thing."

Joanna's face registered her surprise. "How could a blood pressure pill help Mose or a pneumonia pill help me?"

"They couldn't. Joanna. The pills were vitamins, prenatal vitamins."

"What? Why on earth—" She grasped her work bench to steady herself.

"Are you okay?"

"That's unbelievable! It's...it's..."

"It's outrageous and wrong!" Esther cried.

Joanna nodded. Tears sprang to her eyes. "No wonder I'm not getting better. Why would a trained doctor do such a thing?"

"I don't know, but I aim to find out. I also aim to find out who else might not be getting the proper treatment. Now you know why I want you to see someone else." She grasped her companion's arm. "Please?"

"Jah. I'll talk to Reuben tonight."

Esther saw the tears ready to stream down Joanna's face and gave the older woman's arm a gentle squeeze. "Gut."

"There's my little helper." Joanna sniffed hard as Ruth skipped into the greenhouse carrying a bouquet of yellow buttercups, wild violets, and a few ordinary weeds mixed in. "It's a gut thing we really didn't need the trays. My Ruthie can't resist picking the wildflowers. At least she knows they are the only ones she's allowed to pick."

Esther laughed. "What a lovely bouquet."

"For you." The girl beamed and thrust the little yellow and purple flowers at Esther.

"Danki, Ruth. That is very sweet." Esther stooped down to accept the flowers from Ruth's pudgy, little hands. She took a deep breath, pretending to inhale the imaginary fragrance of the wild-flowers. "Ah!" She sighed. The child giggled and threw her arms around Esther's neck.

"I'd say you've made a lifelong freind." Joanna laughed.

With Ruth's "help," the two women quickly removed her cuttings from the basket. Ruth helped pot the new plants in the trays while her snipped cuttings from some of her plants. "Tis gut to share," Joanna re-marked.

"Jah, we can both get different varieties for our customers." Esther placed Joanna's clippings gently into her basket. "Ach! I'd better hurry. Andrew needs to get to work, I'm sure. He came to pick up repaired tools from Zimmerman's and let me ride along to vis-it you."

"I have a feeling he doesn't mind you riding along one bit."

"Now, Joanna, don't go putting two and two to-gether and ending up with five."

"I can add pretty well," her freind teased. "It looks like we finished right in time. Here comes 'your ride' now."

She elbowed the older woman playfully. "You take care, Joanna, and see another doctor. Promise?"

"I will."

"Ready?" Andrew called.

"Be right there." she patted Joanna's arm and leaned down to give Ruth a hug. "You'll be as gut as your mamm at raising flowers." She tickled the little girl under her chin. Ruth giggled and beamed her pleasure at the praise.

Esther placed her basket in the wagon alongside the tools. She climbed in and settled herself on the seat. She turned to wave to Joanna and Ruth as Andrew got the horse moving.

At the end of the driveway, Andrew stopped the horse. Before pulling the wagon out onto the road, he turned to look at Esther. "Is everything all right?"

"Huh?" Esther's mind had already sped off in several directions at once.

"With Joanna. Is everything all right with Joanna?"

"Not really. She needs to see another doctor soon. I hope I convinced her to do that."

"If anyone could convince her, it would be you."

Esther shot Andrew a scowl. Was his remark supposed to be kind or criticizing? Why did she feel the need to question his every utterance?

"What? Why the dirty look? I didn't mean anything bad." Andrew reached as though to pat her arm but quickly rescinded as if afraid he'd get his hand bitten off. "All I meant was you are very persuasive. I'm sure Joanna sensed your concern. That's all. Honest!"

Esther released her tense shoulders. "I gave it my best shot."

"I'm sure you did."

"I've got to find out who else may be getting the wrong treatment or going without any treatment at all." Esther tapped her fingers absently on the wooden seat.

"How are you going to do that?"

"I'm not sure. I'll talk to Barbara Zook, for one." Tap, tap, tap. "I'll see if she visited the pharmacist for advice. Maybe she'll know if anyone else has been given the same pills." Tap, tap, tap.

"Maybe I could ask around a bit, see if the Fishers know anyone who's been sick lately."

"You'd do that?" Tap, tap, tap.

"I'll try."

"Danki. You know, Miriam Esh may have some information. People go to her store and talk about everything under the sun." Tap, tap, tap.

"That's a gut idea." He reached down to still her fingers drumming on the seat between them.

"Sorry." She slid her hand out from under his much larger one. "Bad habit."

"Be careful, Esther. I don't know this doctor fellow, but he may not take kindly to anyone messing with his patients."

"But he's not treating his patients properly. Someone has to stand up for them."

"And you've decided that someone is you?"

"I'm the one who's been trying to piece the information together. I have to speak up." She lapsed into silence for a few moments. "Maybe I was put here for that reason, to help my people." She gazed into the clear, blue sky as if searching for confirmation of that idea. The Book of Esther in the Bible was one of her favorites. That Esther risked her life to approach King Xerxes about the mistreatment of her people. Wicked Haman had plotted to destroy the Jews. Esther's uncle Mordecai reminded Esther that even though she had become queen, she would not be exempt from the evil plot. Mordechai's words—"who knows if perhaps you were made queen for just such a time as this?"—reverberated through Esther's mind. Maybe *she* was put there for just such a purpose as helping her people get the care they needed.

"You got awfully quiet." Andrew drew her attention back to the present.

"I'm thinking."

"Promise you won't do anything, uh, risky?" He patted her hands folded in her lap.

"Why do you care what I do?" she blurted before she could stop the words from tumbling out.

He seemed taken off guard. He hesitated as if trying to formulate a reply. "I...uh, do, that's all. I do care, I mean. I-I wouldn't want you to get into any kind of...uh, trouble or to get hurt."

For once, Esther was at a loss for words. Those funny little butterflies flapped around inside her stomach, inciting her heart to do a little somersault or two. Relief washed over her when her house came into view. Now she could get away from Andrew and the strange, unexplainable reactions her body was experiencing. Flustered and confused, she bolted from the wagon before "whoa" had left Andrew's mouth. She snatched up her basket of cuttings and raced for the house as if being chased by a demon. "Danki, Andrew," she threw over her shoulder and kept going.

"Esther, wait. I..." Andrew's words evaporated into the hot, humid air. Esther was as skittish as a newborn colt. Was she this way with everyone? *I don't think so. At least not as far as I've observed. It must be only me. How will I ever change that?*

Chapter Eleven

"You could have stayed in bed," Esther told Lydia who squinted as she stumbled into the bright, sunny kitchen the next morning. "I've got breakfast under control."

"Where's Mamm?"

"She and Daed ate cold cereal already so they could get an early start. Daed had to see someone about lumber over in Charles County. Mamm went along to visit with some of the women she hasn't seen in a while."

"That's right. I remember Mamm mentioned that. Who got David and Ella dressed?" Lydia's expression softened when she looked at David pouring gluten-free cereal into two bowls and Ella placing napkins and silverware on the table.

"I did. We tried to be quiet so we could let you rest. Is your headache better?"

"Much better. I still feel a little groggy, though. I appreciate your tending to the children."

"My pleasure." Esther slid fried eggs onto four plates and added scoops of hash brown potatoes. Ella eyed the plate of crispy bacon already on the table, obviously fighting the temptation to grab a piece. "Gut job, kinner. I didn't make biscuits, Lyddie. Do you want bread?"

"Nee, this is fine." Lydia searched the special bread box and counter. "Where is the kinners' bread?"

"I had to throw it out. It was growing green stuff."

"Ugh! That was the last of it, too."

"I'm planning to bake them some bread before I go outside to work. They'll be okay without bread for breakfast. They have their cereal."

"I'm sure you're right." Lydia poured herself a cup of kaffi and took a big gulp. "Maybe this will clear my brain fog. I always feel groggy after a bad headache."

"Don't you think you should go see about those headaches?"

"They really are getting better. I think it's mainly stress. And worrying about David and Ella."

"They're going to be fine." Esther tried to inject a positive tone into her voice. She, too, wondered why David and Ella had so many ups and downs while they were ever so careful to monitor their diets. She pasted a smile on her mouth and turned from the counter to give her schweschder a reassuring hug.

"I don't understand the fluctuations in their health." Lydia voiced Esther's own concerns.

"You don't think they could be sneaking into the wrong foods, do you?"

"That isn't too likely. We hover about them whenever they are in the kitchen or near food."

"That we do. And you're sure there is no other medical problem?"

"They were tested for everything under the sun in Pennsylvania. Nothing showed up except the celiac disease. And they were doing so well before we moved here once their diet was corrected."

"Hmmm. There isn't any other treatment for celiac disease except for diet, right? That's supposed to do the trick." What was it about *here* that made a difference in their health? She'd have to ponder that.

"That's what I thought." Lydia took a sip of kaffi and made a face. "Whew! This stuff is strong enough to dance across the room."

"Hey, don't blame me! Mamm made this before she left so it's been sitting here for a while. I think she may have been in a hurry and miscounted her scoops of kaffi, though."

"Have you tried it?"

"Barely. I had to pour it out and get a glass of milk." She paused, considering her next question, then plunged ahead. "Lydia, the kinner aren't taking any medicine, are they?"

"Nee. Only vitamins."

"And I checked that the bottle was sealed." Esther's thought popped out.

"What's that?"

"Um, just...uh, vitamins shouldn't affect them in a bad way." Esther had to think fast to cover her near slip. "So they should be fine as long as they follow the diet. The last time I was at the market at the library, I had to go inside to use the ladies' room. I asked the librarian if she had any information on celiac disease."

"Did she give you anything? I mean, they gave me tons of information in Pennsylvania. I didn't know if there was anything new or different."

"Well, she found information on the computer. I'm sorry I didn't have enough money with me to print all those pages. I did read as much as I could. I am a fast reader, you know."

"And?"

"The only treatment mentioned was diet. I read about people who had relapses only when they ate food containing gluten."

"That's what I thought." Lydia's sigh was big enough to be heard throughout the house.

"We'll get them on track, schweschder. I'm going to bake them some bread and treats. I threw out their cookies, too—what was left of them. They seemed a little stale."

"When did you become a baker?"

Esther shrugged her shoulders. "I found that I really do enjoy getting my hands in the flour and dough. It's kind of like working in the soil. And I really do love those kinner." For some reason, tears jumped into Esther's eyes.

"I know you do, Esther." Lydia squeezed her younger schweschder's arm.

"We're hungry!" David called out as he raced into the kitchen with Ella on his heels.

Esther sniffed and swiped at her eyes. "Well, you've kumm to the right place. Breakfast is ready."

She shooed everyone out of the kitchen after breakfast, even Lydia. "Go spend time with your little ones. You can let me know if I get any customers."

"Okay." Lydia marched the children outside to play before it got too hot to run around. "I can weed the front flower beds while I'm out there."

"Sure. If you feel like it."

"I think some fresh air and some physical work will help."

"Gut." Esther banged around in the cabinets to locate the ingredients she would need. She pulled out the baking pans reserved for the kinners' food and mixed up dough for bread, squeezing it between her fingers to knead it. She knew some people hated to have the sticky dough all over their hands. She equated it with thrusting her fingers into rich, damp soil to plant seeds and seedlings. The correlation hadn't occurred to her until today, but it made perfect sense. She didn't mind getting her hands messy. Dirt or dough under her fingernails didn't bother her.

She left the dough alone, wiped her hands on the checked towel, and stirred up peanut butter cookie batter. She had a few pieces of chocolate candy she'd place on each cookie as an extra treat. She'd read the ingredients and determined the candy was safe for David and Ella. *I've to figure out what's going on in their little bodies and how I can help them, and I need to be quick about it.*

"They were fine when they left Pennsylvania," she mused aloud. "Not long after they moved here, things started sliding downhill. It can't be the weather. That doesn't affect celiac disease."

She popped two baking sheets filled with cookies into the gas oven. She, Lydia, and Mamm were vigilant about adhering to the special diet. What could be the problem? While the cookies baked, Esther whipped up a batch of blueberry muffins using the plump, juicy blueberries she had picked from her overloaded bushes yesterday. She had mixed up enough bread dough for two loaves, so today's baking should produce enough food to last the kinner for a while.

"How's it going?" Lydia poked her head into the kitchen.

"Fine. When the two loaves of bread kumm out of the oven, I'll be done."

"I can watch that if you want to get outside for a while."

"Danki, Lydia. I think I will work outside for a bit."

"I'll make us some sandwiches for lunch. I guess David and Ella will have to have soup today. I won't make it too hot, though."

Esther escaped to her gardens with the intention of enjoying every minute in the fresh air, no matter how hot or humid it might be. She had a bad feeling Mamm was going to make her put up blueberry jam tomorrow.

As much as she loved eating fresh blueberries, after spending Saturday in the stifling kitchen, stirring and canning jam and preserves, Esther didn't care if she never fastened her eyes on a blueberry again. She didn't even eat a slice of the pie Mamm had her bake with the leftover fruit. She had to refrain from dashing outside to yank the bushes out of the ground and hurl them into the woods. Esther knew in a week or so, she'd be ready to eat blueberries again, but right now, she didn't want to think of them. That was pretty hard to do, though, when her hands were stained a purplish-blue color and visions of fat blueberries danced throughout her brain whenever she squeezed her eyes shut.

As preposterous as it seemed, she was actually grateful to sink onto the hard, wooden bench for Sunday's three-hour church service. Even the uncomfortable, backless bench was a welcome relief from standing for hours over a hot stove. She supposed she would grow accustomed to all things domestic if she ever had a home and family of her own. In the meantime, she'd prefer working outside, even if the mercury in the thermometer attached to the white picket fence surrounding the back yard did climb to over ninety degrees.

She attempted to concentrate on Bishop Sol's long main sermon and on the other ministers' shorter sermons, but it was a real challenge. Her lower back ached, and her right hand still cramped from all the stirring. She tried not to think how much harder making apple butter would be when September rolled around. "Sufficient unto each day are the worries thereof," or something like that, if she remembered her reading from the book of Matthew correctly.

At the conclusion of the service at noon, Esther carried platters and dishes to the tables set up in the shade of several old, gnarly oak trees in the Fishers' back yard. For once, she had hoped to remain in the kitchen to gather any snippets of information about anyone who had recently sought out medical treatment from Dr. Kramer. As soon as she entered the already crowded kitchen, Mamm had thrust dishes into her hands to carry outside. Maybe the Lord preferred she didn't eavesdrop but rather spoke to people directly. She would do that, she decided, as soon as opportunities presented themselves to her.

Finally, everyone had eaten until full. The kinner played tag or swung on the rope swing in the front yard. Men sat under trees to discuss crops and whatever else men usually talked about. Women cleared tables and cleaned up the kitchen. Esther finagled a way to work beside Barbara Zook. "How are you doing?" She spoke loud enough for only Barbara's ears to hear.

"I'm ever so much better. I took your advice and talked to the pharmacist. She recommended an allergy medicine I didn't need a prescription for. I'm not sneezing or blowing my nose nearly as much."

"I'm so glad to hear you're better."

"Have you been under the weather?" Miriam Esh obviously overheard the conversation despite Esther's attempt to speak quietly.

"It's my allergies. They seem worse this year."

"I've heard several customers at the store say that very same thing, even some Englischers."

"I'm sure allergies affect us all," Barbara replied. "This new medicine helps a lot. Maybe whenever the plants I'm allergic to stop blooming, I can stop taking it."

"Do you know what you're allergic to?" Esther asked.

"Nee. I never had any testing done. Ever since I was running around playing tag like those kinner in the yard, I've gotten the sniffles in spring and summer."

"I'm glad you found something to help." She patted Barbara's arm.

"Jah," Miriam agreed. "If you tell me what helped you, maybe I can recommend it to folks who come in the store complaining of allergies."

She drifted away and let the two older women chat. She was glad Barbara was feeling better. Still, she wondered who else had been given the peach-colored pills.

"Esther, was ist letz?" Hannah fell into step beside her.

"Nothing is wrong. I'm just thinking." She forced a smile. "You're looking more rested. Are Rebecca's twins in a better mood now?"

"Jah, thank goodness. We were all about worn to a frazzle. I think those teeth have finally poked through the gums. Little Ben and Grace aren't nearly so cranky now."

"I'm sure that's a relief."

"For all of us." Hannah laughed. She sobered and laid a hand on Esther's arm. "Is something troubling you?"

"Why do you ask?"

"I don't know. You seem distracted or something." Hannah waved her hands, apparently at a loss for the right word.

"Like I said before, I'm just thinking."

"So that's it! I thought I smelled smoke!" Andrew exclaimed as he and Jacob caught up with the two young women.

"You're very funny." Esther poked her tongue out at him.

"That's not very ladylike." He shook a finger at her.

"It's not very gentlemanly to say someone so rarely thinks that she short-circuits her brain when a thought does pass through." Her three compannions burst into laughter.

"Gut one, Esther." Hannah elbowed her freind.

"She got you!" Jacob clapped Andrew on the back.

"I guess so. I can't win 'em all."

Esther smirked and cast a sly look in Andrew's direction. Her heart tripped over itself when he grinned and winked at her.

"Hannah, kumm walk with me." Jacob tugged on Hannah's arm.

"I guess we're not wanted." She pretended to pout.

Hannah laughed again and skipped off with Jacob. The love between them was practically palpable. Esther barely managed to conceal her envy.

"Well, Esther, I guess we can take a walk of our own...if it's okay with you, that is."

"I should be getting back to help, with...uh, with something."

"There's nothing to do. Everyone is visiting now."

"Lydia may need help with the kinner."

"They're having a good time playing."

"Well, they have been acting a little puny lately." Why couldn't she simply go with him? Why couldn't she believe he was no longer the devious little bu he once was? Could people really change that much? If she asked him about that last supposed meeting, would he be honest? How would she know?

"Look at them, Es. They're fine now. Kumm. We won't be long."

"I-I suppose it would be all right."

"Only all right?" He put on a dejected face.

She giggled. "You're incorrigible."

"But lovable, ain't so?"

"I don't know if I'd go so far as to say that."

"Essie, you wound me."

She laughed at Andrew's stricken look. For once, she didn't object to his use of her childhood nickname.

"Let's find some shade."

Reluctantly, she set off with him. A furtive look over her shoulder assured her no one was paying any attention to them. She didn't want to start tongues wagging. It took two of her shorter steps to match his long-legged stride. She barely managed to keep up until he noticed her panting and slowed his pace a bit. Esther deeply inhaled the sweet scent of the few small mimosa trees scattered along the tree line bordering the Fishers' property. "Ah." She relinquished the tension and maybe even the fears she'd built up. "I love the mimosa trees."

He reached up and plucked two delicate, feathery pink blooms from a low branch. "Here." He handed her one of the blossoms and reached to tuck the other one behind her ear but quickly pulled his hand back as if he thought better of that idea. Instead, he pressed the flower into her hand. "Sniff away."

"Mmm." She held the blossoms to her nose. "I wish I could bottle this fragrance, so I could enjoy it all year long."

"That's something you can work on, along with the lavender."

"Maybe. I'll think on it."

"So have you found out if anyone else has received pills from Dr. Kramer?"

She glanced around quickly, but only the oak, maple, and pine trees overheard Andrew's question. "Not yet. Miriam Esh did say several customers in her store were complaining about allergies. I don't know if they had seen the doctor, though."

"I tried to ask the Fishers in a round-about way if they knew anyone who had been sick lately."

"And?"

"They didn't know of anyone."

"Oh well, danki for asking."

"Nee problem. I think I'm as curious as you are to find out what's going on."

She quirked an eyebrow. "Really?"

"It's a mystery, for sure. I think I like solving mysteries almost as much as you do. Almost." He smiled down at her, his jade eyes dancing.

She couldn't rationalize the sudden warm feeling that seeped through her marrow at his smile. "I-I'd better get back." Without a watch, Esther had no way of knowing how long she'd been walking with him. She didn't want to be fodder for anyone's gossip.

"So soon?"

"Jah, I think it would be best."

He heaved an exaggerated sigh. "If you must." He turned back toward the house but put a hand out to stop her momentarily. "Esther, I know I've said it before, but please be careful. Don't go off and do something that could be, uh, that could get you into trouble."

"You were about to say 'foolish'."

"Nee. You are definitely not a foolish person. You are a very caring person. I was thinking more along the line of dangerous. I don't want you harmed in any way."

"I-I think I'll be okay…"

"I want to make sure you stay that way."

Esther merely nodded, unsure how she should reply. "Danki." She didn't quite know if she was thanking him for the walk, the mimosa blossoms, or his concern. A blanket 'danki' would cover it all, she supposed. She quickened her pace as they approached the house, leaving him alone with his thoughts. She hadn't been able to ask him about that day. Where was her nerve? *Could it be that I don't really want to know why he stood me up?*

Wee voices called out to her before she reached the yard where kinner of varying sizes ran about. Esther threw back her head and laughed at their antics. She took off in a full gallop, kapp strings flying about her head. She chased the little ones who squealed with glee when she caught them and twirled about with them in her arms. All cares were thrown to the wind while she played with the kinner.

Andrew stopped at the edge of the yard and stared at the scene before him. Gone was the reticent young woman who had strolled along the edge of the woods with him moments earlier. That person had been replaced by a carefree spirit who ran and laughed with abandon.

"She's wunderbaar with them, ain't so?" Hannah spoke his thoughts.

Andrew had been so absorbed in the scene before him he hadn't noticed that Hannah and Jake now stood beside him. "Jah, she is."

"She'll be a great mamm one day." Hannah smiled up at him.

He left that comment alone and remained silent.

"Are you okay?" Hannah touched his arm. He saw the questioning look she shot at Jacob.

"Sure." He paused, then blurted out, "How can I get her to understand I've changed?"

"You're showing her that by your actions."

"She doesn't believe me. She doesn't trust me. I probably shouldn't have teased her earlier. I never know how she's going to take what I say."

"Your teasing now is in fun. It's not hurtful like she thought it was when you were scholars. You have a great sense of humor, and you're fun to be around. Don't change that." She gave his arm a little punch.

"Maybe she would like someone more serious."

"Esther? We're talking about Esther Stauffer?" Jacob laughed. "Look at her!"

The threesome turned again in time to see Esther snatch Ella up and lift her high in the air. Grown woman and little girl giggled in delight.

"You have to be yourself, Andrew. And you are a gut person. I'm pretty sure Esther realizes that." Hannah patted the arm she had recently punched before she and Jacob strolled away.

Andrew remained rooted to the spot, his eyes glued on Esther who still frolicked with the kinner. *Does she? One minute, I think we're making progress. The next, she clams up like she remembers some reason she shouldn't trust me. Teasing is a part of childhood, ain't so?* He didn't mean to hurt her. Or was something else bothering her? He sighed. How did a man figure women out?

Chapter Twelve

July unleashed an oppressive heat and humidity that hovered over Southern Maryland, threatening to smother any breathing creature. Esther tried to accomplish major gardening tasks early in the morning before the dew evaporated from the grass or after supper when the sun's blaze was not so ferocious.

Blue, purple, and green shirts and dresses barely flapped on the clothesline in the practically nonexistent breeze as she weeded her flowers early on a washday. She straightened her back and leaned against the hoe for a moment to catch her breath. She rubbed the perspiration out of her eyes to better focus on the horse and buggy that made the turn onto the driveway. The buggy's occupant couldn't be distinguished at that distance, and she figured it must be someone to see Daed at the mill. Usually, his customers brought their wagons, though.

Esther lifted her face slightly to catch whatever wisp of air may be circulating. With one grubby hand, she loosened the tendrils of dark hair that clung to her neck. She turned back to her work determined to finish before the temperature soared even higher.

"Gude mariye," a woman's voice called from the buggy.

Esther paused, shaded her face with her hand, and squinted in the direction of the voice. "Ach, Joanna! Wie bist du heit?"

"I'm fine, Esther. I wanted to get out and do my errands early, but the time doesn't seem to matter too much with this heat, does it?" She fanned herself with her hand as she spoke.

"What brings you all the way over here?" Esther used the hoe as a walking stick and plodded toward the buggy.

"You do."

"Me?"

Joanna climbed from the buggy and glanced around. "I brought you some plants." She dropped her voice to almost whisper level. "And I had to tell you."

"Tell me what?"

"I did see another doctor. I'm taking real medicine now, and my blood pressure is kumming down. I'm feeling better, too, and I wanted to tell you danki."

"I didn't do anything."

"If you hadn't told me about those pills, I'd be taking a whole handful of them and not getting any better."

"I'm so glad you have improved." A movement near the house caught Esther's attention. Lydia had come outside to shake rugs out. Esther raised her voice a bit. "Let me see what you've brought, Joan-na."

"Kumm. I'll show you."

Esther covered the distance to the back of Joan-na's buggy in a few strides. "How's business?"

"It's fine." Joanna waved at Lydia before turning toward the buggy. "I wanted to tell you about Susan-nah Zimmerman—you know, Timothy's daughter?"

"I know who she is. She must be about ten now, ain't so?"

"Eleven, I believe."

"What's happened to her?" Her heart skipped a beat in fear that something bad happened. She shiv-ered despite the heat. She had such a soft spot for kinner—all kinner, and couldn't stand the thought that something could be wrong with Susannah.

"She's okay now," her freind assured her quick-ly, putting out a hand to steady her. "She was pretty sick for a while, though."

"Timothy didn't say a word to Andrew that day we were out your way."

"It happened after that, I do believe."

"Tell me." Esther lifted a flat of assorted flower-ing plants and carried it to the wooden picnic table in the shade. Joanna followed with a second flat. "I love these Sweet Williams."

"Me too. I had so many this year. I thought may-be you could use some."

"For sure. Danki." Esther motioned for Joanna to sit on the wooden bench. "Would you like a cold glass of lemonade?"

"Not right now. I'll tell you quick-like before someone kumms out."

Esther nodded for her to proceed.

"Susannah complained of a sore throat and had a fever. Timothy and Sally thought it was a cold. When Susannah could hardly swallow anything, they took her to Dr. Nelson's. Only Dr. Nelson wasn't there, of course."

"Let me guess," Esther interrupted. "Dr. Kramer gave her some oblong peach-colored pills."

"He did. And, of course, she didn't get better."

She gasped and clutched Joanna's arm. "The poor girl. What happened? How is she?"

Joanna patted her hand. "Calm down, dear. She's okay. When her throat didn't seem any better after a couple of days on those pills, Sally got one of the Englisch to drive them to the urgent care at the hospital. They took one look at her throat and said she had strep. They did a throat culture to be sure and gave her antibiotics. She started feeling better in a couple of days."

"I'm so glad they took her to the urgent care and got her the proper medicine."

"Jah. The doctor at the hospital said if she hadn't gotten treatment, the strep could have affected her heart or kidneys."

"That's terrible. She should have gotten the proper medicine right from the start. What is wrong with that Dr. Kramer?" She worked hard to tamp down her rising anger.

"I don't know if it's only the Amish patients who aren't getting the correct treatment or if it's the Englisch ones, too."

"Somehow, I have to keep our people from going there," Esther mused aloud. "I've got to keep them safe."

"I'll certainly advise anyone I know to go elsewhere, that's for sure."

"Gut. I appreciate your telling me all this, Joanna."

"I thought you'd want to know. That's mainly why I brought all these plants by. I'm so grateful for the advice you gave me. If you hadn't visited me that day, I'd still be wondering why I wasn't improving."

"I'm glad you're better and that Susannah is better, too."

"I'd better finish my errands and get back home." Joanna rose from the bench.

"Danki for the lovely plants...and for the information." Esther watched her return to her buggy.

How will I ever figure out what Dr. Kramer is up to, and how am I going to keep my people safe? I can't very well visit each family, and I certainly can't take out an ad in the paper. But I have to do something.

Esther shook her head and the damp, dark waves of hair fell to her waist. The tepid shower had felt heavenly after working outside in the heat and humidity and in the equally stifling kitchen. Her brain felt as weary as her body. She padded barefoot across the cool oak floor of her bedroom to the open window. She willed a breeze to blow through. Nature had her own agenda, though, and breathed not so much as a sigh. The vast black sky, heavily peppered with silvery stars, made her feel such a small, insignificant part of creation. Yet, she knew she was important to the Lord Gott.

She padded back across the room, heaving the sigh nature refused to utter, and knelt beside her bed. She poured out her thoughts and concerns, sure the Lord listened to her. She would try to calm her own mind and be still so she could hear His voice.

Instead, she heard muffled whimpering and sniffing. She stiffened and paused in her prayers as she strained to identify the source of the sounds. David and Ella had been tucked into bed hours ago. Mamm and Daed had followed not long after. It must be Lydia, unless one of the kinner was having a bad dream.

Esther pushed to her feet and pulled her robe on over her long, white nightgown. She tiptoed to the door and out into the hallway. She stopped to listen. Sure enough, the sounds came from behind Lydia's door. She crept down the hall and knocked lightly on the heavy door. She only waited a moment before turning the door knob and slipping into the room. Lydia half knelt, half crouched beside the bed with her head on the mattress, which would account for the muffled sound. Her shoulders shook with the sobs she tried to silence.

"Lydia? What is it?" She sailed across the room and dropped to her knees beside her distraught schweschder. She draped an arm around her and stroked her hair with her other hand. "Can you tell me?"

Lydia gulped. "I-I miss Amos s-so much."

"I'm sure you must. Such a tragic loss. Is there any particular reason why tonight is worse?"

"David w-was asking about his d-daed before bed. He asked if he would ever have a daed."

"I know that must be so hard for you." She could see Lydia's puffy, blotchy face in the lamp light. She must have been crying for some time.

"I know we are expected to remarry soon, but Esther, I c-can't. I don't know if I will ever give my kinner another daed."

"*Expected.*" She emphasized the word. "Not required. You would never be forced to remarry, Lyddie. It is totally up to you. If you find someone who would make you happy, then wunderbaar. If you don't, you always have Mamm, Daed, and me to help you with the kinner."

Lydia nodded her head. "I know."

"We certainly can't take Amos' place, but we can offer all the love and support you need."

She nodded again. "I shouldn't be blubbering like a boppli and waking the whole household."

"It's okay to grieve. And I hadn't even gone to bed yet, so you didn't wake anyone." She gathered Lydia into her arms, patted her back, and offered soothing words that could only have been given to her by the Lord Gott because she didn't have a clue what to say on her own. She held her schweschder until the sniffing and shaking subsided and then helped her climb into bed.

"Danki." Her voice was small, her body seemingly drained of all energy.

"I'm here whenever you need me." Esther gave Lydia's arm a final pat and tiptoed back across the room, extinguishing the lamp along the way.

She slipped back into her own room, her weariness suddenly magnified tenfold. She crawled into her own bed and begged Gott to comfort and help her distraught schweschder. As exhausted as she was, sleep took its time claiming her.

Esther cracked one eye open. She seriously considered squeezing it closed and burrowing under the sheet for a few more minutes of slumber. It had been well after midnight when she'd finally dozed off, making it a short night indeed. She groaned and

threw off the sheet. She would have to help get breakfast on the table. Most likely, Lydia would have one
of her headaches after all her weeping last night. She
almost wished she hadn't promised to go with Hannah to Barbara Zook's quilt shop today.

Poor Hannah had been working very hard to
learn how to quilt. Of course, Mamm latched right
onto the opportunity to visit Barbara. She figured
Barbara could instruct Esther as well since her quilting skills were sadly lacking. Mamm had thrown up
her hands in frustration. Esther sighed. She felt sorry
for her mudder for having to put up with her. Mamm
had been so patient, but she could tell that patience
was wearing thin. She sighed again. This could be a
very long day.

Lydia was already in the kitchen. Her eyes were
still a bit swollen and red, but she presented a cheerful countenance for the benefit of her kinner and
probably for their mudder as well. Esther got the
message in the look Lydia shot her: *Not a word to
Mamm.* Esther nodded her understanding.

Hannah arrived right after breakfast, all bright-
eyed and excited to learn more about quilting. Esther
would rather hoe the garden, but she glued a smile
on her face and grabbed up the basket of quilting
supplies Mamm had gathered for her. She climbed
into the Hertzlers' buggy that Hannah was growing
more and more comfortable driving.

"Your skills with the horse and buggy have
greatly improved, Hannah. You seem much more
confident."

"Jah. Old Brownie here is such a gentle soul and
gut natured, too. You, on the other hand, seem quite
tired."

"I suppose I am. I was up with Lydia for a while last night and then had trouble sleeping."

"Is she all right?"

Esther briefly described what had transpired the previous evening, knowing Hannah would keep the information to herself.

"Poor Lydia. It must be so hard losing your spouse, your soul mate. I know how awful I'd feel if something happened to Jacob, and we aren't even married with kinner to think about."

"Jah. I'm sure, though I wouldn't know about that first hand."

"You could if you'd let yourself." Hannah's voice was so soft Esther could barely hear it above the clippity-clop noise Brownie was making.

"What do you mean?"

"There is a certain young man who would like to share his life with you, I'm thinking."

"Hmpf! If it's Andrew Fisher you're thinking about, you might want to think again."

"It's not like you to hold a grudge, Esther."

"I-I'm not holding a grudge. Really. I simply don't trust him."

"Don't or don't want to?"

"What's the difference?"

"Why do you find it so hard to believe that he's changed?"

"He was a mean little bu."

"Mean or a tease?"

"They go together, don't they?"

"Well, some people tease but they aren't trying to be mean. They have a…uh, a playful personality."

Esther stared off into the distance without responding.

Hannah squeezed her arm gently. "Did he hurt you so badly?"

"I...well, I guess I wanted him to-to like me, but he always belittled me." Her voice came out in a shaky whisper. *And he didn't show up when he was supposed to meet me.*

"Ach, Esther! Little buwe pick on girls because they like them. They just aren't smart enough to know how to show that, so they tease or do something else totally dumb."

"Really?"

"Really."

"He, uh, said something like that once."

"When?"

"Several weeks ago."

"And you didn't believe that?"

"Nee, but he was kind of mean to other people, too." 'She attempted to justify her distrust.

"Like who?"

"He teased other kinner. He ran through Kathy Taylor's flower beds and never apologized for breaking up her flowers."

"That's a typical non-thinking bu. You didn't grow up with bruders!"

"Did you?"

"I grew up with a cousin who was like an older bruder. He teased me and Rennie a lot and generally acted mean sometimes, but I knew he really cared about us."

"Jah?"

"For sure. Esther, you didn't have any problems accepting me, an outsider. You defended me to the bishop and the school board. You convinced Jacob to give me a chance. Can't you find it in your heart to give Andrew a chance?" At Her silence, Hannah continued. "Nobody says you have to rush out to plant a field of celery and marry the man, but I think deep down, you like him. Can't you let your guard down at least a little and see what happens — if anything?"

Esther bit her lower lip. "Maybe," she whispered. *If I could ever get the truth out of him.*

"Gut." Hannah pulled on the reins so Brownie would turn onto Barbara Zook's driveway. "It doesn't look like anyone is at the quilt shop right now, so Barbara should be able to help us."

"Great," she mumbled without any enthusiasm.

"This will be fun, Esther."

"About as much fun as a big, fat toothache."

"Think positive thoughts."

"All right. I'm positive I'd rather have a tooth-ache."

Hannah elbowed her freind. "See? You like to tease, too."

"Who's teasing? I'm as serious as the bishop on Sunday morning."

A little bell tinkled when Hannah pushed the door of Barbara's quilt shop open a few minutes later. Esther inhaled deeply. "I do love the crisp, cottony smell of new fabric."

"You and your smells."

"I can't help it if I have an extra-sensitive nose."

"At least you had a positive thought!"

"How is the stitching coming?" Barbara entered the shop from a side door.

"Uh oh," Esther whispered. "This could be a problem."

"Let's see." Barbara approached the younger women.

Hannah pulled her quilt pieces out of the bag dangling from her arm. "I'm really trying, Barbara, but my stitches are far from even. Rebecca is so busy with the kinner that I hate to bother her for help when she gets a free minute."

"Well, none of us is born knowing how to quilt, or anything else for that matter. You weren't born knowing how to teach. Esther wasn't born knowing how to grow plants."

"That's true, but it was a lot easier learning to grow plants." Esther sighed and wished she was anywhere else, preferably in her greenhouse. She wandered around the bolts of fabric while Barbara helped Hannah. Her mind flitted back to the conversation they'd had in the buggy. Could Andrew have changed? Did he really like her years ago? If so, then why didn't he meet her? She jumped when Barbara spoke.

"Okay, Esther. What did you bring?"
She plopped her basket reluctantly on the table and pulled out the quilt blocks she'd agonizingly stitched and stuffed into the basket after Mamm packed it. She hadn't wanted her mudder to see her sorry attempt at quilting.

Hannah's gasp seemed to echo up and down the rows of fabric. "These are beautiful, Esther. They're lovely enough for a wedding quilt." She fingered the blocks gently.

"Ach, Esther! Such wunderbaar combinations. And your stitches are fine and even." Barbara examined all of the blocks, turning them over and over in her hands to scrutinize each one carefully.

"Are you teasing me, Barbara Zook? Because I really tried."

"Not at all, Esther. I am sincere. I was going to ask if Lydia or Leah stitched these."

"I sewed them alone in my room at night. I've been afraid to show them to Mamm or Lydia because I'm sure they would have done a much better job."

"That would not have been possible, Esther dear. Don't you hang your head! These are excellent. I do believe we've found a hidden talent in you."

"You picked such beautiful colors that work so well together," Hannah concurred. "I love them."

Esther felt her cheeks grow warm, unaccustomed to success with any sewing projects. She knew it was wrong to be prideful, but she couldn't deny the teensy bit of satisfaction that bloomed inside her at Hannah's and Barbara's comments.

"You've been hiding your light under a bushel, I'm thinking," Barbara wagged a finger at her. "You are a top-notch quilter."

"Really? Me?" She couldn't believe her ears.

"Didn't you realize how beautiful these blocks were?" Hannah stroked the quilt blocks almost reverently.

"I only knew that I liked them. I didn't know if I was doing anything right."

"It must be an innate talent." Hannah examined each block.

"A real gift." Barbara clapped her hands like a school teacher. "When you girls get your blocks all put together, we'll have a quilting frolic."

Esther had always disliked going to sewing or baking or quilting events in the past. Suddenly, she found herself looking forward to a quilting frolic. Her fingers itched to finish the rest of her blocks and piece them together.

"I may have to get Esther to help me!" Hannah chuckled.

She grinned. "Who'd have thought?" She had even surprised herself. She gathered her quilt blocks and placed them gingerly in her basket. She handled them with a newfound respect. Could it be she did have at least one domestic bone in her body?

They talked of quilting and fabrics a bit longer before Hannah announced they had better get moving in a homeward direction. Esther, still a bit dazed, floated out to the buggy after they bid Barbara farewell.

Once Hannah had Brownie trotting down the road, she turned to Esther. "How's that for changes? You thought you couldn't sew or quilt, and you are actually a great quilter. I'll bet you'll enjoy it more now that you know you are doing it right."

"Maybe." She paused a moment. "I guess you're right. Actually, I am looking forward to working on my quilt now."

"See? Everyone can change — even you!"

She picked at her fingernails. If *she*, of all people, could be gut at something she had never really known how to do, if *she* could suddenly find she liked something she had always found unpleasant at best, if *she* could change so drastically...well, then anyone could change. Couldn't they?

"I hope you don't mind, Esther, but I want to drop these cookies off to Jacob. I made him some oatmeal chocolate chip cookies and packed them in that little cooler back there. I thought it would be a nice afternoon treat. Is it okay with you if we stop for a few minutes?"

"Sure. Oatmeal chocolate chip?"

"Jake couldn't decide if he liked oatmeal or chocolate chip better, so I combined them."

"That should make him happy." *I wonder what Andrew's favorite cookie is?* Now why did that thought pop into her head?

"I hope so. I won't take long. I promise."

"It's okay. It's getting too hot to work out in my garden or flower beds right now anyway."

Hannah stopped the buggy close to the Beilers' furniture shop. She hopped out and reached into the cooler for the plastic container of cookies. "You'd better get out," she said. "You'll roast in here even if I do make this quick."

"I'll be fine."

"Esther, at least get out so you can get a breath of air. You don't have to kumm into the shop if you're afraid of running into 'you know who.'"

"I'm not afraid of running into anyone."

"If you say so. I don't want to have to scrape you off the buggy seat after you've melted."

Esther could tell how eager Hannah was to see Jacob by the way she practically skipped into the furniture shop. This visit was likely to take longer than Hannah predicted. She fanned herself with a scrap of paper she found in her basket, but the movement didn't produce much of a breeze. Finally, she abandoned the attempt and slid out of the buggy to get a breath of air as Hannah had suggested.

Hannah had become such a gut freind even though she hadn't lived in the community very long. She took to the Amish way of life quickly and eagerly embraced their faith and culture. It must truly have been the Lord Gott's will for the tiny, pale-haired young woman to end up in St. Mary's County. Esther was glad.

As lost in thought as she was, she didn't hear anyone approach. She gasped and jumped when a hand touched her arm.

"Sorry, Esther. I called out, but you seemed a million miles away."

"Andrew! You did startle me. I was thinking how well Hannah has adapted to our way of life."

"That she has. I'm sure Jake is glad she came here."

"I'm glad, too."

"How are things with you?"

"Fine." She sensed he was asking out of genuine concern, and she suddenly felt ill at ease. "Hannah and I were at Barbara Zook's quilt shop. Hannah wanted to stop by and bring Jacob some cookies she had baked." For some reason, she felt the need to justify her motives for showing up at Andrew's work place.

"That's nice." He shuffled his feet like a scholar, not a grown man. "It's gut to see you."

Her face heated up hotter than the air temperature. She glanced down at Andrew's shuffling feet and blurted out, "What is your favorite kind of cookie?" Instantly, she wanted to recall those words, but they were already hanging out there in midair.

"Well, I like all cookies, but I'm kind of partial to chocolate chip."

"Nuts?" She clenched and unclenched her fists, upset with her tongue for running off unchecked all on its own volition.

"Nuts?"

"Do you like nuts in your chocolate chip cookies?" She figured since her unbridled tongue had started this conversation, she might as well finish it.

"Nee. I'm partial to plain ones."

"Gut. I mean, uh, I like them without nuts best, too."

He grinned a big, lopsided grin. "Great minds think alike, they say."

She fanned herself with her hand. "It sure is muggy today." She stopped fanning to swat at a fly buzzing too near her face. The last thing she needed right now was to have the offensive creature fly into her mouth and strangle her. She already felt foolish enough.

"It is indeed. Here, let's move under the trees. The shade might help a little." He took her elbow gently and steered her into the shade of the towering oak trees.

She stumbled along beside him, feeling like she was dragging a third leg. What was wrong with her all of a sudden??

"This is a little better," he said once they reached the patch of shade. He still held her arm.

"Jah, it is. Don't let me keep you from your work. I'm just waiting for Hannah."

"Jake said a break was in order. I'm sure he wants to spend a few minutes with Hannah."

"Without a doubt." She wracked her brain for something suitable to say. She wasn't usually at a loss for words. "Uh, what are you working on...uh, in there?" She nodded toward the furniture shop.

"A cherry china cabinet and dining room table for an *Englischer*. She wants a few fancy doodads on it, so I'm trying to add them to the cabinet."

Esther noticed how animated Andrew became when talking about his work. "That sounds beautiful."

"Would you like to see?"

"Sure. If you have the time, that is."

"I'll make the time. Kumm." Andrew led Esther toward the shop. At the door, he seemed to suddenly realize he was still holding her arm. He released his grasp and moved aside to let her enter before him.

Despite the hot, humid day, her arm felt cold where Andrew's hand had been moments earlier. Esther stopped inside the door and waited for him to show her the way. Hannah waved at her and broke into a huge smile. Jacob choked on his cookie and then winked. Now what was that all about?

"Here." Andrew moved to stand beside a tall cabinet with scalloped edges and a leaf pattern carved into the upper corners. "Of course, I'll apply the cherry stain when I'm done."

"It's very nice. I even like the natural cherry wood without any stain. You are quite skilled. I'm sure your customer will be pleased."

His face reddened. She was sure her own face mirrored his. Was she changing in more ways than one?

"Esther, do—" Andrew began but didn't finish his thought since Hannah and Jacob had drawn near.

"Hey, Esther, we'd better go. I'm sure Rebecca could use a break about now."

"Okay." She would never know what Andrew was about to ask but would probably wonder about it the rest of the day. "Danki for showing me your work, Andrew."

"Sure. I'm glad you came by." He spoke soft enough to keep the other workers from hearing.

She nodded. Hannah and Jacob obviously heard Andrew's words if the look they exchanged was any indication.

"You two stay safe going home," Jacob said. "A customer who came in earlier said we were in for severe storms this afternoon. It looks like dark clouds are moving in from across the river in Virginia. But you should be able to make it home before any storms hit."

"We'll hurry as fast as ol' Brownie can go." Hannah flashed one more smile at Jake before they left the shop.

"The wind has started to blow already." Esther raised her face. "It actually feels gut, a relief from the heat."

"But those clouds do look a bit ominous. Let's get going." Hannah hurried to the buggy, and Esther followed.

The leaves had that silvery look she associated with storms, and she smelled rain. She kept an eye on the sky as thunder rumbled in the distance.

Chapter Thirteen

The thunder growled louder as Esther hopped out of the buggy near the house. She snatched up her basket and clutched it to her chest, afraid it would sail away in a gust of wind. Now that she was a real quilter, she didn't want anything to happen to her precious quilt blocks. The sun had completely surrendered to the black clouds. Oaks, poplars, and maples joined the swaying and creaking of the flimsier pine trees.

"Why don't you stay here and wait out the storm?" She glanced at the dark sky and frowned.

"Nee, I don't want Rebecca to worry about me. I think Brownie is spooked enough to make it home in record time. See you soon." With that, Hannah turned Brownie toward the road.

Esther didn't know what her freind had said or done or promised, but the old horse took off faster than a fox with his tail on fire. She offered up a silent prayer for Hannah's safety before sprinting for the back door of the house. She deposited her basket on the kitchen table and raced back outside to help Mamm pull clothes from the line.

After battling the wind for the dresses and pants flapping crazily in the wind, Esther finally filled one of the laundry baskets and hauled it into the house as lightning ripped the sky. "I've got to secure my plants, Mamm." She headed back outside.

"I'll send Lydia out to help you. She should have the kinner up from their naps by now."

Esther didn't reply. She nodded and kept moving. Some of her potted plants had to be dragged inside the greenhouse before the wind sent them soaring into next week. She filled the red wagon quickly with as many terra cotta pots as would safely sit inside. Gasping for air, she yanked the wagon inside the greenhouse.

"Where do you want these?" Lydia yelled to be heard over the explosion of thunder. She pulled a smaller wagon full of plants to the door.

"You can leave it over there." Esther pointed to the opposite side of the greenhouse. She ran back out to fill her arms with the remaining few plants.

"Is that all?" Lydia's breath came in little puffs.

"Jah. Danki. Go ahead and get inside. I'm kumming in a minute."

"Okay, but hurry, Esther." Lydia dashed to the house as rain began to pelt the earth.

Esther secured the greenhouse door and bolted for the house as the drops of rain progressed to a downpour. She was soaked to the skin in the two minutes it took her to run to the house. Mamm handed her a towel as soon as she entered. She dried off briskly, panting from the exertion of the rubbing and the running.

"Why the puckered face?" She chucked Ella under the chin.

"I-I'm scared."

"Let me get dry clothes and we'll play. Okay?"

"Me, too?" David's voice trembled almost as much as Ella's.

"For sure."

She entertained the kinner with games and stories while thunder shook the house and lightning crisscrossed the sky. Trees practically doubled over to sweep the ground and then sprang back to attention when the wind momentarily abated. Mamm cast a wary glance out the kitchen window toward the sawmill as Lydia paced.

The storm set everyone's nerves on edge. Esther had to work hard to distract the children. Again, she prayed Hannah had arrived home safely. "I'm sure Daed and the men are fine." She tried to reassure her mamm.

Somewhere, a siren screamed above the din of the storm. The wail grew louder as emergency vehicles neared the Stauffers' property.

"I wonder what hap—" Mamm began but stopped in mid-sentence at Lydia's frown. Esther caught Lydia's nod toward David's and Ella's panic-stricken faces. Mamm amended her comment. "I wonder what we can make for dessert tonight."

"How about pudding?" Esther tried to think of a dessert the kinner could help make and one they could actually eat. She reached over to tickle both children until giggles drowned out the storm. "Do you want chocolate or butterscotch?"

"Both," David answered. Ella nodded enthusiastically.

"Both?" She pretended to be horrified, and more giggles followed.

Lydia smiled and mouthed her appreciation. Esther heard her whisper to their mamm. "She's so good with the kinner. She needs a house full of them."

She had long ago decided that being an aenti was as close as she would get to having kinner. She pulled mixing bowls, measuring cups, and whisks from cabinets and removed a jug of milk from the refrigerator. She stationed the children at the kitchen table. "Who wants to make the chocolate pudding?"

"Me, me!" David jumped up and down.

Ella's face puckered, and her lower lip trembled. Apparently, she wanted to make the chocolate pudding as well. She simply didn't respond as quickly as David.

Esther had to think fast. "Well, then you, my dear Ella, get to make the very special butterscotch pudding."

The child did not look convinced that this would be anything special. "We'll put whipped cream on the pudding, and I'm pretty sure we have butterscotch chips we can add to the top to make it extra tasty." Esther prayed the chips were gluten free.

As if reading Esther's mind, Lydia scooted over to the cupboard to pull out the bag of butterscotch chips. She scanned the label and nodded.

Esther swallowed her sigh of relief. "What do you think of that, Ella?"

"Yummy." The little girl's eyes sparkled. She reached for a whisk, eager to get started.

"Do we have chocolate chips, too?" David was apparently concerned that plain chocolate pudding might be a bit boring.

"I'm sure we can find something to spruce up the chocolate pudding, too." Esther raised her eyebrows at Lydia, who again rummaged through the cupboard. She eventually produced a little jar of chocolate sprinkles and scanned the ingredients. She handed the jar to Esther.

"Don't these look great?" Esther licked her lips and rubbed her belly. "Now, who's ready to make pudding?"

Both children squealed and manned their stations. Esther and Lydia poured the milk into the bowls and let David and Ella whip in the pudding mix. They guided little hands to ladle spoonfuls of pudding into dessert dishes.

"Sprinkles?" David reached for the little jar.

"We have to let the pudding chill in the refrigerator for a little while first."

"Whipped cream next!" Ella declared.

"You are exactly right." Esther hugged her niece. "But we have to wait for the pudding to thicken a bit."

By the time the pudding was mixed and chilling and the kitchen cleaned up, the black clouds and torrential rain had given way to a light-gray sky and drizzle. Their fears gone, David and Ella played happily in the living room.

"Here kumms your daed." Mamm's eyes had continually strayed to the window as the wild wind and rain beat upon the house. She spotted Daed right away.

"Leah!" he called as he poked his head into the house.

"Thank the Lord you are all right. Let me get you a towel, Daniel."

"Don't bother. Mose, Luke, and I are heading over to Eshs'. I think they have trouble there. I see smoke and firetrucks headed in that direction."

"Should I go along to check on Miriam?"

"I could go, Mamm," Esther offered.

"Nee. I'll send Luke back if we need you." With that, Daed hurried out to the buggy Luke had hitched and waiting for them.

Esther ran to the door and hollered, "Daed, please check to see if Hannah made it home okay."

He nodded and climbed into the buggy. Esther joined Mamm and Lydia in a prayer for their neighbors.

Mamm held off supper as long as she could until the kinner began whimpering that they were hungry. "Might as well all eat now. There's no telling how long your daed will be."

Esther set the table hurriedly while Lydia shepherded her little ones to the sink to wash up.

"Do we get to have the pudding?" David asked.

"After you eat your supper." Lydia tweaked his nose.

Mamm set plates of meatloaf, green beans with boiled potatoes, and pickled beets at each place at the table. She wrapped aluminum foil around a plate for Daed and set it in the oven to stay warm. "I hope he gets home before his food gets too dried out."

They bowed their heads for silent prayer. Only David's growling stomach broke the silence, followed by Ella's giggle. When the prayer was over, Lydia turned a stern look on the little girl. "No laughing during prayer time."

"It's my fault." David defended his little schweschder. "My stomach made a noise."

"You couldn't help that," Lydia said. "But Ella did not have to laugh."

The little girl hung her head. A tear trickled down her cheek. She was so sensitive that any reprimand nearly broke her heart. Esther couldn't stand seeing the poor little thing so upset. She reached over to squeeze Ella's hand. "It's okay. You know better now, jah?"

"Jah." Ella sniffed.

"Okay. Eat your supper so we can get to that yummy pudding." She smiled at her niece.

The little girl picked up her fork and speared a green bean. She smiled back at her aenti before popping the bean into her mouth.

They had only taken a few bites when Luke drove his buggy up the driveway. Daed jumped out and waved his thanks to the younger man. Mose and Luke continued on their way as Daed stomped into the house.

Mamm jumped up from the table to retrieve the plate from the oven and to pour Daed a glass of iced tea. "Was it a lightning strike, Daniel?"

"What happened, Daed?" Lydia asked.

"Is everyone all right, and did Hannah arrive home safely?" Esther inquired.

Daed held up his hands. "Whoa! Let me wash up and I'll tell you everything."

"David and Ella, hurry and finish eating, please." Lydia apparently wanted to get them out of the room quickly to shield them from any possible bad news.

"They're okay, Lyddie. Everyone is fine." Daed scooted his chair up to the table and bowed his head.

Mamm set his plate in front of him. "It's still warm."

"Gut. Danki." He cut his meatloaf and took a sip of tea. "I needed to wet my whistle." Five pairs of eyes locked on his face, waiting for news. He cleared his throat. "Lightning hit Levi Esh's barn. The house and store are fine, though."

"Was the barn destroyed?" Mamm asked.

"Mostly. We may be able to salvage a little. We'll have to see when it dries out."

"Was anyone hurt?" Esther couldn't mask her concern.

"Zeke burned his hand. The ambulance crew fixed him up. Hopefully, he won't have any problems. It's going to be plenty painful, though."

"Sarah and Miriam?" Mamm laid down the fork she had just picked up.

"Sarah was in the house with Miriam. They are both fine, only a little shaken up."

"What about the animals, Grossdaddi?" David loved all animals. He knew Levi had several nanny goats and fuzzy black-faced sheep.

"Zeke and Levi got them all out safe and sound."

"Did you find out if Hannah got home okay?"

"Jah, Dochder. I did. Samuel Hertzler came by. He said Hannah got home right as the storm hit."

"Thank the Lord Gott." She breathed a sigh of relief.

"And thank the Lord Gott there weren't other injuries. We'll pray for Zeke's quick healing," Mamm said.

"And thank the Lord the sheep and goats are fine."

"Jah, David. That, too." Lydia hugged her sensitive son.

"I guess we'll be having a barn raising. Any idea when, Daniel?" Mamm passed the basket of biscuits.

"We're aiming for Saturday. Since this Sunday is not a church Sunday, we won't have to prepare for services on Saturday."

"We'll start getting ready tomorrow."

Esther knew her mamm was already making mental lists.

Saturday turned out to be another hot day, but lower humidity made the heat less oppressive. Freinden and neighbors, including a few Englisch neighbors, gathered at the Eshs' house before the last fuscia and lavender streaks of sunrise gave way to a cloudless blue sky. The men and boys quickly divvied up duties based on skills and strengths, while the women and girls began the noon meal preparations. A lot of food would be required to feed so many hungry workers. The heat of the kitchen would soon match the heat generated by the July sun.

Esther couldn't wait to catch up with Hannah. "I'm so glad you made it home safely the other day."

"*Jah*. Me, too. I just made it to the barn when the rain began to fall in sheets. Samuel took care of the horse and buggy for me so I could get inside to help Rebecca calm the kinner. I got soaked, but no real harm in that!"

"Gude mariye, Sarah. How is everything with you??" Esther turned to the obviously pregnant young woman who joined them.

"Okay." Sarah pushed her glasses up on her nose.

"You seem worried. Is everything okay with the baby?" Hannah asked.

Sarah's puckered forehead smoothed, and a smile tickled her lips. She patted her rounded belly. "The baby is fine. I'm worried about Zeke, though."

"Daed said his hand got burned."

"Jah. It really hurt him all night. I think maybe he needs to get the doctor to check it out and give him some pain medicine, too."

"Won't he go?" Hannah laid a hand on Sarah's arm.

"Nee. He says it will be all right."

"Typical stubborn man," Esther muttered.

Sarah giggled. "I guess so. He says he wants to help with the barn today, but I'm not sure how much he'll be able to do."

"Maybe one of the other men can persuade him to go to the doctor." Hannah patted Sarah's other arm.

"I don't know. Maybe." Sarah didn't sound convinced. "He said the ambulance crew did a gut job. I guess he'll see how the day goes."

"If Miriam doesn't have anything around for burns, I'm sure Sophie has something ." Esther knew aloe might help but couldn't think of any other remedies right off the top of her head. She didn't know how bad Zeke's burn was, but she was afraid if Zeke visited Dr. Kramer, he'd only come away with prenatal vitamins which wouldn't do him any good whatsoever.

"Hello, one and all," a familiar voice boomed. "I'm here to work, so tell me what you want me to do."

"Wilkom, Kathy. It's so gut of you to help." Miriam hurried over to greet their Englisch neighbor.

"I'm so sorry to hear about the loss of the barn, Miriam. We'll do whatever we can to help out. My husband is out helping the men. He's probably getting in the way more than anything else. He's not much of a builder, but he can fetch and help hold boards or whatever else is needed." Kathy blew a wisp of brown hair off her face.

"I'm sure he will be a big help." Miriam patted Kathy's shoulder.

"So, tell me what I can do." She rubbed her hands together.

"Are you feeling better, Kathy?" Hannah asked. "Rebecca said you'd been sick."

"Oh, yeah. I was sick, but I saw the doctor and got some medicine. I'm much better now."

Esther's ears immediately perked up. As inconspicuously as possible, she inched closer so she could discover the details.

"I'm glad you're better now." Miriam smiled and nodded.

"You and me both. Strep throat isn't any fun. Of all things to get in the middle of the summer! My throat was so sore I couldn't swallow food. I lost seven pounds. I'm happy about that, mind you. I actually need to lose a few more, but I don't think getting strep throat is a good weight-loss plan." Kathy finished with a laugh and a toss of her head.

"Which doctor did you see?" Esther hoped her tone was casual.

"That Dr. Kramer. I'll be glad when Dr. Nelson gets back, I'll tell you. I'm not sure about his substitute."

"Why?" Esther probed.

"I can't put my finger on it exactly. There was something a little shifty about him."

"Didn't he help you?" Esther couldn't contain her curiosity.

"Well, he gave me medicine."

"Was it oblong peach-colored pills?"

A look of confusion passed over Kathy's face. "No. He gave me a prescription for an antibiotic. They were red and yellow capsules, not peach."

"Are you sure it was an antibiotic? And you got the medicine from the drugstore?"

"Yes. Amoxicillin. I picked it up at Tideview. I've had it before. That did the trick, I guess, since I'm feeling better."

"Gut." Esther let the subject drop. She figured she'd arouse suspicion if she continued to ask questions. So, Dr. Kramer gave his Englisch patient the right medicine. Interesting. Her mind whirred with possibilities and questions.

"Right, Esther?"

"Huh?" Esther didn't realize Hannah had been talking to her.

"I said we'd set up tables under the big oak trees."

"Okay."

"Where were you?" Hannah elbowed her playfully. "You didn't hear anything I said."

"Wool gathering, I suppose."
"Are you thinking about anything or *anyone* in particular?"

"Not really. I'm trying to figure some things out."

"Do you want to share?"

"Not yet."

"You and your mysteries! Maybe you should be a writer." She chuckled and nudged her again. "After we set up the tables, we'd better take some cold water or tea out to the men. They've got to be thirsty about now."

"I'm sure they are. They're making great progress on the barn." The old, burnt wood had been hauled away. New boards were sawed and nailed in place. Saws buzzed intermittently with the pounding of hammers. She loved how her community worked together, how they were always there to help and support each other. No wonder Hannah wanted to stay and become a part of their group. Who would ever want to leave? Esther couldn't even fathom that.

"Danki." Andrew wiped his mouth on his dirty blue shirt sleeve after gulping an entire cup of water nonstop. "That was exactly what I needed." He smiled at Esther and handed her the cup. His fingers brushed hers, and she felt a tingle all the way up to her scalp.

"More?" She set his cup on a tray.

"I'm fine for now."

"I'll bring more later. How about you, Zeke?" Esther held out another cup to the young man with the bandaged left hand.

Apparently, he wasn't letting a burn stop him. His once white bandage was now mostly gray. He slurped the water and returned the cup to her. He reached to pick up a hammer and nails and winced. The skin around his tight mouth grew white, matching the paleness of the rest of his face. His eyes took on a determination she was sure his body struggled with.

"Zeke, are you sure you're okay?"

"Jah."

"You're in pain."

"Jah."

"Sarah said your hand hurt all night."

"She shouldn't have said anything."

"She's concerned. She's your fraa and doesn't want to see you hurt."

"I'll be all right."

"Maybe you should get the hand checked out and get some pain medicine."

"Leave it, Esther."

"Okay. I'm sorry. I'm only trying to help."

"I know." Zeke grunted before turning his back on her and heading back to work.

She passed water around to more men and walked close to Andrew on her way back to the house. "See if you can talk sense into that mule." She jerked her head toward Zeke. "He's hurting."

He nodded, unable to speak with nails sticking out of his mouth. She hoped nobody clapped him on the back.

The women found time to chat and catch up on news as they scurried around the kitchen. Older girls watched out for the younger kinner, keeping them occupied and out of harm's way. Older boys helped the men by fetching tools and supplies and carrying new boards.

The noon break in the shade provided a welcome relief from work and heat. The men ate as if they'd been fasting for days and gulped down cup after cup of water or tea. Esther and Hannah stayed busy simply refilling pitchers and cups. They were glad when it was finally their turn to sit in the shade and take a little break before beginning the cleanup.

"Ugh!" Sarah sighed as she dropped onto a chair beside Hannah.

"Tired?"

"Very." Sarah pushed her wayward glasses up before reaching down to rub her legs.

"They look pretty swollen." Esther leaned around Hannah to better see Sarah.

"They've been doing that when I'm on my feet a lot."

"Does Carrie know?" Carrie was the Englisch nurse-midwife most of the Amish women used for their prenatal care and delivery. She tried to accommodate the women, whether they wanted to give birth at home or at her local birthing center.

"She knows. She said to rest as much as possible and to put my feet up when I can."

"Have you been doing that?" Hannah used her schoolteacher voice.

"Well…"

"Not today?" Esther interrupted.

"Not today," Sarah echoed. "But my blood pressure and everything has been fine."

"Gut. Let's keep it that way. Esther slid a glass of water closer to Sarah. "Here, drink some water."

"And don't worry about cleaning up. You've done enough work for today," Hannah added.

"But—"

"Nee buts about it." Esther's tone matched Hannah's. "We want a healthy baby in two months."

Sarah smiled, rubbed her belly, and popped a bite of buttered bread into her mouth.

With everyone finally fed, the women could get the cleanup underway. Esther pulled a chair close to the sink for Sarah so she felt included and could chat with her and Hannah as they washed and dried the mountain of dishes.

Before they had completed their task, Kathy Taylor bustled into the kitchen, slightly out of breath from carrying chairs and tables to their storage places. "There you are, Sarah. I wanted to tell you that I'm going to drive Zeke to the doctor's office to get that hand checked. He's been gritting his teeth all day."

"How did you convince him to go?" Sarah asked. "I couldn't do that."

"I guess another man had to prod him," Kathy replied. "Andrew had a little chat with him, I believe."

Esther harbored a tiny smile. They didn't know she had prodded Andrew.

"Do you want to ride along? Then I can drop you two off at your house. It looks like you could both use a rest."

"Sure, Kathy. That will be fine."

"Don't worry about the dishes you brought here," Miriam said. "I'll bring them over later. I'll bring some supper, too, so you won't have to prepare anything."

"Danki." Sarah hoisted herself from the chair and gave her mother-in-law a hug.

By late afternoon, the new barn was completed. Men and women alike were anxious to return to their homes to complete their own chores and to clean up after a hot, tiring day. Esther accompanied her family reluctantly. She really wanted to wait around for Kathy to return. She simply had to find out what the doctor did for Zeke.

"We're ready to leave, Esther." Lydia tapped her on the shoulder. "The kinner are tired and are getting cranky. I know Daed is exhausted. Mamm, too."

"Okay. I'll only be a minute."

"Not much more than that, please." Lydia returned to the back yard, took David's and Ella's hands, and led them to the wagon Daed was hitching.

Esther looked around. There had to be a reason for her to stay a little longer. She felt pretty tired herself but was sure she'd be able to walk home if she could delay her departure. Seconds ticked off in her head.

The kitchen had been restored to perfect order. All tables and chairs had been put away. All toys had been cleared from the yard. The men had cleaned up any debris around the barn and had put all the tools in their proper places. There really was nothing left to do. Yet Kathy had not returned.

Tick! Tick! Tick! Hannah had already left with Rebecca's family. In fact, nearly everyone else had headed home. She would have to do the same. With a sigh, she shuffled toward the wagon. Somehow, she would have to find out about Zeke's doctor visit.

Chapter Fourteen

The Stauffers had a quick supper, more snack than meal since everyone was so exhausted. Esther and her mudder tidied the kitchen in record time. As everyone else wandered off to prepare for baths and bed, Esther slipped outside.

Lydia would be bathing David and Ella and settling them down to sleep. Then Daed would want a bath and then Mamm. It would be a while before she got her turn in the house's only bathroom.

Esther strolled barefoot around the yard, checking on Mamm's flower beds. She'd have to do some weeding on Monday. She ambled over to her greenhouse and peeped inside to ensure everything was in order. Before she could check on her lavender, she heard wheels crunching on the gravel driveway.

"Who would be visiting now?" she said to the calico cat that had trotted out of the barn to receive a pat on the head. She hoped nothing was wrong with Sarah. The mamm-to-be had looked pretty tired and miserable by the time she left with Kathy Taylor. Esther figured the summer's heat and humidity must be extra hard on pregnant women. Would she ever find that out firsthand? Prospects weren't looking promising.

One person occupied the wagon, she noticed as it rolled closer. One man. Andrew Fisher. Whatever was he doing here as the sun sent streaks of scarlet across the sky in its final hurrah for the day? Wasn't he exhausted, too?

"Esther!" he called before he even stopped the wagon. "I'm sorry to kumm by so late." He jumped to the ground, tossed his straw hat onto the wagon's seat, and approached her in long strides. "I'm glad I caught you before you went to bed."

"I'm waiting for my turn for a bath. Is something wrong?"

"Not really. Well, let me say nothing has happened to anyone as far as I know."

She turned a questioning look on the tall, blond man and waited for him to continue. She shifted from one foot to the other and then dug her toes into the grass. Patience was not a particularly strong point for her. She was about to explode when he spoke at last.

"I was still at the Eshs' place when Kathy Taylor returned for her husband."

"Did she say how Zeke was?"

"She said she knew he was in pain but was trying to hide it from her and Sarah. Apparently, the doctor had to re-clean and bandage his hand. Zeke shouldn't have been working on the barn and getting that burn dirty."

"D-Did he get any medicine?"

"I came right out and asked Kathy if she had to stop at the drugstore for medicine."

"And?"

"She said Zeke told her Dr. Kramer put medicine on his hand before he wrapped it and gave him some pills so they wouldn't have to stop at the drugstore."

"Would you happen to know if Kathy saw those pills?"

"I asked her that, too. She said she looked over her shoulder when Zeke showed the pills to Sarah."

"Let me guess. They were oblong, peach-colored pills, ain't so?"

"That's what she said."

Esther stomped her foot in the grass. "That man! Why is he treating us like this?"

"You don't know it's only the Amish."

"Well, Kathy got real medicine when she went there."

"That's true."

"Poor Zeke is going to have another painful, sleepless night. I've got to do something."

"What can you do, Esther?"

"I'm not sure, but I'm afraid one of our people will be seriously harmed — or worse — if we don't stop Dr. Kramer from plying us with worthless treatments."

He moved a little closer and touched her arm tentatively. "You know I'll do whatever I can to help, but be careful, Esther. Don't do anything —"

"Stupid." Hadn't they had this discussion before?

"I was going to say impulsive. I couldn't stand to see you get hurt in any way." He fastened his green eyes on her until she looked down at the ground between them. "I care," he whispered.

Her eyes shot back up to search Andrew's face for any hint of mockery or teasing. What she saw was a sincerity that brought tears to her eyes. "Danki," she mouthed, unable to get sound past the lump that had risen to fill her throat.

His smile lit his face and crinkled his eyes. He squeezed her arm gently. "Gut nacht, Esther."

"Gut nacht."

Esther would have loved a nice, long, relaxing shower, but the last person in the family of six to bathe wasn't left with a lot of hot water. That wasn't a huge issue on such a hot summer evening, but it was quite a different matter in the middle of winter. She tiptoed down the hall to her room since she was certain everyone else was asleep. She dragged out her basket and decided to stitch quilt blocks while her hair dried a bit. Who would ever have thought she would be a gut quilter? She had always hated doing any embroidery or hand stitching when Mamm made her learn years ago. She avoided needlework whenever possible, except for crocheting, which she felt fairly competent at. Now, here she was, actually enjoying quilting. She was amazed at the change in herself.

Change? Jah, she had changed. If she could change something so small as her attitude toward quilting, couldn't people change in much more significant ways? Was Hannah right? Her freind's words sprang into her mind.

Jacob had certainly changed. When he discovered Hannah was an Englischer pretending to be Amish, he turned his back on her. Even though Hannah had been forced into the pretense for her own protection since she had witnessed a crime, Jacob didn't trust her. She, Esther herself, had talked sense into Jacob and reminded him that Hannah was the same loving, kind person he had cared about before the deception was made known. The two had worked things out. Now their feelings for one another would be obvious to even a blind man.

The school board had changed. They were practically ready to run Hannah out of town—or out of the Amish community, anyway—when they found out the truth about her. Again, Esther had defended her freind, even speaking when an Amish woman would normally have held her tongue. Of course, she did get some help from Bishop Sol. But still, those four men changed their attitudes.

Esther laid one quilt block aside and picked up another one. Could Andrew really have changed? Was he sincere now in his words and actions? If she could like quilting, anything was possible! He certainly seemed different—gentle, kind, considerate, helpful. Hannah believed in him. Maybe he had a good reason for standing her up. Could she muster up the courage to ask him about it?

A faint tap at the door interrupted Esther's musings. Before she could call out, the door creaked open, allowing her schweschder to slip inside. Her shadow in the lamplight loomed larger than life. It crossed the room and perched on Esther's bed before Lydia did.

"You need to instruct your beau on the ways of courting unless those ways have changed in the last few years," she teased. "He's supposed to kumm in the dark to your window—"

"Jah, jah. You're so funny. Andrew is not my beau, and he's not courting me."

"I have a feeling any slight encouragement from you could change that."

"Why would you say that?"

"His feelings are pretty obvious."

"Why on earth would he care about me? He could have any Amish woman he wanted, here or in Ohio."

Lydia picked up a long, dark strand of Esther's hair. "You are very beautiful inside and outside. I know we don't compliment one another. Pride and attention to appearance or beauty are frowned upon. But you, my dear schweschder, need to know how lovely you are. You need to believe in yourself. Any man would be blessed to have you for his fraa."

Esther sat stunned, unsure what to make of Lydia's speech. She had never considered herself lovely in any way. Did she really possess the qualities her schweschder mentioned? She knew she cared deeply about her family and her community. Could she love and be loved by a man as well? Was she already?

"Ach, Esther!" Lydia exclaimed, then clapped her hand over her mouth at her outburst in the silent house. "These quilt blocks are magnificent. Did you stitch them?"

Esther nodded. "Surprising, isn't it?"

"I can't believe it. You've been hiding your gift from us."

"Hannah and Barbara called it a gift, too. Honestly, Lydia, if quilting is one of my talents, it was hidden from me as well. I thought I was only gut at growing plants. I just discovered how much I enjoy quilting. I didn't even think I was any gut at it."

"Gut? These rival Barbara Zook's quilt blocks, for sure. We have to show Mamm in the morning, ain't so?"

"I will."

"She will be surprised and pleased." Lydia passed the blocks she'd been examining back to her schweschder, who tucked them carefully into her basket. "Get some sleep, Esther. And think about what I said. You are a very loving and lovable person."

Esther hugged her. "Danki." Her schweschder nodded. She and her shadow slipped back across the room and out the door.

It seems I have a lot to think about.

With no church service, Sunday had been a relaxing, quiet day. Esther had spent time reading, talking to her family, and playing with David and Ella. Mamm had been overjoyed to discover her quilting abilities. Tears had filled her eyes when she carefully examined her quilt squares. She had pronounced them "wunderbaar."

Now, Monday meant back to work and chores. Esther poured kaffi and juice while Mamm finished frying eggs for breakfast. Lydia buttered gluten-free blueberry muffins for David and Ella, who were looking more robust each day.

"I'll start weeding your flower beds after breakfast, Mamm, before I set to work on my flowers," Esther said.

"Uh, Esther, I was going to see if you minded going to the store for me. The kinner are out of their yogurt and gluten-free cereal. I thought I had more cereal, but I guess not."

"Don't you want to pick the things out yourself?" Esther really wanted to work outside before the day grew any hotter. Why couldn't Lydia go to the store for herself?

"I don't need to. You know what they like as well as I do. I was going to bake them some more bread." Lydia paused a fraction of a minute. "I'll help Mamm with the laundry."

"Well..."

"I've already run to the phone and called Kathy Taylor, so you can ride in air-conditioned comfort." Lydia apparently hoped this would seal the deal.

Esther shrugged in defeat. "I guess I'll get my shoes and purse."

"You have time to eat." Her mudder handed her plates to set on the table.

"I'd better re-plan my day," Esther mumbled when she turned away from Mamm and Lydia.

List in hand, Esther scurried through the grocery store, gathering the items Lydia requested. Thank goodness the regular store carried several varieties gluten-free cereal, so she didn't have to go all the way to the health food store.

Kathy tossed the van keys to Esther as she passed her, pushing an extra-full shopping cart. "You can go ahead out and put your food in the cooler," she said. "I'll be out as soon as I can get through the check-out line with all this stuff."

"Okay." Esther clutched the keys in one hand and placed her food on the conveyer belt with the other hand. She hoped Kathy would find a short check-out line.

With all her items packed into three bags, Esther didn't bother to wheel the cart outside. They had parked on the side of the store where there weren't any cart return racks anyway. She hung the three plastic bags on her arms and proceeded to the van to deposit the yogurt in the cooler Kathy had brought along.

She slid the back door of the van open. Before she could raise the lid of the cooler, one of the flimsy plastic bags split open. Yogurt spilled out in two directions. Some containers rolled under the front seat and some under the back seat. Esther prayed the cartons hadn't burst open to leave trails of sticky fruit-flavored yogurt across the carpet of the van.

Quickly, she scrambled inside on all fours to search for the wayward containers. She had to practically flatten herself on her belly to reach all the way under the front seat. Her fingers had almost grabbed a carton of strawberry yogurt when she heard a voice. She sincerely hoped no one was talking to her or could even see her in such an unladylike position. She stopped moving and held her breath to listen. The voice grew closer, but the person was not talking to her. Apparently, the man was on his cell phone.

"Piece of cake," the gravelly voice said. There was a brief pause. "No. No one suspects anything. I should get lots of information, and it's been so easy. They're so trusting. It's like taking candy from a baby."

Esther was afraid to move from her uncomfortable position sprawled half under the seat. She couldn't help but eavesdrop—she had no choice, but she had no desire to be discovered doing so. The voice waxed and waned as if the man was pacing.

"I tell you there won't be any trouble even if they did suspect anything—which they don't. They would never press charges."

Someone must have committed a crime or they were about to. If she could raise up to peek out, maybe she could identify the man. Probably not, though. She didn't know a lot of Englischers, especially men. But that voice... She needed to conjure up all the sleuthing knowledge she'd gleaned from reading her beloved suspense novels.

"I should be able to wrap this up by the time the old man gets back. I'll have all the information I need and can turn this hick town back over to him."

The gruff voice grated on her nerves. Her breathing had become so shallow she feared she'd start hyperventilating and draw all sorts of attention to herself.

"I don't need anything right now." The voice grew quieter. The man must be moving away. "I'll let you know." Another short pause. "Later."

She counted to sixty, wrapped her hand around the carton of yogurt, and pulled herself to her knees. She glanced out the van window but saw only the retreating back of an average-sized man with shaggy brown hair. It could be anyone. What in the world was that all about? She plopped the still-intact containers of yogurt on top of the cold packs in the cooler.

She was fastening her seatbelt when Kathy came around the corner of the building, loaded down with grocery bags. Esther unclicked her seatbelt and leaped from the van to help her situate her bags in the back of the van. Should she mention the overheard conversation? Maybe she shouldn't involve Kathy. Maybe she could figure out this mystery on her own.

Chapter Fifteen

"Hello, Sophie!" Esther called as she opened the screen door to enter Sophie's shop the next morning. She had finished her weeding while the sunrise still painted the sky so she could get there early.

"Esther, dear, it's nice to see you." The older shuffled into the shop from the main portion of the house. "Is this a business visit or a social visit? Or do you have time for more instruction?"

"All of the above. As long as this is a gut time for you." Esther smiled. She noticed the dark skin surrounding Sophie's eyes which made her face appear very pale. "Are you feeling all right?" She reached out to touch her friend's arm. She thought she saw tears shimmering in the older woman's eyes.

"Of course." Sophie blinked and smiled. She grasped Esther's hand and squeezed it. "I'm a bit tired."

"Would you rather rest? I could visit another day."

"Absolutely not. I'd much rather talk to you. Let's see. Where did we leave off?" Sophie dropped her hand and crossed the room to the new cabinet Esther and Andrew had set up for her.

She quizzed Esther relentlessly before providing all kinds of new information on various herbs. Her head whirled. She didn't think she cold cram in one more fact, regardless of how interesting it was. She felt like a scholar again, studying for a big test.

"I've even been jotting down some notes for you." Sophie opened a drawer and pulled out a spiral notebook with many pages already filled with her small, even handwriting.

"Sophie," Esther began but hesitated, unsure how to proceed. "Is there a special reason you want to pour all this information into my head so quickly?"

"Nee. I just…well, jah, there is."

"Do you want to tell me?"

Sophie stared at her fidgeting fingers for a few moments before shifting her watery eyes to Esther's face. "I want you to carry on for me when I'm gone."

"Gone where?"

"I-I have cancer. I-I don't have much time left."

"Sophie, that can't be!" She felt like a mule had kicked her in the gut. "Have you seen a doctor? There are all kinds of treatments. The people will help pay." She couldn't stem the flow of words. If she talked enough, maybe the other woman's words could be erased.

"I have seen a doctor."

"Not Dr. Kramer!"

"Nee. Why?"

"I don't trust him."

"Well, I saw Dr. Nelson before he left to care for his daed. He sent me to a specialist, too."

"When was that? Does anyone else know?"

"It was a few months ago. Only Gid knows about this, and now you."

"Did this specialist tell you about treatments?"

"There really isn't much they can do." Her voice grew hoarse and hushed. "It's pancreatic cancer, and it's already pretty advanced."

"Ach, Sophie!" She burst into tears and grabbed Sophie in a hug. "I-I'm sorry. I-I should be strong for you, and-and here I am crying all over you."

"I've had a while to adjust." Sophie patted her back. Her sobs quieted to sniffs and gulps. The older woman fumbled around on the counter and yanked a tissue from the box. She dabbed at her companion's face, then pulled another tissue from the box and pressed it into her hand. "Now, blow."

Obediently, Esther blew her nose. She dragged in several deep, ragged breaths and willed herself to calm down.

"Esther, dear, I'd like very much to leave the place to you."

"Your business, you mean?"

"Business. House. Everything. You could move your greenhouse here. There's plenty of room for you to grow whatever you want."

"What about Gid?"

"We've discussed this. H-He doesn't want to live here without me." Sophie's voice wobbled a bit. She took a breath and cleared her throat. "Gid plans to move to Lancaster. He has several nephews there."

"But, Sophie, he'd leave his home here?"

"He said it wouldn't be home without me."

"Ach, Sophie." She almost broke down again and struggled for control of her emotions. "I could take care of the house and business, I think, but I couldn't take care of the rest of the farm by myself."

"Gid has thought of that. He has someone in mind that needs a farm of his own. In fact, he has kumm today to meet with Gid, though he doesn't yet know why Gid wants to talk to him." Sophie nodded to the open window.

Esther's eyes followed Sophie's gaze. With all her inner turmoil, she never even heard a horse and wagon rattle up the driveway. But sure enough, there was Gid coming out of the barn to greet the arrival. The man jumped nimbly from the wagon. Esther knew in an instant it was Andrew. Gid wanted Andrew Fisher to farm his land. Her mouth dropped open and she turned to Sophie in shock. "How is this going to work out?"

"I guess time will tell." Sophie gave a soft chuckle.

"Sophie, how are Andrew and I supposed to take over for you and Gid? We aren't married."

"That can be remedied."

"Sophie! I'm serious."

"So am I."

"What? Are you a fortune teller now? Can you see into the future? Andrew and I aren't even, uh, courting."

"That, too, can be remedied."

"Sophie, be serious! Whatever would Bishop Sol say about such an arrangement?"

"We'll talk to him when we know your decision—yours and Andrew's. Sol is a reasonable man. Kumm." She clapped her hands like a school teacher. "We have more work to do. We'll discuss this again later."

Esther wasn't at all sure she could concentrate on any herbs or ailments. She wondered what Gid was saying to Andrew and what his reaction would be. Ach, to be a fly buzzing around their heads about now!

Her head still spun crazily as she hugged Sophie goodbye. She promised to return the next afternoon and agreed to *think* about her freind's request when her befuddled mind cleared a bit. She needed to talk to someone, but Sophie's condition was not her news to share.

She wanted to run faster and faster until she out-ran the specter of death. She wanted to rail at the injustice of the cruel illness that intended to claim Sophie's life. She wanted to cry. Instead, she forced a tremulous smile and waved as Sophie watched her from the front porch. Esther clucked to her horse and prodded him to start down the tree-lined driveway. For once, she paid no attention to the scents of pine and mimosa that she ordinarily delighted in. Tears clouded her vision so that she almost ran into the wagon stopped near the end of the driveway. "Whoa!"

Andrew stepped out from among the trees and approached her buggy. He looked nearly as dazed as she felt. "Would you walk with me for a few minutes?"

Esther nodded, not trusting her voice to speak. She hopped from the buggy before he could offer any assistance. He grasped her arm lightly and led her to the copse of trees. "Did Sophie, uh, talk to you?"

" It's so awful!" She burst into tears and threw herself into his arms. She felt him pat her back and barely heard the soothing words he murmured.

Esther sobbed as if her heart had shattered into tiny fragments. Spent, she gulped in air and struggled to pull herself together. As awareness seeped into her consciousness, she realized where she was and what she had done. Horrified, she pulled back. When she dared to look up into Andrew's face, she saw only concern and compassion.

His hands still rested on her arms. The heat of embarrassment flooded her, and she knew her face must be redder than the geraniums that surrounded Sophie's front porch. How could she have been so bold, so brazen as to throw herself into his arms? Her mortification increased when she noticed the front of his green shirt wet from her tears. She plucked at his shirt. "I-I'm so sorry."

He captured her hand. "It will dry. No harm is done."

"I'm sorry for-for..." She tried to step back and distance herself from this man who had witnessed her tears and shameful behavior. He kept his grip on her hand, and his other hand tightened on her arm so she couldn't flee.

"It's okay. I-I rather liked it. I don't mean I liked seeing you upset." He paused, obviously struggling to put his feelings into words. "What I mean is, uh...I, uh liked holding you."

"Oh."

They stood in silence a few moments. She still wished she could crawl into the nearest hole. "I'm sorry I fell apart," she whispered at last.

He started walking, still clasping her hand which forced her to walk close to him. "That was shocking news for Sophie and Gid to deliver."

"For sure. I-I can't believe it. Maybe Sophie is wrong."

"I asked Gid that. He said several doctors had given her the same diagnosis."

"She seemed so resigned, so at peace."

"Gid did, too. I suppose they've had a while to kumm to terms with it all."

Esther nodded. "Did Gid tell you their wishes?"

"He did."

"What did you tell him?"

"That I'd think on it and give him my answer by the end of the week. I know he wants this resolved so he can spend time with Sophie without the extra concern."

"Sophie told me to think, too. My head is in a whirl."

"I know what you mean. We need to pray about this."

"I'd like to discuss it with Mamm and Daed but can't until Sophie makes her news known."

"Maybe Sophie and Gid want us to figure this out on our own—with Gott's help, of course."

"Maybe."

They shuffled through dried pine needles and broken pine cones. "I'm pretty sure I could take care of Sophie's house and business. I'm certain when the time is right, Lydia and her kinner and maybe a husband will take over Mamm's and Daed's house, so this would be a place for me to live."

"I'm only staying with the Fishers, so I have no claim to any land," Andrew said. "This would give me a farm to work when I'm not building furniture."

Each one thought aloud. Simultaneously, they stopped, looked at each other, and said, "But how…" Esther's cheeks grew warm. They couldn't both live at the Hostetler farm. They shuffled along a few more moments in silence until Esther said, "I'd better get home."

"Jah."

They headed back to their horses, neither one speaking. Esther suddenly realized her hand was still grasping Andrew's. She slid it from his and felt a strange emptiness. She needed to get a grip on herself. She couldn't risk letting him think—what? She didn't know what she thought or felt herself. She gave her horse a pat and turned to climb into the buggy.

"Esther?"

"Jah?" She didn't turn around.

"Look at me. Please."

Slowly, Esther swiveled and dared to look into the jade gaze searching her face. She glanced down quickly for fear she'd get lost in those eyes. A hand cupped her chin, forcing her to look up. His voice was as soft as a caress. "If one night, you saw a light shining in your window, what would you do?"

"Um, I'd see who was outside."

"If it was me?"

"I'd, um…" She tried to look away, but his hand still held her chin.

"You'd what?"

"I'd kumm out to talk to you," she whispered. If her cheeks grew any warmer, they would surely burst into flame.

"Really?"

"Really."

"You wouldn't throw a pitcher of water out the window and try to drown me?"

She laughed. "Do you really think I'd do such a thing as that?"

"You've tried to stomp on my foot a time or two, among other things."

"What other things?
"Several tongue lashings."

She laughed again. "They were well deserved."

"Probably."

"I would not douse you with water."

"That's a relief." His smile stole upwards to crinkle his eyes. She smiled back. "I'll be talking to you soon." He helped her into her buggy, and for once, she didn't shake off his hand.

"Sure." She chided herself for her lack of social skills. Another young woman would have had all the appropriate answers, but she said the first thing that popped into her mind. When she got the horse heading home, she ventured a backward glance. Andrew still stood beside his horse, wearing a huge grin. *Am I setting myself up for another disappointment? I didn't even ask him why he treated me the way he did years ago. Why did I say I would go out and talk to him? I can't even trust him — not with my heart, anyway.*

She'd nearly reached home when she remembered she had wanted to discuss that strange conversation she'd overheard at the grocery store. Since Andrew was her only confidante in the mysterious peach pill matter, she had decided to get his opinion on the odd conversation as well. It would have to wait. Besides, she had no face to put with the voice, but there was something distinctive about that voice, something that raised the little hairs on the back of her neck.

Esther chopped and pulled weeds from between green bean and tomato plants with a vengeance the next morning. If only she could extricate the cancer from Sophie's body as easily as she could weeds from the vegetable garden. When she'd completed her attack on the weeds, she plucked off long, firm green beans and tossed them into a basket.

"If you don't slow down, you're going to spontaneously combust." Lydia stood at the edge of the garden, digging her bare toes into the dirt. "I came to help, but you're almost finished. Why the rush? Was ist letz?"

Esther shrugged her shoulders. "I have a lot on my mind, I guess."

"Do you want to talk about it?"

"Not right now, but danki. I'm trying to finish up here so I can get over to Sophie's for a while."

"Is she training you to be her helper?"

"Um, something like that."

"I'll help you finish up here. David and Ella can snap the beans. David is big enough to do that, and Ella can start learning."

"They're growing up so fast, schweschder."

"Too fast to suit me. Neither one is a boppli anymore."

The women worked in companionable silence until all the rows of beans had been picked. Esther groaned as she straightened. She put a hand to her aching lower back. "I suppose we'll be canning these tomorrow."

"Most likely, unless Mamm decides to do it this afternoon."

"Ugh! At least beans aren't as hard to can as tomatoes. It's still a hot job, though."

"Jah, but we'll be glad we did it when winter rolls around."

They trudged toward the house with their baskets of green beans and set them on the picnic table under the oak trees in the back yard. "Are you planning to sit David and Ella out here to snap beans?"

"That's probably best. It will be a little cooler if this hint of a breeze keeps up, and there will be less mess to clean up afterward."

"I'm going to wash up a bit and head to Sophie's. I don't plan to be there too long today, unless there is something she needs me to do."

"Is she ailing?"

"Uh, I meant she may want my help with something."

Lydia raised questioning eyebrows but asked nothing further. "The kinner have a doctor's appointment tomorrow."

"Aren't you going to cancel it? They seem fine."

"They do seem to be doing well right now. I'll make sure they're no longer anemic, and then maybe they won't have to go back for a while."

Esther snorted. "He'll probably have them return for something," she muttered only half under her breath. She pushed damp tendrils of hair off her neck.

"What?"

"I'm going with you tomorrow."

"I think we'll be okay if you have other things to do."

"Nee. I want to go with you."

"So have you done any thinking about our discussion?" Sophie asked a few hours later.

"Things are kind of going round and round in my head. I walked here today to have extra time to think, but my mind keeps flitting to first one thing and then another."

"I'm sorry to put you in such a quandary." Sophie patted her arm. "Kumm. Let me show you some things in the house. I know you've been here many times, but you haven't looked at it from the perspective of homeowner, or possible homeowner."

Esther swallowed the lump in her throat and followed her through the house. She listened without commenting as Sophie pointed out various idiosyncrasies. Was it her imagination or did the older woman seem a little out of breath? Would she even have noticed if Sophie hadn't told her about her illness yesterday? Was she looking for symptoms or problems? She gathered her courage, took a deep breath, and asked the question that had been searing her brain. "Why me, Sophie? Why did you want me to take your house and business?"

"Because you understand. You're like me. You love the land and the plants. You're smart. You've learned a lot about herbs and remedies very quickly. You care about our people. They know that and will trust you. You are my *only* choice."

The speech surprised her. She was pleased to be held in such high regard by this woman she respected and looked up to. Yet, she feared she wouldn't live up to Sophie's expectations. "What if I make a mess of everything? What if I fail?"

"I know you, Esther dear. I've watched you grow up. I believe you can do all things with Gott's help. Trust Him. He will never leave you or forsake you."

She nodded. "But a single woman living alone?"

"That isn't totally unheard of. There have been others, but you won't always be single, I daresay."

"Whatever makes you say that?"

"I see the sparks. You just need to fan them into a flame."

Esther's cheeks grew hot enough to start that fire. "You're imagining things."

"I don't think so. I'm pretty astute."

"Are you trying to play matchmaker, too?"

"I don't think I need to."

"Well, Daed and almost everybody else seems to be throwing Andrew and me together."

"Maybe they see what I see, what everyone sees except you."

"Is that why Gid asked Andrew to take over his farm—to throw us together?"

"Nee. We would never do that. Gid knows every young man wants his own place. Since Andrew doesn't have parents here to work with, and with no farm land for sale now, we thought he'd be interested in this place."

"How is that supposed to work with me living here?"

"We can stipulate that you have the house and surrounding land and Andrew has the rest of the property or something like that. We can work out the details when you two make your decisions."

"It sounds a little odd to me."

"Promise you'll pray about it."

"I have been praying and I'll keep praying."

"Gut. Let's have some of those molasses cookies you brought. I have some iced tea already made."

"The cookies are for you and Gid."

"I think we can spare one or two for you. It was sweet of you to bring them. I haven't done any baking lately."

"Is there anything else I can do for you, Sophie?"

"Not right now. I will admit I've been getting weaker, but Gid has been helping me. I take naps when I'm too tired." She exhaled in a long, deep sigh.

Esther blinked hard to squelch the tears that threatened to flow.

"Don't you go being sad, Esther." Sophie reached out a trembling hand to pat her arm. "I have had a happy life, and I'm ready to meet the Lord Gott. So smile and dry those tears."

She smiled and tried to comply. "I'll miss you so much."

"And I will miss you, but we will meet again. I'm sure of it."

She nodded. "I'm sure, too."

"Here, dear, have a cookie."

Chapter Sixteen

Early the next morning, Esther helped Lydia get David and Ella fed and cleaned up before piling into the buggy. She hoped the doctor's appointment went well. She also hoped they wouldn't have to return for more visits. The past couple of weeks, David and Ella had been healthy and active. They had not complained of tummy aches. They had not been unusually tired or irritable. They even seemed to have filled out a bit. Surely they must be on the right track now. Even Lydia seemed less stressed and suffered fewer headaches.

David and Ella bounced along in the back of the buggy and watched Englischers zoom by in their cars as the buggy rolled along on the shoulder of the busy highway. They could have asked Kathy Taylor or another Englisch driver to transport them, but Lydia wanted to save the money. Esther thought the outing in the fresh air—albeit hot air—would do them all gut. The traffic would be lighter on the way home, so she would be able to relax a little then. Right now, she had to be extra alert to watch for automobiles that might turn or swerve into her path.

She tied the horse to a hitching post in the shade. He, too, seemed relieved to be away from the cars whizzing by in their frantic dash to reach their destinations. Esther lifted Ella out of the buggy as David hopped out the other side and took Lydia's hand. Only a few cars dotted the parking lot at this early hour. She hoped they would get in and out of the office quickly.

"It looks like there are only two people ahead of us," her schweschder whispered when they had entered the waiting room. Esther signed the children in at the receptionist's window while their mudder settled them with puzzles at the little child-sized table.

Esther settled herself the best she could on the hard, plastic chair next to Lydia. "I hope this is the last time we have to bring the kinner her for a long time." Lydia nodded.

At last, the familiar medical assistant, wearing animal print scrubs, called them back. Today, her name badge faced outward. Mindy. What a cute name, Esther thought. Mindy had each child step on the scale. Ella had gained one pound and David had gained two.

"Hurray!" Mindy cried. "They must be eating well." She led them to the lab where the technician would again draw a blood sample. The children weren't happy, but they stoically complied.

Mindy ushered them into an exam room after they'd had their arms poked. "I'll bring the results in when they're ready. The doctor will be in shortly." The door didn't quite shut all the way when Mindy left the room, allowing Esther and Lydia to hear muffled, one-sided phone conversations from the front office.

"Well, hello." Dr. Kramer pushed the door open and entered the examining room.

Esther found herself clearing her throat as if that would clear the doctor's voice. That voice. That gravelly voice. Why, it sounded like the man outside the grocery store! Could it be one and the same?

Dr. Kramer consulted the charts. "It looks like they've both put on a little weight. That's good."

Lydia smiled and nodded.

"Their blood work is better, too. Their hemoglobin is in the normal range today."

"Does that mean they aren't anemic anymore?" Lydia's voice was filled with hope.

"They aren't at the moment. Are they following their diet okay?"

"They always have been." Esther jumped in before Lydia could answer. She hoped she didn't seem too abrupt. Sometimes words shot out of her mouth without her brain's knowledge.

"Yes. Well. Let's see. Are they still eating the bread and cookies you got here?"

"Nee," Lydia said. "We ran out several weeks ago. We've been making our own."

"Using gluten-free ingredients, of course," Esther added.

"Of course. I do have some bread and cookies today that I can give you. That will save you from baking in this hot weather."

"It's nee problem to make their foods." Esther wasn't sure she trusted the doctor's supply. "We have to cook and bake anyway, regardless of how hot it is."

"Oh. I guess so, but please let me get those items for you."

Before either of them could protest further, Dr. Kramer slipped out of the room.

Esther turned to her schweschder to whisper. "Do you ever want to offer to wash that lab coat to get the ink stain out or to iron his shirt?"

Lydia covered her mouth to stifle her giggle. "Or comb his hair."

Esther snorted. She struggled to compose herself when footsteps alerted them to the doctor's approach.

"Here we go. At least maybe this can be a treat for the ride home." Dr. Kramer's arms were full of the packaged food. He thrust three packages of cream-filled sandwich cookies and three loaves of brown bread at Lydia. "I'll have Mindy find you a bag."

Why was the doctor so insistent they take his food?

"Dr. Kramer, can you come help, please?" the receptionist called.

"What's wrong?" The doctor heaved a sigh.

"Mindy, the lab tech, and I are trying to help a patient out of the car. His wife can't do it, and I'm afraid even the three of us need reinforcement. He is, uh, rather large."

"Excuse me. I'll be right back." Dr. Kramer sighed again as he shuffled from the room.

Esther waited a few seconds then crept over to the door.

"Where are you going?" her schweschder asked.

"I'll be right back."

"Esther, what are you up to?"

"Shhh! I'll be back in a minute." She slipped out of the examining room and tiptoed down the hall. A quick glance out the window assured her the entire office staff remained occupied with the man in the car. "Perfect!"

First, she sneaked into the doctor's office. Stacks of files filled one corner of the big, oak desk. A ledger of some sort sat opened near the phone. She'd take a quick peek. Her lips formed soundless words. "Forgive me, Lord, if this is wrong. You know I only want to help. I believe You want me to help."

She saw sets of initials--SZ, DK, EK MT, JK, EE--with brief notes beside each set. Esther could think of Amish names to go with each set of initials. Quickly, she scanned as much as she could and tried to commit the words to memory. She tiptoed back to the hallway and paused to listen. No one had entered the office yet, but she would have to hurry.

Esther slipped into the lab area. A scrap of cellophane paper on the floor caught her attention. She crossed the room and peered into the trash can. "What?" She pulled out empty cookie and bread wrappers from name-brand products found in the grocery store. She scanned the labels. Regular foods. The first ingredient on each was wheat flour. A box of plastic bags sat on the counter next to a seal-a-bag type contraption.

She gasped. "He's had us give David and Ella regular food. Gluten-containing food. No wonder they felt sick sometimes but not other times." Her words, though whispered, seemed to echo around the room. Her brain scrambled to review the pattern.

She thought back to a few weeks ago when David and Ella were tired and cranky and complained of tummy distress. At that time, they had been giving the kinner the cookies and bread from Dr. Kramer.

She wanted to stomp her foot and yell. It was bad enough the man didn't provide proper treatment for adults, but he deliberately gave David and Ella foods that would hurt them. He must have been purchasing regular foods and repackaging them before giving them to two trusting, unsuspecting Amish women. What was wrong with the man? He was supposed to help people. He was a doctor. Didn't doctors take some kind of oath to do no harm?

The slam of a car door ended Esther's internal tirade. Hastily, she grabbed the wrappers and folded them as small as possible. She scurried back down the hall to the examining room where Lydia waited with the kinner.

"What in the world were you doing?"

"Shhh! I'll tell you later." Voices in the waiting room and footsteps on the tile floor made her heart skip beats. She snatched her handbag off the chair and thrust the food wrappers deep inside. Was this stealing? She'd never stolen anything in her life. But these papers were in the trash can on their way out to the big green dumpster. Taking trash couldn't be stealing, could it? She sent up a prayer asking for forgiveness, just in case.

Esther dropped onto the chair, clutched her handbag to her chest, and tried to control her trembling. Dr. Kramer pushed the door open. He looked slightly more disheveled than before. she hoped her expression was serene even though her heart pounded beneath the handbag. She dropped her eyes to study the blue and gray tile floor, afraid the doctor would read the guilt she knew must be written on her face.

"Well, now," Dr. Kramer began. "I grabbed a bag for your food on my way in. Looks like you folks are all set. You can schedule an appointment for next month."

She wanted to throw the food at the man and demand an explanation. And why did David and Ella have to come back next month if they were doing so well today? Was it to see how sick they got eating the doctor's "special foods?" She didn't trust herself to speak.

"Why do they need to kumm back in a month?" She wanted to hug her schweschder for being brave enough to ask the question.

"Well, uh…" The doctor obviously searched for a reason to justify his decision. "To make sure they stay on track."

"Oh, I—" Lydia stopped when she elbowed her sharply in the ribs.

"Let's go." Esther spoke in Pennsylvania Dutch. "No appointment, schweschder. I'll explain later." She grabbed Ella's hand and Lydia took David's. They led the kinner through the waiting room and to the door.

"What about your next appointment?" the receptionist called out.

"We'll let you know." She herded everyone out the door as quickly as they could move.

"Why didn't you let me make the appointment?" Lydia asked as soon as they were all settled in the buggy.

"I don't think the kinner will need to kumm back next month."

"Why?"

She hesitated, not sure how much she should tell Lydia.

"Mamm, can we have a cookie like the doctor said?" David took advantage of the lull in the conversation.

Lydia reached for the bag of food and pulled out a package of cookies. Esther's hand clamped around her wrist before she could tear the package open.

"What are you doing?" She turned a puzzled look on her schweschder.

"They can't have those."

"If I say they can, they can." Lydia folded her arms across her chest as if preparing for a showdown.

Esther reached for a plastic grocery bag beneath the seat. She pulled out two bananas and handed one to each child. "Here you go." They seemed as pleased with the fruit as they would have been with cookies.

She turned back to Lydia and switched to speaking in Englisch since David and Ella didn't understand that too well yet. It would be much harder to have secrets or even a private conversation once they knew the language. "Those foods aren't appropriate for David and Ella."

"What do you mean?"

"They aren't gluten free."

"How would you know that?"

"Well, uh, I have the labels."

"You what? How did you get the labels? I've never seen a label on the foods Dr. Kramer has given us."

"Exactly. He didn't want us to know, I'm sure."

"Where are these labels?"

"Look in there." Esther pointed to her handbag. "Down in the bottom."

"So that's what you were sneaking around the office for? You suspected something?"

"I felt something hasn't been quite right."

Lydia hauled the purse onto her lap and fished around inside. She pulled out the crinkled papers, smoothed them, and stared at them for a moment. "Whole wheat bread. Cookies made with wheat flour. This is what I've been feeding my kinner?"

"I'm afraid so."

"I've been giving my bopplin foods that made them sick?" Lydia covered her face with her hands.

"You didn't do it intentionally. You — we — trusted the doctor. We thought he was being helpful. Don't blame yourself."

"Why would he do such a thing? He knew they couldn't have foods containing gluten."

"I don't know, Lyddie, but I aim to find out."

"How are you going to do that?"

"I'm not sure yet, but I'll figure out something. Put those labels in the bag with the food. I want to save them all."

"Whatever for?"

"For evidence, of course."

"You know gut and well we won't go to the authorities or press charges."

"I know that. For my own peace of mind, I need to find out Dr. Kramer's motive."

"I think it's best if we get rid of this food and not go back to the doctor until Dr. Nelson returns. I can give the bread and cookies to neighbors."

"Can you wait a little while? The food is sealed up with the doctor's bag-sealing contraption, so they will keep a while. Let me try to figure out a few things. Please?"

"It's against my better judgement, but okay."

"Danki. Oh, and maybe we shouldn't say anything to anyone else yet."

Lydia hesitated before answering. "Okay."

Esther had a hard time concentrating on anything else the rest of the day. She alternated between feeling angry and hurt. She was sure Lydia must be experiencing the same emotions. Despite the heat, she worked outside after the noon meal. She attacked weeds like they were some great enemy to be defeated until sweat poured down her face and back. Her blue work dress clung to her body. Whatever wasn't soaked with perspiration was covered with dirt. When she found herself gasping to catch her breath, she abandoned the weeds and performed calmer tasks, like repotting plants and straightening her potting shed.

The kinners' squeals from the back yard brought a smile to her face and chased away the frown. Apparently, nap time was over, and David and Ella had been turned loose to play in the shady yard. Esther knew she should wash up and help with supper preparations, but she couldn't resist taking a few minutes to play with her niece and nephew. How she loved them!

The thought that someone would deliberately try to hurt them pained her greatly. She forced those thoughts from her head as she jogged to the back yard. She pushed first one and then the other on the wooden swing suspended by thick ropes tied to a sturdy oak branch. She had loved swinging as a girl. To be completely honest, she still enjoyed swinging and sometimes stole outside as the sun sank in the sky to climb on the big swing. Something about soaring in the air was so freeing. Cares flew away, at least for a time.

"Push me! Push me!" Ella demanded.

"I will. David gets two more pushes. Then it's your turn."

"One! Two!" Ella shouted.

Esther laughed. "I haven't pushed him yet. Be patient." Maybe the child was too much like her. "Why don't you pick me some of those little blue flowers while you wait?" She pointed to a clump of tiny flowers growing wild near the edge of the yard. Ella scampered off. The little girl loved flowers almost as much as her aenti did.

Ella returned shortly with a fistful of flowers, some with roots clinging to the stems. "Two?"

"Jah. I've pushed David two times. It's your turn. You can lay the flowers on the picnic table. We'll put them in a cup of water when we go inside. Danki for picking them. They're very pretty." David hopped off the swing so Ella could have her turn.

When they grew tired of swinging, Esther chased the kinner around the yard and played silly games with them. She was so glad to see them strong and healthy and having fun. She soon lost all track of time.

"David! Ella! You need to wash up," Lydia called.

Esther slapped her own forehead. "I didn't get inside and help with the meal. Mamm will have my hide." She'd better apologize right away.

She scrubbed her face and hands, wishing she had time to shower and change her dirty clothes. She rushed into the kitchen with moisture still gleaming on her face and hands. "Ach, Mamm! I'm so sorry. I got so caught up with the kinner that I forgot all about the time. I meant to help and was on my way in here. I stopped to play for a minute and well…" She knew she rambled but couldn't seem to stop.

Lydia burst out laughing, and even Mamm cracked a smile. "It's all right. I saw you out the window. I figured the little ones could use some aenti time."

"Danki. I'll set the table."

"It's done. We're just waiting for Daed," here schweschder said.

For once, Esther was at a loss for words. Like everyone else, she waited.

With supper and clean up as well as Bible reading and prayers behind her, Esther could finally take a much-needed shower. She let the water run over her for as long as she dared, luxuriating in the fragrant soap and shampoo. When she could prolong the experience no longer, she turned the water off and dried on the big, fluffy towel. She pulled her nightgown over her head, threw her dark blue robe around her shoulders, and slipped down the hall to her room. She combed the tangles out of her waist-length hair before kneeling beside her bed to ask for guidance. What should she do with the evidence she had acquired?

A flicker of light distracted her from her prayers. She glanced at the lamp on her nightstand to make sure it wasn't sputtering and about to go out. The flicker came again but not from her lamp. It came from across the room. From the window?

She pushed herself to her feet and padded barefoot to the window. Blackness greeted her. Strange. As she was about to turn away, the flicker came again. This time, she saw the source. Andrew's face shone momentarily in the last flicker of light. Her heart did a funny little dance. Did he have news? Had something happened to Sophie? He would have knocked on the door if that was the case. Could he possibly be here to see her? She nodded her head at the window.

With fumbling fingers, Esther rolled her hair back into its customary bun and pinned her kapp into place. She pulled clothes on quickly and tiptoed downstairs, praying the back door wouldn't creak when she pulled it open. "Andrew?" she whispered into the darkness.

"Jah," he whispered back. Silently, he crossed the yard from beneath Esther's window to where she stood on the back steps. "I know it's not Saturday, but…uh, I…uh, wanted to see you."

She smiled at his nervousness. "Do you want to sit on the front porch?"

"Sure. That would be fine."

Neither one spoke as they walked side-by-side to the porch. The sat on the old wooden swing suspended from the ceiling, their arms barely touching. Andrew set it in motion. Thankfully, it didn't squeak tonight.

Finally, he broke the silence. "I can't explain it, Esther, but somehow, I got the feeling you needed me, needed to talk to me or something." His hushed voice trailed off.

"Ach, Andrew! I don't know what to do."

"About Sophie's request?"

"That and something else, too." She jumped from the swing and grabbed his hand. She tugged until he, too, was on his feet. "I forgot all the windows were open. Let's walk."

"Okay." He followed her in the darkness.

She wandered through the yard and out to the gravel driveway, still clinging to his hand. Halfway down the driveway, she spoke. "I went with Lydia to the kinners' appointment with Dr. Kramer today." She paused briefly and then, in a rush of words, told him everything that had transpired. "I'm trying not to be angry, Andrew. Really, I am. And I'm trying to be forgiving, but it's so hard. How could that man deliberately hurt little ones? Why is he mistreating our people?"

"I can't imagine."

"I have to find out."

"And do what with the information? It's not our way to press charges."

"I'm not going to the police or anything. I only want to know why he's doing these things. I can't stand by and watch him hurt any more of our people."

"What do you propose to do?"

"I-I think I'll have a talk with the man."

"Do you think a confrontation is wise?"

"I have to hear an explanation for his actions. He had at least six sets of initials with notations beside them. Those initials matched up with David, Ella, Mose, Zeke, Joanna King, and Susannah Zimmerman. There may be others or there may be more to follow. I have to stop him."

"Esther, you don't really know what this man is capable of. I don't want you to get hurt." He squeezed her hand.

'I'll be careful. Maybe I'll even get Kathy to drive me. I can make a quicker getaway."

"Do you want me to go there with you?"

"I appreciate the offer, but it's probably better for me to go alone. That way, he won't suspect anyone else is on to him."

"You'll let me know when you talk to him?"

"For sure."

They strolled to the end of the driveway, still hand-in-hand. A slight breeze rustled the tops of the oak and maple trees. "Mmm. That breeze, small as it is, feels wunderbaar!" Esther lifted her face skyward to feel the tiny breath from Gott. "And look at all those stars. I love a moonless night when the stars have a chance to shine their brightest."

"Me too. There's the Big Dipper." He pointed to the constellation.

They turned back toward the sleeping house under the canopy of stars in companionable silence.

"This is nice," he commented.

"What is?"

"This walk with you beneath all these stars."

"Jah. It is nice."

"Have you made any decision about taking Sophie's place?"

"Not really. I mean, I'm still thinking and praying."

"Me, too."

"Andrew, do you get the feeling this may be what the Lord Gott wants us to do? Maybe agreeing to Sophie's plan would give her some small measure of comfort during, uh, her last days." She sniffed and struggled not to do a repeat crying-on-the-shoulder performance.

"Maybe so."

"I think I'd like taking over her business and combining it with my own nursery business. I've always had a fondness for her house..." Her voice trailed off. She sniffed again. "But I hate the circumstances!"

"I know." He squeezed her hand. "I'd like to give Gid some peace of mind about the farm. He loves his land, and I know he wants it taken care of. I believe I'd like the chance to do that."

"But you are such a skillful furniture maker."

"I think I could do both. Especially if, uh, if there was someone special there to work alongside me." He stopped walking, forcing her to halt as well. "D-Do you know what I'm saying, Esther?"

"I'm not sure." She was glad the darkness hid her burning cheeks.

"I think we could manage Gid's and Sophie's place together."

"Well, that's why they asked us both, I'm thinking."

"I mean really together. You and me—together."

"You mean together as in…"

"Jah." Andrew's whisper was close to Esther's ear.

She felt him lean even closer and then his lips brushed across hers. His action totally surprised her, but even more surprising was her response. She enjoyed his lips on hers. She actually closed her eyes and returned his kiss.

Esther opened one eye to peek at the sky. Surely the stars had exploded, but they still hung suspended exactly where they had been a few moments ago. The fireworks were inside her!

Andrew pulled back. "Forgive me if I've been too bold. I don't mean any disrespect. In fact, Esther, I have higher regards for you than for anyone. I-I-lo— care about you very much."

"Really?"

"Really."

"I haven't been very nice, you know."

"I think you've been afraid. You've been cautious. You've been protecting your heart, ain't so?"

"Maybe." Her voice wouldn't project any louder than a whisper. Her emotions were in such turmoil. First the kiss. And now—did he almost say he loved her? She couldn't prolong her questions. She'd never know any peace or feel totally comfortable with him until she understood why he set her up for heartache. She took a deep breath. She didn't know how to broach the subject. Words danced around in her mind. "There's something I need to know, Andrew. Why did you deliberately ask me to meet you all those years ago and then not show up? And why did you laugh about it later?"

Chapter Seventeen

"What in the world are you talking about?"

Esther swiped a hand across her eyes. *I will not cry. We will discuss this like two adults.* "How could you forget such a thing?"

"There isn't anything to forget. I never asked you to meet me."

"I got a note from you telling me to meet you in the school yard at dusk the day before you left Maryland. I slipped away from home and ran there, thinking you really wanted to, uh, to see me, that you liked me."

"I did like you, but I never sent a note. I wish I had been brave enough to do that, but I didn't."

She stomped her foot. "I got the note."

"How do you know it was my writing?"

"It was a scribble like I remembered seeing on your school papers."

"All buwe scribble."

She hesitated. That was true from what she re-membered from school. Most of the handwriting papers on the wall belonged to girls. "But . . ."

"Anyone could have done that. Some of the fellows loved playing tricks, you know."

"But you laughed about it with several other buwe later."

"I didn't, Esther. Honest."

"I saw you talking to the others and laughing about how pitiful I was standing there, waiting for you to show up." She sniffed hard.

"I didn't. Really. That day, I had to help pack up the whole house. I didn't stop until I dropped into bed. I didn't go anywhere."

"Then who —"

"Did you see the fellows clearly?"

"I-I suppose not. It was getting dark. But I saw your straw hat. I knew it was yours because it was always bent up in the back."

"My hat was missing the next morning when we left. I never had a chance to go looking for it."

"So you're telling me some other bu wrote the note and took your hat to fool me—actually, to make a fool of me."

"It sounds like it. I'm sorry, Esther. I liked to tease, and I'll admit I did a lot of dumb things, but I would never have stood you up like that. Please believe me." He reached for her hand and squeezed it.

"I guess I could have been mistaken. All these years, I thought you deliberately tried to break my heart."

"Never would I have done such a thing. I'm sorry that happened and you were hurt. I wish you had asked me about this when I first returned. We could have cleared up your mistrust of me."

"Maybe. I still had to work through all your teasing. I felt so clumsy and inadequate."

"I'm sorry." After a few silent moments, Andrew
whispered, "Have you forgiven me?"

"I think so. Jah, I forgive you."

"Do you really believe I've changed?"

She got the feeling he was holding his breath as
he awaited her answer. "You are no longer that
pesky, bratty little bu."

"What am I?"

She knew her face would be beyond crimson. It
might even be glowing in the dark like the last em-
bers of a bonfire, but she forged ahead. "You are a
caring, kind man." There. She said it. She might kick
herself all day tomorrow, but she voiced the feelings
that had been hiding under her gruff façade.

Andrew blew out a breath. He pulled her to him
in a hug. "You've made me very happy." He kissed
the top of her head which fit very nicely beneath his
chin.

Esther's arms acted on their own volition and
wrapped themselves around his waist. She pulled
back to try to see his face. "I'd better go back now."
To her surprise, she found she didn't really want to
leave the circle of his arms, but she pulled away anyway. On the way back to the house, the stars danced
in the black sky over their heads, and hope bloomed
in her heart.

"It looks like someone has had a change of
heart." Lydia winked at her schweschder as they
washed the breakfast dishes the next morning.

Esther pulled her attention back to the present.
Her mind had been revisiting the events of the previous evening. Had Andrew really shone his flashlight

into her window? Had he really held her hand as
they walked? Had he actually kissed her and said he
cared for her? No one knew she had longed for that,
dreamed of that when they were younger — before he
started teasing her, that is. Maybe the teasing really
had been his immature way of showing he cared.
Who could understand the mind of buwe?

"Hmm? What are you talking about?" She
passed a freshly washed plate to Lydia to dry.

"Someone — I'm not naming any names, but her
initials are E.S. — had a late-night visitor last night."

She gasped. How did Lydia know? They tried to
be as quiet as two people could possibly be. "How
would you know that?"

"I had trouble sleeping. I got up for a drink of
water, and I heard voices outside."

"You did, did you? And what did you hear?"

"Not any actual words, but I'm almost positive I
heard Andrew Fisher talking to you. It couldn't have
been, though. I mean you loathe the ground he walks
on, ain't so?"

"I never said that."

"So it was Andrew!" Lydia's face split into a
huge grin.

Esther hesitated. "I'm thinking that's my business." She twirled the wet dish rag and whacked
Lydia with it.

"Ach, Esther! You got me all wet!"

"Gut."

"You know I'm only kidding around. I think it
would be great if he was here to see you last night."

"Really?"

"Jah." Her schweschder paused, but Esther could tell
she wanted to say more. She gave Lydia a sideways
glance while scrubbing the next plate. "Here, give me

that plate." Lydia_tugged the plate from her hands. "You're going to scrub it in two."

Esther immediately dropped the dish rag into the soapy water, rinsed the plate, and thrust it toward her schweschder. Lydia chewed on her lower lip as she dried it and stacked it with the others.

"And you're going to chew a hole in your lip."

Lydia released it. She studied Esther for a moment before blurting, "Well, did you have a nice chat?"

"We did."

"And?"

"A very nice chat."

"There's nothing like dragging information out of someone!" Lydia sputtered.

"You know some matters are private."

"Courting is private. Are you two courting?"

"I never said that."

"That's just it! You haven't said anything!"

"I've never known you to be so nosy." Esther laughed.

"I can't help it. I want to see you happy."

"I haven't been unhappy."

"You know what I mean!"

She swirled suds around in the cast iron skillet but kept mum. She wished she could discuss everything—her feelings, Andrew's kiss, Sophie's request—but that just wasn't usually done. Besides, some things *were* private.

"Now do you believe Andrew has changed?"

"If I can change and discover I actually like quilting and baking, I suppose Andrew can change, too."

"It seems he's turned into a right nice man."

"Seems so."

"You aren't going to tell me more, are you?" Lydia elbowed her playfully.

"Probably not."

"Oooh, you! At least tell me if you like him."

"I do." Esther dropped her gaze to the soap suds in the sink lest her companion read all the emotions on her face and see the sudden tears collecting in her eyes.

"I'm glad." Lydia gave Esther a brief hug.

"You are?"

"Of course. It's about time you were courting."

"I didn't say we were courting." Were they? Is that what the kiss meant? Was that Andrew's intention? Hope burned in her heart. Flames spread to her cheeks. She pressed her wet hands to her face.

"It's all right. I won't say anything to anyone."

"You'd better not. I'm not even sure of anything myself."

"Ach, but I think you are." Lydia gave her arm another little squeeze.

Esther hung the dish rag up and escaped outside to putter around with her plants. She needed to think—as if she hadn't spent most of the past night doing exactly that.

Since Mamm hadn't planned any canning or extra chores for the afternoon, Esther set out for Sophie's place. She wanted to spend as much time as possible with the dear woman. Although she couldn't ever hope to be as wise as Sophie, maybe a little of the older woman's knowledge would rub off on her. She still didn't have a definite answer yet, but Sophie wouldn't push. That wasn't her way.

"Wie bist du heit?" Sophie called. She stopped pruning her lavender plants and watched Esther approach.

"Ser gut." Was it hurtful to say she was very *gut* when Sophie's health was failing? She hoped not.

"I can tell you are." Sophie smiled.

"How's that?"

"You're different. You have a spring in your step."

Esther grinned. "You must be imagining things, Sophie. I'm the same as always."

"Nee, I don't think so. I think something is cook-ing."

"Go on with you! Whatever makes you think such a thing?"

"I saw the same bounce in the step of a certain young man a bit ago." Sophie looked toward the barn.

She followed Sophie's gaze. Her cheeks burned when she spotted Andrew talking with Gid.

Sophie chuckled. "I can read the signs. I'm not so old I can't remember being young and in love."

"Sophie! I'm not... I'm not..."

Sophie laughed harder. "Kumm. Let's look at some of these plants. I want to tell you about this lav-ender."

She had a hard time concentrating on her men-tor's words. Her eyes kept straying to the barn where Gid and Andrew remained in deep discussion. Was Andrew having a difficult time focusing, too? Her attention snapped back to Sophie's instructions on caring for the lavender plants.

"You know, I think the lavender could turn into a gut business for you. It has so many uses, and many people are interested in the oils and such."

"Jah," she mumbled. *Pay attention, girl.*

"Maybe we can go over this later." Sophie fol-lowed her wandering gaze.

"I'm interested, Sophie. Honest."

"I believe you are, but I think your mind is occupied elsewhere." She winked. "Let's take some tea and lemonade out to the picnic table. The men will probably welcome a little snack. We can talk more afterward."

"Okay." She trotted behind her to the kitchen and poured lemonade while Sophie fetched cookies. She hoped she hadn't hurt her freind's feelings. Stupid heart and roving eyes! "Sophie, I'm sorry I was distracted. I really want to learn."

"I know you do, dear. You have nothing to be sorry about. We'll get to all that business talk. Let's visit first."

They carried refreshments outside to the big oak picnic table in the shady yard. As if on cue, the men headed in their direction.

"You'd think they smelled the snickerdoodles clear across the yard." Sophie set the plate of cookies on the table.

Esther laughed. "It sure looks that way." A sudden shyness crept over her as Andrew and Gid drew closer. She heated from the blush that stained her cheeks and, embarrassed by her reaction, quickly looked down at the table.

"Ah, just what we need." Gid dropped his straw hat onto a bench.

"Danki, Sophie." Andrew removed his hat, too. "Hello, Esther."

"Hello." She didn't dare give him more than a quick glance.

"Sit." Gid looked at Sophie and patted the bench beside him.

"I believe I will." With a sigh, she lowered herself onto the bench next to her husband.

Andrew walked around the table to stand beside Esther. "Are you going to sit down?"

"Sure." She set the pitcher on the table and sat on the bench across from Gid and Sophie.

Andrew wiggled to fit his long legs under the table and brushed against Esther as he did so. She jerked. Her heart fluttered, and her arm felt tingly.

"Sorry," he mumbled. "I didn't mean to bump you."

"It's okay."

Esther caught the amused glance Sophie gave Gid. She knew their conversation was an attempt to put her and Andrew at ease. Soon, they all talked and laughed until the cups and cookie plate were empty.

Sophie looked at Esther. "Are you ready for another lesson?"

"Sure. I'll gather up the cups."

When Andrew handed her his cup, his fingers brushed hers. Startled, she looked into his jade eyes. He winked and smiled a smile that melted away any fears and doubts she harbored. She smiled back at him.

It was late afternoon by the time Esther and Andrew started walking home. Her mind reviewed the information Sophie had imparted, trying to sort and store facts.

"It looks like some storm clouds in the distance." He pointed at the darkening sky.

"Maybe a storm will cool things off a bit. August has sure been a hot month."

"Fall is right around the corner."

"Did you give Gid your answer?"

"Not yet, but I've only got a couple more days."

"Me, too."

"What are you..." they began at the same time and laughed.

"I think I'm going to accept Gid's offer."

"I think I'll accept Sophie's, too." Her voice came out as faint as a whisper. He reached for her hand and squeezed it. He didn't let go as they walked along the deserted road. When the next farm came into view, she slid her hand from his. "I also think I'm going to have a talk with a certain doctor tomorrow since I'll be so close to his office when I go to the market."

Chapter Eighteen

Last night's storm washed away much of the heat and humidity that had enveloped Southern Maryland, leaving market day warm but not sweltering as previous days had been. Esther was happy to have Lydia accompany her to the big market. She thought her schweschder needed to get out of the house more and appreciated the help today.

Sales had been gut. Esther's reputation for quality flower and vegetable plants was well known. Customers generally flocked to her stand early in the day to select choice plants. They snapped up Mamm's jams and jellies in record time. Even Lydia's crocheted dish cloths and potholders sold well.

"I'm going to take a little break," Esther announced shortly after noon. "Will you be all right here for a bit?"

"Where are you going?"

"Just for a little walk."

"Esther, what are you up to?"

"Nothing bad. I'll be as quick as I can."

Lydia rolled her eyes. "You'd better be. I'm not packing this stuff up all by myself!"

"I'll be back way before then. I won't leave you alone that long. Most people are probably grabbing lunch now anyway."

"If you say so."

"Danki, Lydia. I'll hurry."

She wound her way through vendors selling fresh fruits and vegetables, household items, tools, jewelry, and squawking chickens. Once she reached the parking lot, she quickened her pace. She tried to plan the right words to say while she walked. She synchronized her puffs of breath with her rapid foot-steps and was all but running by the time she reached the two-story brick medical building. At least it was within walking distance of the market, so she didn't have to hire a driver or hitch up the buggy.

She forced herself to slow down so her breathing would return to a more normal rate. She yanked the heavy glass door open and needed to pause for a mi-nute to allow her eyes to transition from bright sun-light to subdued indoor lighting. As she climbed a flight of stairs and made her way to the end of the hall, her black sneakers made no sound on the blue and white tile floor. She pushed open the door to find an empty waiting room and no one at the reception-ist's desk. Could everyone be at lunch? She hadn't thought of that possibility before making the trek here.

Esther hesitated only a moment to consider her options. Queen Esther in the Bible could have been killed for approaching the king unbidden, but she had to take that risk to save her people. She had prayed and fasted and left everything in Gott's hands. Esther had prayed. She hadn't fasted unless she counted not eating since her quick bowl of cereal this morning as fasting. But like Queen Esther, maybe she had been born for such a purpose as this.

She took a deep breath, summoned her courage, and slowly turned the knob on the door leading to the examining rooms. The smell of alcohol and cleanser immediately assailed her nostrils. Had they cleaned the office and gone home? Not likely, since the doors were all unlocked. She let the door close softly behind her. *Dear Lord, let me do the right thing. Please let this place be empty if you don't want me to talk to the doctor. Please —*

A voice interrupted Esther's prayer. It was that rough, gravelly voice, the one she'd heard outside the grocery store. She sucked in a breath and held it.

"I've run into a little glitch." Dr. Kramer's voice came from the direction of his office. Esther heard no response, so she assumed the doctor was speaking to someone on the telephone. "Some of them aren't re-turning for follow-up appointments. Maybe it's a money thing."

There was another pause. Esther dared to exhale slowly and pulled in another gulp of air.

"Yeah, yeah," the doctor continued. "One group has been coming back. I guess I'll have to make house calls for the others. You know they don't have phones."

Esther sought to comprehend the man's words. Apparently, some Amish weren't returning to see Dr. Kramer. It was probably the people she had warned. It must be those in other districts that still relied on the doctor's so-called care. She'd need to find a way to alert them as well. Why was Dr. Kramer targeting the Amish?

"I told you before. I should have everything we need by the time the old man gets back, so relax." Another pause. "I'll get back to you later."

She heard the doctor slam the phone receiver. It was time to make her presence known. She stomped a little harder so she wouldn't appear to be sneaking around and cleared her throat. "Is anyone here?"

She reached the office with the big desk where Dr. Kramer sat before he had time to answer her. He appeared more disheveled than ever. Obviously, he'd been running his hands through his shaggy, brown hair since it stuck out from his head in several directions. He pushed the heavy, dark-framed glasses back up on his nose.

"Ms..."

"Stauffer. I'm David and Ella Kauffman's aenti."

"Yes. Of course. I remember."

"I'm sorry to barge in on you. There wasn't anyone out front."

"They're probably still at lunch. They must have forgotten to lock the door. I'll have to talk to them." He muttered the last statement as if talking to himself. "What can I do for you?"

Esther really wished he would clear his throat or take a sip of water. His raspy voice made her throat ache. "I needed to ask you some questions." She squared her shoulders. She had to be more assertive, even if she did feel like racing for the door.

"Is there a problem with your sister's children?"

"Not right now. But I want to know why you keep giving them foods you know they aren't supposed to eat." The man at least had the decency to look startled though not actually guilty.

"What are...what do...what on earth are you talking about?"

"All those cookies and loaves of bread. They weren't gluten free."

"Why would you think such a thing?"

"I don't think it. I know it."

"You don't have any idea what you're talking about."

"I'm Amish, Dr. Kramer, not stupid."

"I never said you were stupid."

"But you don't think I'm smart enough to figure out you are mistreating Dr. Nelson's Amish patients?"

"I think you are grossly misinformed. I tried to help you out by giving you some ready-made foods so you wouldn't have to bake everything yourself, and this is the thanks I get." He crossed his arms across his puffed-out chest and assumed a self-righteous demeanor.

"Foods that were like poison to David and Ella."

Dr. Kramer's chuckle sounded forced. His condescending attitude told Esther he considered her a mere child who couldn't possibly understand his sophisticated world.

"Forgive me, Doctor, but I don't see the humor in deliberately giving the kinner foods that made them sick."

"You have no proof…"

"But I do. I saw the food labels. Regular cookies and bread. The first ingredient was wheat."

"Oh, come on, Ms. Stauffer—"

"I know what I saw. I have the labels and the food." She saw the shocked expression that crossed the doctor's face briefly before he could mask it with an angry expression. "And I also know Amish patients were given oblong peach-colored pills to treat serious illnesses. Peach-colored prenatal vitamins!"

"That is totally ridiculous!" The doctor slammed his fist onto the desk. "You are making false allegations." His raspy voice grew louder.

Esther forced herself to remain calm. "Don't worry. We won't sue you or press charges. That's not our way. I just want to know why. Why are you out to hurt my people? What do you have against us?"

"I believe our conversation is over." Dr. Kramer waved a hand in front of his face as if he could prevent the crimson stain from creeping up from his neck.

"I only want to understand, Dr. Kramer," Esther persisted. "We came to you with needs and trusted you to help us. Why would you deliberately do something to harm us, or at the very least, not help us? If you don't like Amish people, why would you agree to fill in for Dr. Nelson?"

Her questions were met with a tense silence. Esther spun around and strode to the door. Obviously, this fellow had no explanations. She choked back tears of frustration as she made her way down the hall. She paused at the shrill sound of a phone ringing in the doctor's private office and heard him snatch the phone off the hook.

"What?" She heard him rasp into the phone. "I believe I've identified at least part of the problem here. I'll take care of it!"

She nearly jumped out of her shoes at the slam of the phone and the pounding on the desk. She scurried out of the office as fast as her feet would move. She stopped only long enough to close the outer office door silently, then dashed down the hall to the door with the red exit sign over it, galloped down the stairs, and raced outside. She sighed in relief when she emerged into the bright sunshine. What did Dr.

Kramer mean when he told the person he'd take care of it? Take care of what? She shivered despite the hot August day.

"Where in the world did you go?" Lydia demanded when Esther arrived out of breath at the market stand.

"An information-seeking adventure." She panted to catch her breath.

"Did you get it?"

"Get what?"

"The information. What else?"

"N-Not really."

"What does that mean?"

"Nothing. Were you busy?"

"Nee. You were right. Most people seem to be more interested in finding lunch right now. I did make a couple of sales, though."

"Gut." She sought a topic of conversation to take the focus off of her escapade. "It looks like you've made progress on your crocheting."

"It's progressing." Lydia held up the green and white blanket. "It's for Sarah's boppli."

"That's so nice of you. The blanket is very pretty."

"Danki. You aren't going to tell me, are you?"

"Tell you what?"

"Why is it always so hard to get information out of you?"

"There's nothing to tell, actually."

Lydia's exasperation came out in an exaggerated sigh. "Okay. Have it your way." She reached into her bag and pulled out a peanut butter sandwich. "Here." She thrust the plastic-wrapped sandwich into Esther's hands. "I'm sure you didn't eat while you were gallivanting about doing who knows what."

"Ick! It's warm!"

"What did you expect? Eat it anyway. You're probably starving."

"I'm not *that* hungry." She laid the sandwich down. "Do you have an apple in that bag?" She let Lydia pack their food that morning while she loaded the wagon, so she had no idea what she'd brought along. Hopefully, there was something besides a melted peanut butter sandwich.

"David and Ella like gooey peanut butter sandwiches." Her schweschder rummaged through her bag.

"I'll save this one for them."

"You're in luck!" Lydia pulled out a large, red apple.

"Do you want it?"

"Nee. I had a sandwich and a banana."

Esther took the apple from her. "This will tide me over until we get home."

"We'd better leave soon, then, or you'll starve."

She smiled. Lydia had been sad for so long. Her bantering was a pleasant change. She took a huge bite out of the apple. "Mmm. This will hit the spot."

"I'll remind you of that in an hour when your stomach is grumbling."

Saturday began as one of those cloudless, brilliant blue-sky days. The few white, wispy swirls on the blue backdrop could hardly be called clouds. A brief thunderstorm the previous evening had washed away most of the humidity. For August, the day was perfect, in Esther's opinion. She actually enjoyed working outside, and her dress wasn't soaked with sweat by noon as it had been on other days lately.

She helped Mamm and Lydia prepare some food for the after-church meal the next day and then slipped off on a leisurely stroll to visit Sophie. The dear woman's health seemed to be declining more each time she saw her. Although Esther had gleaned a wealth of information from the wise woman, she had much more to learn. She needed to give her answer today. Sophie deserved peace of mind over this matter.

Please, Gott, direct my thoughts and let my decision be Your will, she prayed as she ambled along the fields leading to Sophie's house. My house? She tried the thought out to see how it fit. She smiled. A sudden peace settled over her, wrapping around her like a warm hug. She took a deep breath, relishing the feeling and enjoying the sweet scent of late-blooming honeysuckle.

"Yoo-hoo, Sophie!" She stood outside the screen door.

"Kumm in. I just washed the floors, but they should be mostly dry by now."

She tiptoed across the linoleum floor of the kitchen. Clattering from the mud room meant Sophie must be rinsing her bucket. If Esther had been a little earlier, she could have performed the task for the older woman. She had the distinct feeling, though, that Sophie wanted to handle things for herself, in her own way, for as long as possible.

"Here I am," her freind sang out as she entered the kitchen.

Was it Esther's imagination or did the older woman look a bit thinner? Bright blue veins glowed like neon lights– beneath the surface of the parchment-like skin of Sophie's arms. Esther crossed the room in a couple of strides and hugged her. "How are you feeling today?"

"I'm hanging in there. I'm glad to see you."

"Sophie, you know all you have to do is holler and I'll be here to help you, don't you?"

"I know. You're such a gut girl."

Esther gave a little laugh. "I'm sure there are folks who would disagree with that assessment."

"I can't think of even one."

"That's because you don't have an unkind thought in your head. Do you have some other chores that need to be done?"

"Not right now. Let's visit a bit."

Sophie seemed a little out of breath. When did talking become difficult? Maybe she was still a bit winded from her scrubbing. "Would you like to sit in your shop or outside or here in the kitchen?"

"I have some notes and books in the shop to show you."

"Okay. Why don't I bring some water or lemonade while you get the books?"

"That would be fine."

Sudden tears sprang to Esther's eyes as she watched her mentor shuffle toward her beloved shop. She blinked and gulped to swallow the lump clogging her throat. It wouldn't do for her freind to see her upset.

She plunked ice cubes into two glasses before filling them with lemonade. She snatched a few oatmeal raisin cookies from the cookie jar and wrapped them in a napkin. Sophie looked as though she needed to eat a dozen or so cookies. Esther's heart ached at the thought of her deteriorating health. She straightened her shoulders and pasted a smile on her face. She had to be brave.

She thought she made plenty of noise to warn Sophie of her approach, but the older woman must have been lost in thought as she sat on a stool behind the counter. Such a tired, sad expression resided on her face. She jumped when she did hear Esther and smiled quickly.

"Here we are." She forced a cheeriness she didn't feel into her voice. "I brought you a few cookies, too." She set a glass and the napkin filled with cookies in front of Sophie.

"Danki." Sophie patted the other stool next to her. "Sit a while."

Esther set her own glass down and wiggled onto the stool. Thank goodness it was padded and she didn't have to sit on the hard wood. She must be losing weight, too. Her backside had been protesting when she sat on hard surfaces lately. Perhaps she should snatch one or two of those cookies. "Did you bake the cookies?"

"Nee. Hannah and the little girls brought these by yesterday. She said the girls helped bake them. Rebecca sent along a loaf of bread, too. I think people are getting the idea that I've been ailing."

"I haven't told anyone," Esther quickly assured her. "I'm pretty sure Andrew hasn't either."

"I believe you. I'm sure folks can guess something is wrong simply by looking at me. I'll have to tell everyone soon. I don't want pity, though."

Esther squeezed Sophie's hand. "Not pity, Sophie. Love. We all love you and want to help."

She saw tears flood her companion's eyes as she whispered, "I know."

Esther took a gulp of lemonade. "Now, where are the notes you wanted to show me. I'm trying to be a gut scholar."

"You're the best." Sophie's smile returned. "I have no doubt you'll be a fine source of knowledge for the community."

The two women pored over the notes and books. Esther asked questions to clarify information she didn't quite understand. Sophie seemed pleased with her progress. She stacked her papers and returned them to file folders before closing her herb book. "That's enough for now."

Esther reached for her glass and drained it dry. "Eat your cookies."

"I've had one."

"You nibbled at one."

"Same thing."

"Not quite. Try a few more bites." She knew she sounded like a parent trying to coax a picky child to eat. But Sophie did pick up a cookie and took a healthy bite.

"Here." She slid the napkin toward Esther. "You look like you could use some cookies yourself."

Esther picked one up but didn't bite into it. "Sophie, I've made my decision." She laid her snack back on the napkin and looked in the eye.

"Jah?"

"I've decided to accept your very generous offer." She swiped at a tear that threatened to trickle down her cheek.

"That's wunderbaar!" Sophie cried, leaping from the stool with surprising agility. She wrapped her arms around Esther and nearly pulled her off the stool. "That makes me so happy — and relieved."

"Hey, is this a private party or can we fellows join in?"

The women looked toward the door. They hadn't heard Gid's approaching footsteps. He entered the shop, pulling Andrew in behind him.

"Soph, Andrew—"

"Gid, Esther—"

They all burst into laughter. Sophie recovered first. "Esther agreed to take the shop."

"And Andrew wants to farm the land."

"What about Bishop Sol? Will he approve?" Esther frowned. "He may not be happy about a single woman living here and...well, the whole situation."

"Gid and I will talk to him tomorrow."

"I don't know what Mamm and Daed will say either."

"You are a baptized adult and can make your own decisions, but I know you want their blessing." Sophie patted her arm.

"Jah."

"Daniel and Leah are reasonable people. I don't think this will be a problem for them." Gid spoke with confidence.

"We'll make sure they know I'm still living at the Fishers' house. I'm only farming here when I'm not at Beilers' Furniture."

Esther's face grew warm. She nodded again.

"Let's celebrate. I have a peach pie Gid picked up at the market." Sophie clapped her hands and smiled broadly. "I've been waiting for a reason to slice it up."

They talked and laughed until the peach pie had been completely demolished. "I'd better get home and help Mamm with supper—not that I'll have room for much myself." Esther patted her stomach.

"You only had a tiny sliver of pie. I think you need to bulk up a bit," Sophie said. "You're feeling all right, aren't you, dear?"

"I'm fine. I've just been working hard." *And worrying about you and how to help our people.*

"I'd better get home, too, and get cleaned up." Andrew stood up to leave. "Tomorrow is church day."

"Church is at the Zooks', ain't so? I didn't get around to making anything for the meal." A frown wrinkled Sophie's brow.

"That's okay." Esther knew Sophie always helped with church day meals. "I'm sure there will be plenty of food. We prepared some dishes, and I'm sure Barbara's been cooking."

"Gid picked up two pies. You didn't eat the other one, did you?" She wagged a finger at her husband. He shook his head. "We can take that along for dessert."

Esther started to protest but realized her freind needed to contribute. "That would be fine, I'm sure."

"If you're ready, I'll walk home with you." Andrew turned toward Esther and smiled.

She hugged Sophie and thanked her before joining him.

"We are grateful to both of you," Sophie said. "You've relieved us of a huge burden, ain't so, Gid?"

"For sure." The men shook hands as the women hugged again.

"We'll talk to Bishop Sol either tomorrow afternoon or Monday and let you know his response."

"That's fine. Get some rest now, Sophie. We'll see you at church tomorrow." Esther felt tears threatening and knew she'd better hurry and leave.

They strolled toward home, enjoying the less humid day and each other's company. Esther didn't protest or try to pull away when Andrew reached for her hand and interlocked his fingers with hers. A sudden warmth at his touch travelled from her fingertips, up her arm, and into her heart. A gentle squeeze assured her he felt that same tingling. She glanced into his jade eyes and smiled. Her shyness around him was gradually being replaced by a comfortable, contented feeling.

"Do you think Bishop Sol will agree to the plan?" She couldn't imagine how the bishop would respond to the Hostetlers' plan.

"It's hard to say. You probably know him better than I do. He seems a stern man but a fair one."

"That about sums him up. But he did approve of Hannah teaching our scholars even though he knew she wasn't Amish. He defended her and protected her."

"Maybe we stand a chance then." They ambled along in silence for a few more paces. "What about your mamm and daed? What do you think they will say?"

"That's a very gut question, but I *am* an adult."

"True, but you are still under your daed's care. I'm almost more afraid of his reaction than of Bishop Sol's."

"Daed trusts me. He knows I wouldn't do anything against the Ordnung."

"But he doesn't know me so well."

"I think he knows you fairly well. He certainly tried to play matchmaker, which isn't like him at all, so he must trust you."

"Matchmaker, huh? For you and me?"

"Jah."

"That makes me feel a little better. All the same, you're his dochder, and he would want to protect you."

"I'm not a little girl anymore."

"You definitely aren't. You are a beautiful woman." A cherry stain flooded Andrew's neck and face and even reached both ears mostly hidden by his hair.

Esther nearly stumbled. She felt the heat rise in her own cheeks, too. "Danki."

He cleared his throat. "Let's hope and pray the bishop and your folks will accept Gid's and Sophie's plan."

"I'd really like to put their minds at ease." She swallowed a sob that tried to rise. "Have you noticed Sophie seems to be failing?"

"She definitely looks thinner."

"She never complains, though. She's so b-brave." She felt her lip tremble. He squeezed her hand. "It's going to be so hard when she—" Her voice broke.

He stopped walking and pulled her into his arms. "I'll be here with you, I promise. I'll help you however I can."

She nestled into his arms, amazed she could finally accept the fact that Andrew the man was quite different from Andrew the bu. After wrestling with her fears and misgivings, she trusted him now and drew comfort and strength from him. His tenderness stroked her aching heart. She nodded into his chest before pulling out of his embrace. He looked down at her with such caring and concern in his eyes that tears of joy mixed with her tears of sadness. He raised one hand to brush the tears away gently.

By some silent agreement, they resumed their walk toward the Stauffer house. When the house and barn came into view, they unclasped hands and continued on side by side.

At the end of the Stauffers' gravel driveway, they stopped. Andrew looked down at her. "You know, there is a way we can be sure we'll both get to carry out the Hostetlers' wishes."

"How?"

"If we got married, that would clinch the arrangement so no one would object."

Esther felt a spark of anger burst into flame. She stomped her bare foot, ignoring the pain. "Andrew Fisher, marriage is not an arrangement. All this time you've acted like you cared about me when all you wanted was to seal an arrangement? Like buying a new horse to make the plowing easier?" Before he could utter a word, she continued. "And here I let my guard down. I believed you had changed. I-I thought I m-meant something to you, but—" Her voice broke on a sob. She took off at a full run toward the house, not paying any attention to the rocks that tore into the soles of her bare feet. *How could I have been so foolish again? Why didn't I trust my original feelings? I believed him. I thought he had changed. When will I ever learn?*

"Wait! Esther!" Andrew called. "I didn't mean..." She had gotten too far away to hear him. He slapped his straw hat against his leg in frustration. "I didn't mean it that way," he said, even though there was no one around to hear him. "I said it all wrong. Women!" He stomped off toward the Fisher place, wondering how or if he could straighten out this mess he'd made of things.

Chapter Nineteen

Esther stumbled into the mudroom adjoining the kitchen, panting for breath. The sound of voices from the kitchen made her pause to gain control. Who was Mamm talking to? It wasn't Lydia's voice she heard. A few slow breaths calmed her enough to enter the kitchen.

"I think everything will work out," Mamm was saying to Naomi Beiler.

"I hope so. I like Hannah. I really do. I just don't know if she's right for Jacob. She only recently became Amish. Who knows if she'll stay? Then what will happen to Jake?"

Esther couldn't help it. She had to intervene and defend her freind. "I'm sorry, Mamm. I wasn't trying to eavesdrop. I heard your conversation when I came in. Naomi, you can trust Hannah. She's honest and gut. She and Jake will make each other happy."

"Jah, but—"

"I know she just joined us, but she *chose* to join us. She wasn't born Amish and merely decided to stay. She actually chose our faith, our lifestyle, out of her own free will. She may have to learn more of our ways, but she's Amish in here." Esther patted her chest, right over her heart.

"You make gut points, Esther." Naomi's frown fled.

"I think the Lord Gott brought Hannah to us," Esther continued. "I believe Jake feels that way, too."

"I do believe you are right." Naomi sighed. "I'm a worrying mamm, that's all. I will try to remember to trust Gott. And I will wilkom Hannah into our family if she chooses to join us."

"I think she'd make an excellent fraa for Jacob, if that's their plan." Esther felt pretty sure that was the couple's intent, but marriage plans were kept secret until the couple was published in church.

"I feel better. Danki, Esther. I'd better get along home now and put supper on the table for my always-hungry men. I'll see you both at church."

As soon as the door closed behind Naomi, Mamm turned to Esther. "Now, dochder, do you want to tell me why you look so down in the mouth?"

"N-Nothing to tell, Mamm. I only wanted Naomi to think well of Hannah."

"Your eyes tell me different. They are a little puffy and a lot sad."

"I have something on my mind that I need to work out."

"Okay. I can tell you don't want to talk about it. Remember, I'm here when you're ready to share." Mamm gave her a brief hug that was almost her undoing. "We'd better get ready to feed our own brood so we can all get cleaned up for church tomorrow."

Despite splashing her face with cold water, Esther's eyes still felt gritty and her face still felt puffy after a night of sobbing into her pillow. She wiggled on the hard, wooden bench and forced her eyes to stay open and focused on the ministers. Not for a moment did she let them stray to the men's side of the Zooks' barn during the three-hour church service. Well, maybe for a fraction of a minute, her gaze wandered. She had snapped her eyes back to Bishop Sol when they connected briefly with Andrew's sad, green eyes. He started to mouth something to her, but she turned away, feigning disinterest. Her heart warred with her head, begging her to turn back to determine his message. She pressed her lips together, crossed her arms over her chest, and refused to give in to her heart.

When the service finally concluded, Esther hightailed it to Barbara Zook's kitchen where she stayed until her family decided to go home. She didn't even go outside to sit at a shady table for the noon meal. Instead, she stayed in the sweltering kitchen and nibbled at a carrot stick. She didn't feel like eating anyway.

"A baby rabbit would eat more of that carrot." Hannah held out her hand. "Let's go out and get some real food."

Esther shook her head. "I'm not hungry."

"Kumm outside with me anyway. I'm not going to eat much either."

"Nee, you go ahead."

"Please, Esther. Kumm out and talk to me."

"I'm not gut company right now."

"Did something happen with Andrew?" Hannah moved closer so she could whisper her question.

"You might say that."

"Let's go for a walk. We don't have to eat."

"Not if he—"

"Andrew left. He didn't eat either. He looked like a lost little bu."

"Huh!"

"Kumm, Esther. Get some air."

Esther allowed her freind to lead her outside to walk along the shade of the trees at the edge of the Zooks' property. She broke her vow of silence and shared Andrew's remarks with Hannah.

"Did you let him explain? I can't believe he meant what you think."

"He didn't have to explain. I got it. I'm not stupid."

"Of course not. But you might be, uh, mistaken."

"I think I was mistaken to trust him and to give him my heart—" She broke off and tried hard to choke back a sob.

Hannah clutched her arm. "I'm so sorry, Esther. I hate to see you hurting. Maybe if you talk to Andrew, this can all be resolved."

She shook her head so hard her kapp bounced and the strings flew around her face.

"Well, promise me you'll think about it."

Esther remained silent.

"Esther?" Hannah squeezed Esther's arm a little harder.

"All right. I'll think about it. Tomorrow. On my way to the Charles County district."

"Why are you going there?"

"I have a little business I need to take care of."

"Will you still be able to help with the school clean up?"

"Sure. I'll probably be a little late."

Monday dawned as one of those late August days that should put anyone in a positive mood. White, billowing clouds hung suspended in a cerulean sky. Robins, wrens, and jays performed an impromptu bird concert. A whisper of a breeze stirred the oak and maple leaves. A few honeysuckle bushes near the potting shed still sported white, sweet-smelling blossoms.

Mamm and Lydia chattered as they packed the wagon with cleaning supplies. David and Ella ran around getting in the way in their anticipation of playing with the other kinner at the school while their mamms cleaned.

"If everyone shows, we should be able to spruce up the school right quick." Mamm put her last bundle in the wagon.

"It's hard to believe school will be starting up again in a few weeks and that my David will be attending this year."

"They grow up in a blink of an eye." Mamm sighed. "It doesn't seem that long ago that you and Esther were scholars heading off to school with your books and lu+nch boxes."

Esther remained silent, her mood as gray as a rainy day. She planned to take the buggy alone to complete her mission. She should have gone to the Charles County community last week after her talk with Dr. Kramer, but she'd needed a little time to mull things over in her mind. She hoped she wasn't too late to warn them.

"Esther, you are planning to help at the school, ain't so?" Mamm asked.

"Jah. I need to take care of an errand first."

"Why are you so glum?" Lydia searched Esther's face.

She shrugged but didn't reply.

"Maybe the work at the school and the company will lift your spirits." Lydia patted her schweschder's arm.

"Maybe. I'll be at the school soon."

She waved the others off and tried to mentally prepare herself for her mission. She rolled her head from side to side to try to ease the tension from her tight muscles. A nagging headache pounded behind her eyes. Lack of sleep had left her tense and achy. She took a deep breath and let it out slowly. Time to get moving.

She gave a final glance to the rows of chrysan-themums that would soon be ready for potting and advertised for sale. They were her biggest seller for late summer and early fall. She loved their big deep-red, white, gold, and rust blooms. To Esther, mums meant fall. She'd better hurry to the buggy Daed had hitched for her before leaving on his own errand so she could do what she needed to do and get to the school.

The sound of tires crunching on the gravel and a car's purring engine grabbed Esther's attention. She shaded her eyes and squinted. She wasn't expecting anyone, but she supposed it could be a customer this early. She didn't recognize the fancy-looking, silver car as belonging to one of her regular Englisch cus-tomers. The car jerked to a stop. The driver threw it into reverse and zoomed backwards out of the driveway, slinging rocks as it backed toward the paved road. A man leaned out the window and waved in her direction. Esther shrugged her shoul-ders. He must have made a wrong turn and needed to turn around. Maybe he was looking for the nearby race track. All kinds of vehicles zoomed up and down the road on race days.

Something gleaming in the sunlight near the chrysanthemums caught Esther's eye. "Ach! My tools. I always put my tools away. Where is my head today?" At least the unexpected vehicle caused her to notice her tools. She trudged toward the hoe and rake lying in the dewy grass. Her legs felt as heavy as concrete pillars. She knew exactly where her head was—back on that walk home from Sophie's house. "I'm not going to rehash that yet again. I'm not!" she whispered to the mums. She bent to retrieve her tools.

Intense pain exploded through the back of Esther's head. She had no time to turn around to find what had caused it. She couldn't stop herself from falling forward, but she could hear a voice behind her.

"Too bad you can't help them," the voice sneered. "You won't win. I won't let you best me."

Esther's knees hit the damp grass. She wanted to throw her hands out to break her fall but could only manage to turn slightly so that her right side took the brunt of the impact. A sharp sting pierced her upper left arm. Before darkness overtook her, she heard his muttering as if from far away. "She's heavier than I thought. I'll have to move the car closer."

"Where is Esther?" Hannah asked after the women had been scrubbing and scouring the schoolhouse from top to bottom. "I know she had an errand to take care of, but it's nearly lunch time."

"You know that girl. She probably got distracted by something and lost all track of time." Leah gave a little laugh but worry shone in her eyes.

"I'm sure she's all right, Mamm." Lydia patted her mudder's shoulder. "Would you like me to go look for her?"

"Nee. We don't even know what or where this so-called important errand was."

"Let's give her a little more time," Hannah said. "I'm sure the kinner are hungry after all their running around and playing. Maybe we should set out the food."

"That sounds like a gut idea. I don't know about the little ones, but I, for one, am starving." Naomi Beiler patted her stomach.

The other women laughed and nodded in agreement. Their hard work produced a hearty appetite.

They had spent the morning scrubbing walls and floors, washing desks, dusting shelves, and unpacking materials. They'd made steady progress but were in need of nourishment and rest.

As they cleaned up after everyone finished eating, the women heard a cart rattling along the school driveway. The big, brown horse snorted as the cart kicked up a cloud of dust.

"It looks like Jacob." Naomi shielded her eyes and squinted in the direction of the approaching cart.

Hannah turned quickly to look at the approaching horse and cart. "Jah, it is Jacob." She reached to smooth her hair and straighten her kapp.

"You look fine," Lydia teased.

Hannah's cheeks warmed and no doubt took on a bright red glow. "Who's with him?"

"It looks like Andrew." Sarah pushed her glasses back into place. She had been sitting with her feet propped to reduce the swelling in her ankles. She dropped her feet to the ground and prepared to stand.

"You sit," Hannah instructed the former teacher in her own best teacher voice.

"I'm getting tired of sitting."

"It's the best thing for you and the boppli, ain't so?"

"You don't have much longer now, Sarah," Lydia said. "You'd better rest now while you can."

"This can't be over with soon enough! I'm ready, but I think I'm actually a bit nervous, too."

Lydia smiled. "That's completely normal. You'll do fine."

Hannah practically skipped over to the cart when Jacob stopped the horse near the school. "My tables! You finished my tables!"

"Right in time for school, too." Jacob grinned at Hannah's excitement. "Just show us where you want them."

Hannah had requested two work tables where scholars could work on projects or where she could stack extra supplies. Jacob had made two tables with shelves that could serve both purposes. She was delighted with the finished products.

"They look nice." Lydia watched as the two men prepared to unload the first table. "They should be very useful, too."

Andrew paused to scan the group of women. He looked back and forth at each green, blue, or purple dress.

"She's not here." Lydia dropped her voice to a whisper. "I can't tell Mamm, but I'm worried."

"I'll be right back. Let me help Jake get these tables inside."

She waited near the horse and wagon while the other women returned to the school to ooh and aah over the new tables and to get back to their cleaning.

Little ones had been put down for naps on blankets while older kinner played or helped.

Andrew bounded down the steps and jogged over to Lydia. He pulled a handkerchief from his pocket and mopped his brow. "Where is Esther?"

"I'm not sure. She said she had an errand to run and then would be right here. Andrew, she should have been here long ago."

"I'll see if Jake will let me take the wagon and go look for her."

"You can take our wagon so Jake can get back to work, but I'm coming with you."

"Okay. I'll hitch up."

She pointed out the right wagon. "You know the horse. I'll run tell Mamm to keep an eye on David and Ella for me."

He had the wagon ready to roll by the time Lydia flew out of the building. She climbed into the wagon, panting. "Let's go. But I'm not sure where to look."

"I have an idea, but let's check your house first in case she returned there for some reason."

They lapsed into silence as he urged the horse to trot faster. "There's your buggy. It looks like she did return home." He nodded toward the buggy as they drove up the driveway.

"Nee. It's in the exact same spot. I don't think it has been moved since Daed hitched it for Esther this morning." The horse whinnied and pawed at the ground at their approach.

Andrew leaped from the wagon before "whoa!" had barely left his lips. "Wouldn't your daed have noticed anything amiss when he came in for lunch?"

"Daed had business elsewhere this morning. He left with Luke Troyer when we left for the school. Mamm packed them a lunch and water because they planned to be gone most of the day."

"Then Esther must be here somewhere." He looked around the greenhouse, then shaded his eyes and turned in every direction to survey the yard and fields.

Lydia jumped down and quickly joined in the search. "Esther!"

"Look! There's a hoe and a rake in the grass." He pointed to the rows of chrysanthemums. "Maybe she got started working and lost track of time."

"Nee. She did that earlier this morning before it got too hot. That's when she usually does her weeding or else she does it in the evening. Andrew, Esther *never* leaves her tools out. Never!" Lydia ran her hands up and down her arms. "Something must be terribly wrong."

Chapter Twenty

Esther recognized scents before anything else as consciousness began to return. The overpowering smell of damp earth, basil, oregano, and rosemary filled her nostrils until she thought she would suffocate. A pebble that felt more like a boulder tore into the soft flesh between her spine and right shoulder blade. Her entire right side throbbed.

From somewhere, a soft moan rose in crescendo, filling the air with sound. She rocked her head to and fro in time to the moan. Gradually, the fuzz cleared from her brain, and the realization dawned that the moan came from her own lips.

Becoming more alert, she struggled to move and then to keep from moaning with the pain each slight movement brought. Her head pounded, threatening to explode. A burning pain seared her wrists. She tried to rotate them but couldn't. Something rough surrounded them. Rope. A rope bound her hands together across her abdomen. Her legs moved a bit more freely. They must not be tied as tightly. Where was she, and how had she gotten there?

She fought to suppress the rising panic. She tried to slow her breathing in an effort to calm her nerves. A Bible verse floated just out of reach until she could finally reel it in. It was one of her favorite verses from Second Timothy. "God has not given us a spirit of fear; but of power and of love, and of sound mind." She said the words over and over in her brain until hope and strength filled her. *Gott has given me power, love, and strength. He has given me a gut mind. Use these! Focus!*

Bits and pieces of memory seeped in around the throbbing in her head. She had been on her way to Charles County. She was going to warn the community about Dr. Kramer. Some of them had appointments with him this week, if she had been right about the initials she'd seen on the paper in his office. She couldn't die there in that dark place. She had to help her people.

Her brain rewound and replayed a sneering voice. *Too bad you can't help them. You won't win.* Esther tried to sit but couldn't. She wiggled her hands, hoping to loosen the rope. That voice. Even though it had been disguised, certainty shot through her battered being. She knew who that gravelly voice belonged to. She could not let *him* win.

She fought against the rope, gasping in pain at each movement. *Think, Esther!* She tried to take a deep breath and focus on her dark surroundings. The smells. A mixture of herbs. Dirt. She must be in her potting shed!

Esther blinked several times, hoping her eyes would adjust to the darkness. She had to get her bearings. The shed wasn't that large. If she could figure out her position, she could try to roll or scoot toward the door, even though the movement would be painful. Was she at the back or along one side? Maybe she could wiggle her legs loose since they weren't tied as tightly. He must have been in a hurry.

How did he know she would be alone when he arrived? Was it a lucky guess? Where did he kumm from? Had he been lurking about on the property, waiting for the opportunity to strike. Why did he choose today? Esther had confronted him on Wednesday. Had he been watching her since then?

All the questions and speculations made her head pound harder. She had to find a way out of this hot, dark shed. She had no idea how long she had been suffocating in there. The workers at the mill would never hear her if she hollered, and there was no one at the house. It was up to her. *Give me strength, Lord. Give me power and wisdom.*

Esther jerked her feet hard to stretch against the rope. She grunted at the pain that shot up the side of her body and culminated in her head. She must have fallen awfully hard on her right side. She would endure the pain if the knot loosened a little more. Was it loose enough that she could pull her feet up and get free of the rope? She'd have to make the effort.

She rested for a minute to gather her courage and strength. She would have to convince her body to move again. At least the blow to her head and wherever else she'd been struck did not paralyze her. Slowly, painfully, she bent her knees and scooted her feet up toward her head. The rope slackened a bit more. She wiggled her feet. She could almost shake one foot out of the rope's loop but not quite. Frustrated, she let her legs flop back down. She panted to catch her breath. This was taking longer than she had hoped. What if her attacker came back? That thought spurred her on. She'd have to bite her lip and work harder to escape.

Enough rest. Esther flung her legs out as far as she could in one direction. They met no resistance, touched no objects. She pulled them back to center and flung them in the other direction. Her feet banged against a wall. Now she had to figure out which wall.

Rest. Just that simple effort of moving her legs seemed so great. It completely stole her energy. She felt woozy. Her legs must weigh fifty pounds each. Maybe she'd close her eyes and give in to the fatigue. Her eyelids were almost as heavy as her legs and slammed down over her eyes.

No! No! No! You can't sleep! The shrieking voice somewhere in the recesses of Esther's brain forced her to open her eyes. *Think, Esther! Use that sound mind the Lord Gott gave you!* Scents. Drying herbs. If she could determine which direction the smell came from, she might be able to orient herself. She twisted her head one way and then the other, ignoring the hammer pounding against her skull and threatening to send her back into oblivion. She swallowed the bile rising in her throat and prayed the nausea brought on by the intense pain would subside.

Left. The herb scent was stronger on her left side. She thanked Gott for her keen sense of smell. Often, she thought of it as a curse. Today, it proved to be a blessing. She had hung the herbs on the right side of the potting shed, right inside the door. Her feet had stuck the wall when she swung her legs to the right. That must mean her head was toward the back of the shed. If she could slither closer to the wall, she could inch along toward the door. Then, if she still had some strength, she could kick the door open and at least get fresh air. Maybe someone would hear her if she could eventually yell.

This would all be so much easier if she could manage to stand and hop toward the door. She was fairly certain, though, that standing would intensify the pain in her head, and hopping would jar her battered body. Why did she hurt so much? She remembered falling on her right side, but the rest of her body felt scraped and bruised. He must have dragged her into the shed. Did he kick her, too? Her ribs said so.

Time to move again. Esther was much too determined, too stubborn, to give up. She *would* get out of this shed, even though the heat combined with every little effort she put forth left her thirsty, queasy, and drenched in sweat.

Lydia raced through the house, calling Esther's name every five seconds. She checked every bedroom upstairs as well as the cellar and laundry room. No sign of her schweschder. Andrew searched every nook and cranny of the barns and outbuildings and even climbed the ladder to the hay loft. No Esther. They reunited near the chrysanthemum bed.

"Do you think she could have gone to the mill to talk to Mose about something?" Lydia was unable to keep the panic out of her voice.

"I suppose it's possible, but why would she leave the poor horse hitched for so long? I was going to unhitch him but thought I'd wait in case we need the buggy for something. If you want to check with Mose, I'll put Esther's tools away and search the woods. Maybe she went for a walk and fell or hurt herself. If we don't find her, I'll unhitch the horse, and we can be on our way."

"Okay." Lydia sped off toward the mill.

Andrew trotted over to retrieve the tools. "Esther!" he called. His heart pounded in fear. What could have happened to her? *Dear Gott, please take care of her and show me where she is.*

Esther managed to get to the door of the shed by bending her knees and propelling herself forward with her feet. The rough wood floor scraped her back through the thin cotton fabric of her dress, but she kept pushing and scooting. Tears of pain trickled down both cheeks, but she couldn't wipe them away. Progress was slow, and she nearly gave up before finally reaching the door. She paused for a shaky gulp of stale air and rested for a minute until the pounding in her head subsided and her heartbeat slowed. When the roaring in her ears quieted, she strained to listen. She must be hallucinating. Had someone called her name? She kept perfectly still. There it was again.

Esther raised both feet and pushed as hard as she could against the door. It refused to budge. Her attacker must have turned the lock on the outside. Tears of frustration and pain increased. "Help me!" The words she tried to shout came out in a pitiful whimper.

She heard the scratchy sound of the latch turning. Had her attacker returned? She was completely at his mercy. There was no place to hide, even if she could scramble out of the way. She couldn't even force a scream to climb out of her parched throat. She squinted and tried to focus when daylight suddenly burst into her dark prison.

Andrew stooped to retrieve the hoe and shovel and crossed the field in long strides. He knew Esther had been upset with him, but she would never simply disappear and worry her family. She was a thoughtful, responsible person. And she kept her word. If she said she would help at the school, then she would have been there. Even if her errand had been visiting the Charles County district as he suspected, she should have made it to the school well before lunch time.

Before reaching the shed, he heard a thumping noise. It sounded like it came from inside the building. "What in the world?" He stopped to listen for another sound. All was quiet. Had some animal gotten trapped there? A trapped creature might be pretty surly, especially a possum. At least he could use the tools in his hand to fend it off, whatever it was.

He approached the shed door cautiously and turned the latch. He grabbed the door handle and flung the door wide as he leaped back to let out whatever lurked inside.

"Ach, Esther!" He rushed to the whimpering young woman just inside the shed. "What happened? Are you all right?" He dropped to his knees and brushed the silky, dark hair off her dirty and tear-streaked face. "I've been so worried. Where do you hurt, lieb?" His fingers fumbled at the tight knot securing the rope at Esther's wrists. "Who did this to you?"

He wanted to gather her in his arms to comfort her and to soothe her pain. First, he had to get the ropes off her wrists and ankles so he could determine the extent of her injuries. His desire to free her quickly and his anxiety over her condition made his fingers clumsy with the small, tight knots.

At last, the rope fell away from her wrists. He ran his fingers gently over the rope burns. The blood from the torn skin had already dried. "If I help you, do you think you can sit up?"

"I-I'll try."

He slid his hands beneath her shoulders and lifted her upper body.

"Oooh! My head."

He probed the back of her head and let out a low whistle when his fingers encountered a huge knot. "No wonder your head hurts."

"Dizzy," she mumbled.

"Do you want to lie back down?"

"Nee."

"Are you okay sitting here for a minute so I can free your legs?"

"Jah."

"I'll be as quick as I can."

She swayed when he let go of her. He steadied her and tried to help her lie back down.

"I-I want to s-sit." She gasped for breath, then hunched over as if in great pain.

"What else hurts besides your head?"

"Ribs, back, wrists…"

"I'll get the rope off your legs then holler for Lydia to call 9-1-1. Your daed wouldn't have taken his work cell phone with him, would he?"

"Nee. I-It's strictly f-for the mill. Lydia's here?"

"Jah. Jake and I were delivering tables to the school. Lydia told me you hadn't shown up. We were going to drive to Charles County to look for you but decided to check here first. It's a gut thing we did."

He gradually pulled his hands away from Esther's shoulders and gave her a moment to stabilize herself. "I don't think this knot is as tight. Let me get you free." He moved his hands to the rope around her ankles and picked the knot loose.

"Andrew! Andrew! Where are you?" Lydia yelled.

"Potting shed!"

"Andrew, Mose hasn't seen—Esther!" She rushed into the shed as he pulled the rope off Esther's legs and slung it aside. "Esther! Are you all right? What happened?"

"She's not all right. Can you run to the mill and call for an ambulance?"

Lydia stooped down to touch Esther's shoulder. "I'll get help, Es. I'll be right back."

"I-I don't want an ambulance." She could do little more than croak.

"You have a big knot on your head and I don't know what else. You might have a concussion or broken ribs. Let them check you over at the hospital."

"I-I'll be f-fine."

"That's my stubborn Esther! Let's let the professionals tell us you're fine." Andrew crawled over beside her. He gently pulled her close and pressed her head against his chest. "I was so worried, Essie, and so scared when I first saw you lying there. I thought I'd lost you. Even though you don't want anything to do with me, I still…uh, care very much for you."

She sniffed but made no reply.

"I said everything all wrong before on the way home from Sophie's house. I didn't mean I thought marriage was a business deal. Marriage is a union between two people who love each other." He tipped her face gently upward so he could look into her large, chocolate-brown eyes. "Do you understand what I'm trying to say?" He sighed. "Ach! I'm saying it all wrong again."

"Nee. Y-You're saying it just right." She winced as she reached a shaky hand to Andrew's cheek. "I-I'm sorry I didn't give you a chance to explain."

"Shhh, lieb. It's all right." He rocked her in his arms. "Esther, do you possibly feel the same way I do?"

"I think so."

"I love you, Esther."

"Then, jah, I feel the same way. I do love you, Andrew."

He bent to brush his lips across her forehead. He wanted to hug her tightly but didn't dare. With a thumb, he wiped the tears that trickled down her cheeks. "Are you in a lot of pain?" It hurt him to think so.

"A-A fair amount. The tears are those of joy, too."

"You've made me so happy, Esther. I want to know what happened to you, but I'm sure Lydia does, too. I don't want to make you tell it twice."

She gave a slight nod as if anything more would be too unbearable.

"I want to know, too," a strange female voice said from the doorway.

Andrew turned toward the open shed door.

Esther struggled to sit up straighter so she could put a face with the voice. She tried not to groan as she did so. The voice sounded familiar, but it didn't belong to a family member or neighbor. Of that she was certain. Andrew shifted his arms to help her sit up a bit more.

A tall, slender woman with auburn hair curving under at her shoulders entered the little potting shed. Esther was glad she wasn't claustrophobic because the little shed was getting awfully crowded. She squinted to make her eyes see through the thick cloud that still enveloped her, making her feel woozy.

"I know you!" She rejoiced that her memory was still intact. "You're from the drugstore."

"That's right. I'm one of the pharmacists at Tideview. I'm Meredith Cole."

"I remember. You told me about those peach-colored pills." She exhaled shakily and gasped for another breath.

"Why don't you rest a moment? Is it your sister you're waiting for? You can tell us what happened when she gets here." Meredith reached into the pocket of her khaki pants to pull out her cell phone. "Should I call for the rescue squad?"

"That's where Lydia went," Andrew replied. "She should be back in a minute."

"I-I really don't want to go the hospital. I'll be f-fine."

"You might have a concussion or broken ribs." Andrew's voice was calm but firm.

"I don't think so."

"I think your young man here is right. You need to be checked out," Meredith concurred.

"Ugh!"

Lydia burst through the doorway breathless. "The ambulance is on the way."

"Actually, the sheriff should be here momentarily, too," Meredith said.

"Sheriff? Why?" Esther winced as she tried to sit up better.

"I believe he will have some questions."

"Esther, can you tell us what happened?" Lydia sank to her knees beside Andrew and Esther.

"I'll tell you what I can." Haltingly, she described how she was struck on the head when she bent to pick up her hoe and shovel. Despite her attempt to keep from falling, she landed hard on her right side. She told them she remembered feeling a pinch or sting on her left arm before everything went black. When she woke up, it was in the hot, dark shed with no recollection of how she got there or why she felt so bruised and battered.

"I figured out where I was by the smell of the herbs and dirt."

"You and your nose!" Lydia clicked her tongue.

"It helped me this time. I was able to tell my position and then inch my way to the door. I couldn't open it, though."

"I'm so sorry, Esther." Her schweschder looked near tears. "Those rope burns look pretty nasty."

"That's because I kept trying to work my wrists free." She struggled again to push herself up. "I've got to warn the other folks. That's where I was going."

"You can't go anywhere right now." Lydia patted her arm.

"If you mean you need to tell the other Amish communities about those pills and Dr. Kramer, don't worry. I got the word out." A storm cloud crossed the pharmacist's face.

"How did you know?" Esther asked. "I didn't give you any names."

"You were very careful not to incriminate anyone that day we spoke, Esther, but I put things together and figured out who was mistreating the Amish patients."

"Danki, I was afraid I was too late." Esther paused for a moment. "Ach, the horse! Is he still hitched?"

"I asked Mose to tend to him," Lydia said. "Don't worry."

The distant sound of a wailing siren grew louder as an emergency vehicle drew nearer. Sheriff Carmichael arrived first in his black and white cruiser with the red-and-white ambulance close behind. Meredith stepped to the door of the potting shed and signaled to the sheriff.

"May I speak with you for a few moments before the rescue squad takes you, Ms. Stauffer?"

"Go ahead, Sheriff. I'd like to get this over with." She repeated her story as the sheriff made notes.

"Did your attacker say anything?"

"He said something like, 'too bad you can't help them' and 'I can't let you win.'"

"Did you recognize the voice?"

"It was rough, sort of gravelly or hoarse, like..."

"Who?" the sheriff prodded.

Esther looked at Andrew, then at Lydia and Meredith Cole. Finally, her eyes travelled back to the sheriff's face. "Like Dr. Kramer."

The sheriff nodded as though he wasn't even surprised at the mention of the doctor's name. "Any idea why he would do such a thing?"

She told the sheriff of her discovery of the peach-colored pills, of her visit to the pharmacy to confirm her suspicions, and lastly, of her visit to the doctor.

"Why didn't you come to me?" Sheriff Carmichael looked concerned, not angry.

"That's not our way. I didn't want to get anyone into trouble. I wanted to help my people. It seemed he targeted the Amish. I thought if I could keep my people away from the office until Dr. Nelson returned, everything would be okay." Her voice faded. She felt totally spent.

"I think we need to assess our patient now, Sheriff," a paramedic called from the doorway.

"Certainly. Thank you, Ms. Stauffer. I needed to hear your story, but I want to let you know we have already taken Dr. Kramer into custody. We had other suspicions about him. When we found certain evidence on him, he admitted to the attack on you and injecting you with Versed."

"With what?"

"It's a sedative. It's given to people before medical procedures to render them unconscious," Meredith explained hurriedly. "If he gave you a heavy dose, as I suspect, it will take a while for the total effect to wear off. You may feel dizzy or lightheaded or groggy for a while."

"Why did he do it? Why did he want to hurt us?"

The paramedic shifted from one foot to the other, obviously anxious to do his job. Sheriff Carmichael gave a brief reply. "It seems Dr. Kramer was doing some sort of research to prove people could heal themselves, sort of mind over matter. As long as people thought they were getting treated, they would improve. He was testing his theory on the Amish because—"

"We wouldn't sue him for malpractice," Lydia sputtered. "He could have caused real harm for my kinner. He could have killed someone!"

"He won't be practicing medicine again, I'm sure." The sheriff sounded almost as angry as Lydia.

"I do have some good news," Meredith announced. "I heard Dr. Nelson is coming back soon."

"Gut." Lydia and Esther spoke in unison.

"I'm going to let this very patient paramedic have a look at you now." The sheriff backpedaled toward the door.

"I-I won't have to testify or anything, will I, Sheriff?" Esther never intended to get the sheriff involved. She would never have contacted him on her own. The thought of appearing in court made her stomach churn.

"You shouldn't have to. We have a confession."

She sighed. Meredith and Lydia followed the lawman out of the tiny building so a stretcher could be wheeled in. Esther groaned as two men lifted her onto it. One wrapped a blood pressure cuff around her arm and checked her pulse.

"C-Can Andrew go with me? Please?"

Andrew looked from one man to the other.

"Sure," the paramedic with the blood pressure cuff said.

"Lydia will tell your parents. I'll tell her to call Kathy Taylor to bring us home." Andrew trotted out of the shed behind the stretcher. He spoke to Lydia as the men loaded it into the back of the ambulance.

"No sirens, please." The slam of the vehicle's rear door was all the noise Esther could handle at the moment.

Chapter Twenty-One

It felt strange to watch the women set out foods for the picnic on this off-church Sunday instead of helping them. The Beilers were hosting the picnic, and most families were in attendance. Mamm insisted Esther sit and rest, even though she felt much better. The dizziness and woozy, wobbly feeling disappeared when the drug had completely worn off the day after the attack. Her mind and vision were clear now.

Unused to being idle and watching other people work, she began to push up from the chair in the shade of a big oak tree in the Beilers' back yard when a large hand clamped down on her shoulder, aborting that plan.

"Going somewhere?"

Esther looked up into Andrew's jade eyes. Crinkly smile lines fanned out at the corners. "I thought I would help a little."

"What did the emergency room doctor tell you?"

"I've been taking it easy for days now. I'm not used to being inactive."

After several hours in the emergency room and multiple x-rays and scans, Esther had learned she had a mild concussion, bruised ribs, and multiple bruises and scrapes. Her open wounds had been bandaged and she'd been offered pain medication which she refused to take. She had been allowed to go home and admonished to take it easy for the next week. The inactivity grated on her nerves.

"I know it's hard for you to sit still but give it a few more days. For me?" He gave her a smile that melted her heart.

"Okay, but I don't like it. Why don't you go eat?"

"I'll bring you a plate and eat with you."

"I can wait. Mamm or Lydia or Hannah will bring me something. For that matter, I can walk to the table and eat with the women, you know."

"You sure don't like to be pampered, ain't so?"

"I'm not used to it."

Lydia sailed by with a bowl of coleslaw and slowed long enough to say, "Maybe Daed should have planted more celery." Esther knew her face must be as red as Andrew's.

"I'll go eat with the men, if you'll be all right." Andrew patted Esther's shoulder.

"I'm peachy. Wait until I get my hands on Lydia!"

He gave a lopsided grin. "I'll be back soon."

She wasn't alone for long before Hannah sidled up to her chair in the shade. "He certainly is very attentive."

"It seems so."

"You're looking better."

"I'm feeling better."

"I'm glad. Now, tell me about Andrew."

"He's about this tall." Esther raised her arms as high as she could. "He has blond hair and jade-green eyes."

"You know exactly what I mean, Esther Stauffer. You two seemed pretty cozy." Hannah dropped to her knees in the grass.

"Cozy? That must be one of your Englisch expressions. And you know we don't talk about our relationships." She brushed imaginary wrinkles from her purple dress and pasted on a prim and proper expression. She couldn't quite hide the smile lurking beneath her mock-stern demeanor, though.

"Amish girls discuss their beaus just like Englisch girls. They only pretend they don't."
Esther burst out laughing. "Is that so?"

"For sure. So talk. You two have apparently resolved your misunderstanding."

"I suppose so."

"Suppose so?"

"He has been very gut to me since the, uh, since I was injured."

"Just since then?"

"I guess he's been gut to me ever since he returned to St. Mary's County." She cut her gaze over at Hannah who grinned but kept silent. "Go ahead and say you told me so and that I've been too stubborn to realize that."

"I wasn't about to say any such thing."

"You were thinking it."

Hannah laughed. "You know me too well."

"How are things with you and Jacob?"

"Great."

"Are you and Rebecca working on celery recipes?"

"Maybe. And maybe we'll have extra celery for you, too." Hannah squeezed Esther's hand. "Would you like me to bring you a plate?"

"I think I can walk to the table to get my own food." Esther winced only slightly as she pushed herself out of the chair. Hannah scrambled to her feet to offer assistance.

Before the young women reached the two picnic tables pushed together and overflowing with cold cuts, cheese, breads, coleslaw, potato salad, and other assorted vegetables, they turned their attention to the gravel driveway leading to the Beilers' house.

"I wonder who that could be." Hannah watched the dark-green jeep drive slowly up the driveway.

"It must be someone who doesn't know we don't do business on Sundays." As the vehicle neared, Esther could identify the driver. "It's Dr. Nelson."

They reached the table but did not pick up plates and watched as the doctor slid out of the jeep. It seemed that all eyes were fastened on him as he approached the assembled group.

"Hello, everyone. Esther, how are you?" The doctor crossed the yard quickly to stand before her. Dr. Nelson stood almost as tall as Andrew but had a thinner build. His dark hair had begun to recede, making his forehead appear wide. His kind eyes looked her over.

"I'm fine Dr. Nelson."

"I am so very sorry this happened to you...to all of you." Dr. Nelson turned so his gaze could encompass everyone. Tears welled in his eyes. "I apologize sincerely for the actions of Dr. Kramer. I hesitate to call him a doctor. He certainly cast a black mark on the whole profession. He came highly recommended to me. I knew him as a young, new doctor. He was very conscientious and dedicated back then. I had no idea he had changed so completely."

"It's not your fault." Bishop Sol spoke for the group.

"I feel that it is. I thought I was leaving my patients in capable hands, not with someone who planned to use them as human guinea pigs! The man was so wrapped up in his ridiculous research he lost all sight of the oath he took to do no harm."

"We are all okay now." Esther spoke softly.

"Thanks to you, Esther. If you hadn't put the clues together, checked with the pharmacy, and warned your neighbors, someone could have been even more seriously harmed than you all were." Dr. Nelson paused to scan the crowd. "Mose, glad you're recovered, and you, too, Zeke." Both men nodded. "Lydia, the children..."

"They are fine, Dr. Nelson."

The doctor sighed. "Thank the Lord. Anyway, I humbly beg your forgiveness."

All heads nodded. Before anyone could speak, Dr. Nelson continued. "I don't expect you all to return as my patients, and I completely understand. That isn't my intention today. I simply want to apologize." Dr. Nelson's voice broke.

"We do plan to see you for our medical needs," Bishop Sol stated. Again, all heads nodded. "You are not at fault. We have always trusted you and will continue to do so. We're glad your father has improved and you've returned to be our doctor."

Dr. Nelson swiped at his eyes with the back of his hand and seemed at a loss for words.

"Now, Dr. Nelson, please pick up a plate and join us," Bishop Sol invited.

A huge grin spread across the doctor's face. "Thank you. I certainly can't pass up the opportunity for some good Amish food. I surely missed it."

The women bustled about, ladling food on Dr. Nelson's plate and pouring him a cup of tea. They inquired about his family and filled him in on local happenings. When he had eaten two platefuls of food and assured himself that Esther was indeed healing, he sought out Sophie and sat for a while with her and Gid.

Andrew returned to Esther's side after she had nibbled at her coleslaw and potato salad. The remainder of her food sat untouched. "Aren't you going to eat?"

She shivered at his nearness and the tickle of his breath in her ear. "I'm not terribly hungry."

"Try to eat a little more."

"You sound like my mamm."

"Mamms are smart. And you haven't been eating."

"You've been talking to my mamm, apparently." She scooped up a forkful of coleslaw and then handed her plate to him. "You can finish it."

"Well, I hate to see food go to waste." Andrew polished off the cheese and ham before tossing the paper plate into the huge trash can.

Esther glanced at Sophie and Dr. Nelson. Tears instantly flooded her eyes. She didn't think her beloved freind and mentor would be with them much longer.

Andrew's gaze followed Esther's. "Let's go sit with Hannah and Jake a while." He wished he could erase the sadness from her eyes and heart. He would be there for her, though, when Sophie's time came. If anything could cheer her up, it would be laughing with the couple who obviously loved each other as much as he loved Esther. One day — soon, he hoped — he would spend every day caring for here and doing everything possible to keep her safe from harm. He knew in his heart she now believed him, trusted him, and loved him. He would spend the rest of his life nurturing those feelings. As if she could read his mind, she reached to clasp his hand, her big, brown eyes expressing all the love in her heart.

Epilogue

The mid-November sun shone brilliantly, illuminating the burnished gold and deep-red leaves still clinging to tree branches. Its warmth barely held the chill of approaching winter at bay. The laughter and love filling the Hertzlers' barn chased away any remaining cold. There, the community had gathered to share in the wedding of Hannah Kurtz and Jacob Beiler. Hannah's teary eyes and trembling lips during the solemn service gave way to broad smiles and laughter during the wedding meal.

She had chosen purple for the color of her dress and the dresses of her attendants. Her pale blonde hair was pinned expertly beneath the white kapp with no stray strands dangling down her neck. Though she was still learning new things all the time, Esther had trouble remembering Hannah was not born Amish. She knew her freind would be the perfect fraa for Jacob.

Hannah's Englisch family attended the wedding as they had her baptism into the Amish Faith. Her happiness was practically palpable, and Esther was happy for her.

"What was that big sigh for?" she asked as she sidled up to the bride.

"I'm so happy."

"Gut."

"And next week, it's your turn." Hannah squeezed Esther's arm.

"Can you believe it? I'm finally getting married."

Hannah giggled. "What a change, ain't so? From avoiding Andrew at all costs to marrying him. You'll be a beautiful bride and a wonderful fraa to him."

"I hope so. I only wish…"

"What?"

"I wish Sophie could have celebrated with me." The beloved wise woman had passed on at the end of September. Gid had moved to live with his relatives.

"I know you do." Hannah patted her arm. "I like to think she's smiling down on us."

"Me, too."

All the women had worked hard the last few weeks, preparing for two weddings and getting the former Hostetler house in shape for its new occupants. Esther and Andrew would move into the house after their wedding the following week.

"She's happy, too." Hannah nodded to Sarah who rocked her new little bu in her arms.

"That could be you this time next year." Esther squeezed her friend's arm.

"Or you."

Her mouth dropped open. "I suppose it could be."

"Are you two having a solemn conversation on this festive day?" Rebecca had put the twins down for a nap in the Beilers' spare bedroom. Her other kinner played in the yard, so she finally had a few free minutes.

"Not really," Hannah replied. "Danki, Rebecca, for all you've done for me. You took me in, a stranger, and treated me like family."

"You were never really a stranger, dear Hannah. The Bible says strangers may be angels, and you have certainly been one to me."

"I'm going to miss teaching school, but even more, I'll miss helping you with the little ones and the house. I'll still help you whenever you want."

"You will have your own home and husband to care for now. And, the Lord Gott willing, you will have a houseful of your own little ones to tend to." The three women laughed. "Besides," Rebecca continued. "A letter came in the mail this very day from my little schweschder. It seems KatieAnn wants to kumm to St. Mary's County to stay for a while."

"Ach!" Samuel slapped his forehead in mock horror. The women hadn't even heard his approach. "Another maedel to put up with!"

"Was I so bad, Samuel?" Hannah paused. "Wait a minute. Maybe I was." She knew there had been some rough times and that Rebecca and Samuel had had a few disagreements because of her when they learned the true reason she had come to their community.

"Nee. There were some misunderstandings along the way, but you, Hannah *Beiler*, have been a blessing to us."

Tears threatened to spill from Hannah's eyes. Even Esther teared up. What a change this man had undergone — from not trusting Hannah to considering her a blessing.

"Let's hope KatieAnn has put aside her mischievous ways." Samuel winked at his fraa.

"I'm sure she has grown up considerably and has changed into a wunderbaar young woman." Rebecca smiled. "All will go smoothly with her visit, Samuel. You wait and see. We will all be glad she came to visit."

"Ahh!" Esther exclaimed. "Change is in the air." Her eyes sought out her beloved. "I've discovered change can be very gut."

About the Author

Susan Lantz Simson has been writing stories and poetry ever since she penned her first poem at the age of six. She has always loved the magic of words and how they can entertain and enlighten others. Her love of words and books led her to earn a degree in English/Education. She has taught students from Pre-kindergarten to high school and has also worked as an editor for the federal government. She also holds a degree in nursing and has worked in hospitals and in community health.

She writes inspirational stories of love and faith and has published a middle-grade novel (Ginger and the Bully). She lives in Maryland and is the mother of two wonderful daughters. She is a member of ACFW and Maryland Christian Writers Group. When she isn't writing, she enjoys reading, walking, and doing needlework.

Acknowledgements

Thank you most of all to God for giving me the ideas and the words for my stories and for allowing my dream to come true.

Thank you to my daughters, Rachel and Holly, for believing in me and dreaming along with me. (Rachel, you patiently listened to my ideas and ramblings, and Holly, I couldn't have done any of the tech work without your skills!)

Thank you to my family and friends for your continuous love and support.

Thank you to my mother who encouraged me from the time I was able to write. I know you are rejoicing in heaven.

Thank you to Mennonite friends, Greta Martin and Ida Gehman, for all your information.

Thank you to my friends at Mt. Zion United Methodist Church for all your support and encouragement and for patiently waiting for this book. I hope you aren't disappointed.

Thank you to my wonderful agent, Julie Gwinn, for believing in me from the beginning and for all your tireless work.

Thank you to Dawn Carrington and her staff at Vinspire Publishing. I appreciate all your efforts to make my dream a reality.

Dear Reader,

If you enjoyed reading *Plain Discovery*, I would appreciate it if you would help others enjoy this book, too. Here are some of the ways you can help spread the word:

Lend it. This book is lending enabled so please share it with a friend.

Recommend it. Help other readers find this book by recommending it to friends, readers' groups, book clubs, and discussion forums.

Share it. Let other readers know you've read the book by positing a note to your social media account and/or your Goodreads account.

Review it. Please tell others why you liked this book by reviewing it on your favorite ebook site.

Everything you do to help others learn about my book is greatly appreciated!

Susan Lantz Simpson

Plan Your Next Escape!
What's Your Reading Pleasure?

Whether it's captivating historical romance, intriguing mysteries, young adult romance, illustrated children's books, or uplifting love stories, Vinspire Publishing has the adventure for you!

For a complete listing of books available, visit our website at www.vinspirepublishing.com.

Like us on Facebook at
www.facebook.com/VinspirePublishing

Follow us on Twitter at
www.twitter.com/vinspire2004

and join our announcement group for details of our upcoming releases, giveaways, and more! http://t.co/46UoTbVaWr

We are your travel guide to your next adventure!

Made in the USA
Monee, IL
17 February 2021